By Michelle L. Rusk

Route 66 Dreams

Route 66 Dreams
Copyright © 2022 by Michelle L. Rusk

ISBN: 978-0-9837776-9-4
Library of Congress Control Number: 2021914155

info@chelleheadworks.com
505-266-3134
Albuquerque, New Mexico

Book design by Megan Mickey

Printed in the United States of America
First printing February 2022

Michelle L. Rusk

For my parents,
Robert and Marianne Linn,
who taught me to appreciate the past.

*J*ana Danielson stood at the side of the pool and noticed how light acted as a mirror over the water. She could see her hands on her hips, her clear sunglasses with the mirrored frames on her face, and her dark blonde ponytail on top of her head. Her tennis shoes were hidden from the mirror image by the worn concrete pool coping, but her white shorts and pink t-shirt were obvious in the reflected image.

The Midwestern air was hot. No, she thought. That's an understatement. The air in Southern Illinois was more like an oven. No matter which way she walked or moved, it was like slicing through it. Jana always heard the stories from her parents, "It might be warmer down south in the winter but that means it's always warmer in the summer. And more humid."

Steamy, she thought. Yuck. She wriggled her nose and noticed how she could see the trees surrounding the pool area– loungers and other chairs showing up as mirror images as well. She had never met anything but humidity in all the summers of her fourteen years.

The Breezy Corner Motel– not feeling so breezy at that time– wasn't crowded and she stood there by herself, a leftover yellow spiral-bound Mead notebook in her left hand–college ruled, of course, so she could write more on each page. She'd used the notebook in her social studies class but her mother had taught her to never throw away paper– "Always use it for something else," she would say, "We are such a wasteful society." But that meant no new notebooks for Jana's writing. There was always plenty of leftover paper from something else, the partially used notebooks and notepads stored on a shelf in the linen closet in the hallway of their home. Jana always thought it was an odd place but she finally realized that it was easily accessible to the entire family. And so, extra paper and pens resided with the towels and sheets that the family used on a regular basis.

The one-story motel, with a big kidney-shaped green sign with white neon lettering, sat off old Route 66 on the Illinois side of St. Louis. It had been a long, slow drive through Illinois that day, the trip her dad's idea to rediscover Route 66, this time with his family.

For as long as she could remember, Mike Danielson told the story about the trip he'd taken with his best friend Danny after their college graduation in 1964 from Chicago to Los Angeles via what he always called "The Mother Road."

Sometimes he'd pull out the slides and make the family watch them, Jana and her sisters Katie– who was sixteen– and Lisa who was eight– often fell asleep during the production. Jana thought her mother often fell asleep, too.

"I've made a decision about our summer vacation this year," he had announced at the dinner table in February, watching his wife Donna pass the bowl of mashed potatoes to Lisa. "We're going to drive Route 66 to Los Angeles and spend a week there before coming back."

"Ugh," Katie instantly said, making a face at Jana who was about take a bite of the chicken breast on her plate. "Do I have to go?"

"If you find a summer job, you don't," her mother reminded her.

"Great. I'm not sure which is worse."

She'd gotten a job at the local Dairy Queen that didn't need her until they would be back from their trip. Jana secretly wondered if one of her parents had called and told the manager Katie needed to go on vacation with the family and arranged it but she knew she'd never be able to confirm that because she'd never have the courage to ask.

"Convenient," Katie had said, puckering her lips at the dinner table. "Family vacation, Danielson style, 1986."

Every other family vacation– at least as far as the girls could remember– involved boarding a plane and flying to Florida where Mike golfed for a week and Donna and the three girls either frolicked on the beach or at the pool. But this year for reasons he didn't explain– nor did they ask– he wanted to pile them into the car and head west.

"At least we're going to California," Katie had lamented, flopping onto Jana's twin bed one evening before they left, *Seventeen* magazine in her right hand, her blonde bobbed, curly hair stuck in place from all the mousse she'd worked into it earlier that morning, part of an elaborate routine to prep for the day ahead. "Maybe we'll meet a movie star and not have to come back. Or a rock star would work, too. Hmm."

Jana looked up from where she sat on the floor leaning against her bed, writing in her journal, and shook her head, not sure how meeting a movie star or rock star would change anything for them. But she let her sister dream anyway.

Now, here they were, the first evening of a nearly two-week trip ahead of them. Jana wasn't quite old enough to work but she had committed herself to being available to several neighborhood moms for babysitting while they ran errands in the afternoons.

"It's your last summer before you'll need to find a job," her mother had reminded her when school ended. "You'll be fifteen in the spring so you can plan that you'll need to do something more substantial next summer."

Work was expected, Jana knew. As she watched her sister, who the past summer worked at McDonald's, Jana tried to figure out in her mind how she could get past those jobs. It wasn't the work that she would mind– or the paycheck– it was that she believed she was bound for bigger things in life. Her parents constantly reminded her that she needed to start somewhere and that one day she'd look back with fond memories of whatever her first job was. Jana didn't believe them.

They'd left early that morning, in the dark, because, as her father said, "You've seen everything nearby. Let's get an early start."

He also had slightly cheated, not driving them into the city to the exact spot in The Loop–Downtown Chicago– where Route 66 began, instead choosing to start from their house in the western suburbs.

"This is where Route 66 begins for us," he said as he put the station wagon in reverse and pulled out of the driveway of their residential street.

Donna had successfully managed to wake all three girls and get them– and their luggage– to the car while Mike packed it. Katie's eyes resembled slits as she fell into the backseat behind their father, Lisa the most excited because she was still young enough to appreciate a family adventure, and Jana feeling somewhere in between.

"Embrace it," Donna had told the girls at the drugstore two nights before when they picked up all their necessities, Donna loading the shopping cart with suntan lotion.

"We don't need that," Katie informed her as she pointed at the brown Coppertone bottles in the cart.

"Yes, you do," Donna said, crossing her arms in front of her chest to let Katie know there wouldn't be any discussion. "When you don't have wrinkles when you're my age, you'll thank me."

Katie did her signature eye roll and walked around the corner to find the mascara she liked.

The first part of the drive had been quiet, Lisa curled up in a ball between Katie and Jana, the two girls on the outside using their pillows to rest against the doors of their mother's light brown wood paneled station wagon that Mike and Donna had bought just a few months before.

"At least it's not a mini van," Katie had whispered to Jana when their parents showed it off in the driveway after bringing it home from the dealership. "Have you seen those? They're awful. I'm never going to have one. I'll drive my kids around in a two-seater convertible if I have to."

They left the familiarity of their suburban Naperville neighborhood behind, everyone clearly still asleep, houses looking dark, only the newspaper delivery person driving around throwing copies of the *Chicago Tribune* onto the paved driveways.

The territory became less familiar as they headed south toward Joliet and the hospital with a big red bulb on top of it– Katie calling it a gum ball when she was younger– making it easy to find, especially in the darkness.

Everything looks different in the dark, Jana thought.

From the front seat– as Jana drifted in and out of sleep– she could hear her parents talking about the drive, about how far their father planned for them to go that day, and the radio, WGN's morning talk show playing, the show she knew her father listened to each morning in his drive to Baxter Healthcare where he worked as a sales rep, traveling to doctors' offices and hospitals most days.

Jana's white and yellow, thick striped, tote bag held a few notebooks and pens, the pens brought home by her father, that she could use for her writing.

"It's probably some weird drug for colons," Katie always joked, squinting as she looked at the names printed on the sides, then shrugged her shoulders. "But if it helps you write, we should support you so one day you can support all of us when you're a famous writer."

The sun had risen enough that Jana could see the growing cornfields they traveled by, this part of the trip on the interstate because it ran directly over where Route 66 had been. She fully expected that at some point her father would act as a tour guide, as if they were on a tour bus, and tell them facts about Route 66, where they were traveling, and his trip all those years ago. She could tell he was excited to share by the way his brown eyes lit up when he started to talk about it.

Then he'd nervously run his hand through his short curly brown hair– the curly brown hair that to Donna's dismay none of the girls inherited. Every few months she went off to the beauty salon and read *People* magazine while tiny plastic pink rollers – they were the smallest ones at the salon– were rolled onto every strand of her brown hair and solution poured on to make the short, tight curls stay longer.

Now Jana watched the back of both of their heads as they sometimes talked, sometimes were quiet, her father fiddling with the radio station because they had drifted so far from Chicago. "We should be getting something from St. Louis soon," she heard him say, taking what looked like an endless stream of sips of his coffee in the yellow gold and brown plastic cup he used each morning to start the day with a fresh cup on his way to work. They'd made a quick trip to Dunkin' Donuts right when it opened and an orange and pink box with all of their favorite donuts sat on the arm rest between the two front seats.

As she looked at her parents, not really sure what they were talking about, her headphones with the round black sponges covering her ears. Hence, drowning her in her latest favorite songs that she had taped off the radio, mostly from Kasey Kasem's Top 40 countdown that previous Sunday morning.

The mix tape inspired her a bit, giving her energy even in her sleepiness. The songs were short stories in some ways. And while Jana never felt attracted to poetry, she admittedly loved song lyrics. And yet she didn't understand how they were written. For her, it made more sense to write an entire novel. Something she had yet to do but she knew she would accomplish. Sooner than later, she hoped.

"Everyone wants to write the great American novel," she once heard, but also wondering how many people actually did it.

I'm going to be someone who does, she thought, fast forwarding past "West End Girls" by The Pet Shop Boys– not really sure why she had included the song because they seemingly played it on the radio every hour and she'd become bored by it. Madonna's "Live To Tell" came up next and Jana took a look at Katie, still wearing her sunglasses even in the darkness and her headphones, and Jana wondered how many times Katie had played that very song already since they'd left the house.

4

Katie loved Madonna and notoriously rewound certain songs off her most recent "True Blue" tape, especially "La Isla Bonita," always exclaiming that Jana and Lisa would understand better when they took Spanish in high school.

"Tell her that you're taking French," Jana would say to Lisa, wanting to tease Katie who just assumed the details about everyone.

"Why would you take French?" Katie would then ask Lisa, her right hand on her hip, one foot forward, giving a slight pout. "How will we ever have a conversation if you speak French and I speak Spanish?"

Jana always made sure she had turned the corner when this conversation took place, knowing that Katie had taught Lisa well, that Lisa was growing into her own person.

"Because we'll be speaking English," Lisa would say, mimicking Katie with her hands on her hips, her long blonde hair pulled back in a ponytail by Donna earlier that morning. "Duh."

Katie could never come back from that one.

Jana thought mostly about her parents on that morning though. They always shared aspects of their lives but Jana and Katie admittedly didn't really listen.

"Yeah, we know you walked two miles to the schoolhouse every day with no shoes in the snow," Katie would say to their father. "But you got this great job selling drugs so we didn't have to do that. So I don't get why we have to hear that story over and over again."

If Jana had to write an essay about her parents, as she sat there in the car knowing they had a long way ahead of them, she decided that she would write about how they were especially good at staying out of the girls' lives. She didn't mean that in a sense that they didn't care because she knew they did. She meant it in the sense that they were allowed to do things, to experience life, and, quite honestly, fail.

"Then if you didn't study, that's your consequence," Donna said the one time Jana came home with an F on a math test. "What were you doing that you didn't study?"

Donna barely looked up from the onions she was browning for spaghetti sauce for dinner that night.

It was enough that Jana never did it again.

Jana remembered her dad teaching Lisa to ride a bike on their block a few years ago. Lisa fell down and Mike not running to her, instead, called out to her, "Get back on the bike! That's the only way you'll learn!"

Lisa was crying, then sniffling, but she got back on the bike and kept riding.

It obviously wasn't that way with suntan lotion– Jana saw that firsthand by what Donna had loaded the cart with at Osco– but her parents chose their battles with them. Sunburns were one thing Donna felt the need to protect them from, and yet math tests were another. That, Jana would learn, her mother felt she needed to figure out on her own.

It was as if her mother said, "It's not okay to burn but I'll let you get an F because I know that one F will change your outlook. One burn won't. You won't see the consequences for far too long."

And that consequence was her Aunt Hilda who lived in Arizona. Aunt Hilda had left Chicago in her early thirties when she married a man named Earl. The story went that Aunt Hilda loved to play golf and that wasn't something she could do in the winter in Chicago. So she met Earl, who lived in Arizona, quickly declared her love for him, and moved there with him.

Every year she sent a photo of them and every year she looked more and more weathered from the sun. Donna would cringe when she opened the Christmas card, afraid of how leathery Aunt Hilda's skin looked. While she had quit warning, "Don't end up like your Great Aunt Hilda," because one day Katie snapped back that she didn't care about Great Aunt Hilda, they all knew where the threat was coming from.

The only way Jana knew to give any depth to her parents was to compare them to the parents of her friends and others that she knew. And when she did that, her parents seemed rather…normal.

She dozed off while OMD's "If You Leave" song played, realizing she wasn't sure what to expect from the trip but she hoped it was at least interesting. And fun. Maybe she'd have a few good stories for her friends when they returned home right before the July 4th holiday.

Donna hadn't seemed that excited about going to California and Jana wasn't sure why. Whenever they made their Florida trips– which were always by plane– she seemed to have an extra spring in her step. The only part that Jana knew she appeared happy about was taking a trip by car.

"Too many plane crashes," Donna had said one day on the phone with her mother, Jana happening to be walking by the kitchen on her way to find her navy blue sweatshirt in the laundry room. Donna was sitting at the desk in the kitchen– designated her desk– the long cord from the phone hanging on the floor, Jana wondering when her parents would get a cordless phone as seemingly everyone else had. Donna had taken out the gold hoop earring from her right ear because it hurt against the cradle of the phone and held it in her right hand.

"Driving will be fine," she was saying. "But I wish we were going to Florida."

She didn't ask her mother if she preferred Florida for some reason that Jana didn't know. Maybe she didn't like the slide shows Mike insisted they watch either. But Jana didn't feel comfortable enough to ask her mother anything about it. That was something best left to Katie although if Katie didn't do it, Jana realized, she might never know. Jana knew she didn't have the nerve.

Jana thought about her friends who had taken family vacations, most of them to go visit grandparents and other relatives during the holidays because everyone lived in other places.

Their suburban town was a transient place filled with corporate employees whose typical stay was four years.

One day a friend would announce they were moving, a for sale appeared in the front yard, and dad was already working in the new place, leaving mom to pack up the kids and house for the move. That wasn't the case for Jana's family. Both her parents grew up in the Chicago area and they had no intention of leaving. Donna had made clear that she didn't want to live anywhere else. Mike traveled some for his job but not all the time. Somehow their lives were different than others they knew.

The vacation, though. Does a vacation ever change things? Jana wondered, thinking about how many movies she had seen with some sort of drama where everything goes wrong and then somehow brings everyone back together. That wasn't what she wanted. She wanted it to be a good experience for everyone. Was that too much to ask?

The reality was if they could return home not hating each other, it had gone well.

She looked over at Lisa whose long hair was strewn everywhere, including across her face. Katie had left the house in the dark, with her sunglasses on, but they were now angled the wrong way, Katie clearly asleep not having noticed yet.

"You always wear your sunglasses at night?" Jana had teased her sister, using song titles to form a conversation, much to the aggravation of everyone around them.

"Why can't you two speak like normal teens?" Mike would ask at dinner as he rolled his spaghetti onto his fork.

"Like, really, Dad?" Katie would tease him, rolling her eyes at Jana who would giggle.

"That's not normal either," he would say.

"Like yes it is," Katie– the one with the courage to speak up– would continue. "And if we're going to California, like we'll both be speaking like this by the time we get home."

He would shake his head and keep eating.

Now here they were, the first day into the trip. She already missed her best friend Marcella, knowing she'd only get to talk to Katie and Lisa for the next two weeks.

"At least send me a postcard from LA," Marcella begged. "You think you don't want to go but you're lucky your parents are taking you somewhere. My mom said I can go visit my grandma. In the city." She'd turned up her nose. "She doesn't have air conditioning and it's awful. Stinky and humid. My Uncle Jose lives with her and he never showers."

Maybe I'll find something to write on this trip, Jana had thought hopefully, now staring out the window. It had been a relief to stop in Springfield– conveniently along Route 66– for a few hours to visit a few sites, all related to Abraham Lincoln. Walking around felt good after they had been smashed like sardines in the station wagon.

"How come we never did this before?" Jana heard her mother ask her father as they walked back to the car after they all visited a house where Lincoln had lived.

"I don't know," he had said, placing his black sunglasses back on his face. "It's not like it's that far away."

"If we had done it before does that mean we would have had to do it again?" Katie had whispered, sidling up to Jana who covered her mouth to keep from laughing. "And how is this related to Route 66? I don't remember this from the slide shows. I was always awake at least until he got to St. Louis."

Now as Jana sat down in a lounge chair by the pool, her sisters having gone for a walk to the convenience store up the street to get sodas, she opened the notebook and tapped the light blue pen on the blank page.

What do I write? She wondered, looking thoughtfully at the empty pool, hoping they would swim after they came back from dinner. *What story do I tell?*

"Jana!" She looked behind her where the voice was coming from and saw her mother walking toward her, waving something in her hand.

Donna Danielson's brown hair– slowly going gray– had been cut and permed before they left on the trip. She walked purposefully toward Jana, wearing a long brown geometrical sundress and brown heeled wedges. Donna opened the gate on the chain link fence and walked over to her daughter, sitting down sideways on the lounge chair next to Jana. That's when she presented her with a notebook.

"I got so caught up in packing I forgot to give this to you before we left home," her mother said proudly of the spiral-bound Mead notebook. In pink.

"Brand new?" Jana asked, sitting up straighter and looking through the blank pages.

"Yes," her mother said. "And in pink. I don't think we've ever seen a pink notebook. It was in a pile at Osco. I usually don't go down that row but I was trying to avoid an elderly lady and her shopping cart who was taking too long. And there it was. I guess it was meant to be."

"For me?" Jana was surprised.

"Yes." Her mother reached over and placed her hand over Jana's wrist. "So you can become that writer you want to be. So you can write on this trip. So you can go into high school feeling as if you're on your way."

"Thank you, Mom," Jana said, feeling excited over the small gift.

Her mother smiled at her and Jana took the opportunity to ask her something that had been on her mind.

"Mom?" She asked.

"Hmm," Donna said, now standing up, her hands on her hips, staring at the pool as if she had dropped her grocery list and the wind had blown it into the water. Jana noticed she wore the gold earrings with a yellow hard plastic ball at the end of each one– a gum ball Lisa had called them at one point not understanding why she couldn't have the earrings and had to buy a gum ball from a machine for a penny instead. Jana guessed they were her mother's favorite earrings because she wore them the most.

"Do you believe you have to suffer to be a writer?" Jana asked, feeling shy, not usually asking her mother– or her father– a question like that, a question that she thought a lot about but had no answer to.

Donna shrugged her shoulders and then looked at Jana. "Well, I suppose to some extent. No, maybe not."

She paused and while she did, Jana thought about what her mother read: romances. Specifically, Harlequin romances. Maybe she wasn't the right person to pose this question to.

"Donna!" A voice called out from across the parking lot, by the car, and they both looked to see Mike waving a piece of paper in his hand and calling her to him.

"Oh," she said, suddenly, seemingly forgetting Jana's question and heading right toward him.

I guess that's okay, Jana thought, disappointed but then wondering if her mother was glad she'd been distracted. That way she didn't have to answer a question she clearly didn't have an answer to.

But then Jana thought about something else. Not long ago she hadn't been invited to the eighth grade dance. It was a couples gig, as if to prepare them for the high school dances where it was expected one went with a date. First would be homecoming in the fall, then spring dance, and, of course, prom. It felt as if everything in junior high was preparing them for high school. And beyond.

Jana didn't have a date that night and stayed home watching tv on the set in their parents' room while they went out to dinner, leaving her home with Lisa who had fallen asleep watching "The Parent Trap"– the 1960 film with Hayley Mills– for the millionth time on video. After Lisa refused to budge in her sleep from the couch in the family room, Jana had sighed, and gone upstairs to their parents' room to watch "Miami Vice" instead. Katie was out with her friends at the movies and not due back until midnight, the luxury of a late curfew for Friday night.

While Crockett and Tubbs chased drug dealers around Miami in great-looking clothes, Jana wrapped her arms around one of the brown-patterned throw pillows from their bed and felt overwhelmed by sadness. She didn't really know *who* was going to the dance that night but from the discussions in school that day, it felt like everyone.

Except her.

And somewhere in her sadness about what she didn't have, she began to weave together a story. She pulled it from a very small piece of string, like that small piece of thread that one has to cut off after sewing a button back onto a shirt. She took that small thread and ran with it, creating a story about a dance, a fairy tale of sorts maybe, but with a twist.

There would be sadness but not for that reason. The girl would be the one who would win. And she would win because she was the strong one, stronger than any boy would ever know. That would make her realize that she didn't need him. Because there would be someone better out there for her.

By the time her parents came home at 10:00, Jana had filled up several pages with her story.

"Writing again?" Mike asked, looking tired, when he walked into the room, Donna coaxing Lisa downstairs to her bed.

"Yeah," Jana said, feeling shy as she always did about her writing, closing the notebook before anyone tried to look into it. She didn't know if her parents knew there was a dance that night. She hoped they didn't. She didn't want them to think less of her because she didn't have a date.

She went off to bed and hadn't looked at that story since that night, glad she had written it, but not sure what she would do with it. While each time she wrote something, she felt good about it, nothing felt quite right that it was what she was supposed to write. Yet she kept writing because it brought her comfort and sometimes lifted her out of a depression that might have set in because of an event in her life that she couldn't control.

After her mom left the pool area, Jana thought about how it was just a small gift– not an expensive one by any means– but it was the thought that her mom had picked it up for her when she easily could have kept her cart rolling to the shampoo aisle where she was headed.

Just two weeks ago Jana had walked out of her junior high school and officially into the summer as an incoming ninth grader.

"You know I'm going to pretend that I don't know you," Katie had teased her, but really handing Jana one of her old school folders with the map of the high school on the backside. "Here," she said, holding it up so Jana could see the map, before pushing it into Jana's hands. "The best gift I can give you is what no one did for me. Memorize the map so you don't look like a freshman. You'll never be lost, you'll never be late. And you'll always thank me."

But something even more important had happened just days before that when Jana had been recognized with the newspaper award always given to an eighth grader. Maybe she hadn't been aware of the award, she didn't know, so she was surprised when Mrs. Gallagher called her name and handed her a trophy in the all-school ceremony. That's when she looked into the crowd of parents and saw her own, smiling and happily cheering her on along with her classmates.

Mrs. Gallagher had what Jana always thought was a happy-sad look on her face, as if someone could experience more than one emotion at the same time. Jana felt as if Mrs. Gallagher had a story to tell about her life but Jana never had the courage to ask her. After all, she was only fourteen. How could she expect that Mrs. Gallagher might share any pain in her life with an eighth grader?

"Good luck," she told Jana, shaking her hand and then pulling her toward her red print dress for a hug. "I'll be rooting for you."

Jana had spent a lot of time with her over the past three years, since that day in sixth grade when Mrs. Gallagher had been assigned to her for English class and had announced she was also the school newspaper adviser.

After class that day, Jana had shyly approached her. "What I really want is to write books," Jana said, not knowing more than that.

Mrs. Gallagher, with her long black hair piled high in a bun on top of her head, tapped her red pen on her desk. "Well," she said, her face looking kind. "You should know that it might take a while for you to make money writing books. In the meantime, you'll need a way to support yourself. If you pursue journalism, you can write newspaper articles during the day, keep the bills paid, and write your novels in your spare time."

Jana stood and watched her, holding her new folder, notebook, and textbook in her left hand, careful not to let them drop to the floor. She nodded, absorbing it all. "Okay," she said.

"And in the process, the more you write, the better writer you'll become."

On the bus ride home that afternoon– the bus traveling back to her subdivision from the school– Jana looked out the window and told herself that she would begin writing then.

If I get a head start now, she thought maybe life might be easier later.

"So you want to be a writer," her dad said at dinner that night, everyone looking supportive around the kitchen table.

"You can tell stories about your great older sister," Katie teased, still wearing her freshman cheerleading skirt from practice earlier that day with a t-shirt on top.

"No, she can tell stories about her fun little sister," Lisa said, a big smile spreading across her face– with spaghetti sauce stains making her look like she had a clown mouth.

"I'm sure Jana has lots of ideas," Donna reminded her girls, also looking happy at the announcement.

What Jana couldn't tell anyone– because she didn't understand it herself– was that she didn't know what she was going to write. She just knew this was what she wanted to do. But in the next three years, Mrs. Gallagher was there to encourage her in any way she could.

"You should get pen pals in other countries," Mrs. Gallagher suggested one day out of the blue. "Whatever you write, it's all going to make you a better writer."

By seventh grade, Jana knew what she enjoyed most were reading stories about other people. Her mother didn't question it when she came home with biographies and autobiographies from the library. She didn't even bat an eye when she found Jana laying on the living couch reading *Mommie Dearest*, the back-stabbing book Christina Crawford wrote about her mother, the actress Joan Crawford.

"She was a great actress," was all Donna said, leaving the room with the magazine she had left on the coffee table and had come looking for.

No one knew that it came from Jana stumbling on the television movie based on the book. That was what peaked her interest.

In eighth grade, Jana found herself– luckily, she thought– in Mrs. Gallagher's class again.

"They need me to teach eighth graders this year," she said, looking happy to have some of the same kids back again. "At least now I can see if you've learned anything from what I taught you two years ago."

And when, that spring, she assigned them to write an autobiography of a person they admired, Jana immediately chose Marilyn Monroe.

"Marilyn Monroe," David Mills teased her, looking over her shoulder as she scanned the *Reader's Guide to Periodical Literature* for magazine articles in the library. "Why?"

"Why not?" Jana shot back, David, running his hand through his thick black hair that curled as it went down his neck, backed off.

She couldn't find any articles though and then remembered that Marilyn had died too many years ago.

"You need an older *Reader's Guide*," suggested Mrs. Nolan, the librarian. "You should try the college library."

That afternoon, Jana walked through the snow to North Central College, the small liberal arts campus not far from her junior high. She easily found the green bound books and settled into a chair in front of those from 1960 on, hoping the last few years of Marilyn's life would give her the information that she needed to write the paper. Mrs. Nolan and Mrs. Gallagher had taught them enough about how to use a library that Jana didn't flinch at the idea of finding old magazines– bound together like books– or the microfilm rolls.

It was *Life* and *Look* that gave her exactly what she was looking for, the stories about Marilyn who was at the height of her fame and thus interesting to the public even though she faced many internal struggles.

But who was she? Jana kept asking herself as she flipped through the magazines taking her to another era that wasn't just about Marilyn. Why did she feel so drawn to the clothes and the décor? she wondered, losing track of time as she flipped through the big bound hard-covered books of a year's worth of magazines in each one. She treasured the black and white photos that helped her sense what it was like then, nearly the same time her parents were in college, meeting, falling in love, and getting married. But something about her parents' lives didn't resonate with her like these magazines did.

Yet as she now lay at the swimming pool on a trip through another time– a time her dad wanted to revisit– she could see it was the same time.

The early 1960s, she thought. Why do I want to be there? She looked at the swimming pool, still believing the answers might be written in the water. She closed her eyes, pen still in hand, until her chatty sisters walked into the pool area, laughing.

"You totally missed it," Katie laughed, Lisa right next to her, looking up at the older sister she idolized. "There was this dweeby guy in the convenience store." Katie's hair looked just like their mom's– blonde permed– except that hers was cut in a bob that made it poof out at the edges. Trendy. "Total loser. He tried to ask me on a date."

Lisa started to giggle.

"He's like, 'Hey, wanna go to the movies tomorrow night,'" Katie said rolling her eyes as she made up a voice that Jana knew probably was far from what the guy's voice actually sounded like. "I was like, 'Dude, I don't even live here.'"

Lisa kept giggling, then sipped her soda.

"Are we going swimming?" Katie then asked, looking over at the pool.

"After dinner," Jana said. "You should go tell them you're back– maybe we can go eat now."

"I'm not sure where we're going to eat in this hole of a town."

"I guess there are places near the interstate," Jana said, not wanting to upstage her sister's sarcasm that was her trademark in the family.

"It would have been nicer if we'd stayed by the interstate," Katie said, looking toward their room and turning up her nose. "I'm sure there's a nicer place than this crap hole."

Jana didn't disagree with her sister. The room smelled musty and like people had smoked in there for years. The only good news was that the rooms were so cheap their dad had splurged for a separate room for the girls. However, what Jana liked was the pool and the cool motel sign at the edge of the property by the sidewalk.

"You know why," Katie had joked, nudging Jana who gave her sister a look.

"I don't want to think about that. Or hear anything."

Jana often found herself watching her family as if she were on the outside, as if she were watching them on television. Her parents argued frequently and it seemed as if it was about nothing. One time she heard her mother blow up at her father because he was mad she hadn't gotten him shaving cream.

"But you didn't tell me you were out! How was I supposed to know!" She yelled back, Jana hearing it down the hall in her own bedroom. These were the moments when Jana wished she could climb out her bedroom window and go hide somewhere down the street until they were speaking to each other again. Usually her father was upset about money so it surprised Jana that he was willing to spend the money on the extra room.

"It must have been cheap," Katie said out loud with a snort as she carried her pillow with her to their room when they had arrived.

"Thanks, Dad," Jana told him as he held the door open to their room and handed Jana the key with the plastic fob on it, giving the room number and the motel information.

Try to be thankful when Katie isn't, she often told herself.

She also expected her sister to be somewhat moody on the trip for several reasons: one that they would be separated from their friends for two weeks.

"Can I call them?" She asked her parents one night at the dinner table not long before they left on the trip.

"No," Donna said, cutting her off before she could say anything else. "Absolutely not. Do you know how expensive long distance is?"

"But doesn't it get cheaper the further away you go? And if you call in the middle of the night?"

"How does she know these things?" Mike asked his wife, not looking thrilled that his daughter had figured this out.

Jana bit her lip to keep from laughing, not able to take another bite of her pizza that her father had picked up from Oodles on his way home from work– Mike called when he was leaving from work and Donna had learned to gauge when he would be twenty minutes– barring a tollway accident– away and she would call the pizza in for him to pick it up before he arrived home. Other times they ate at Oodles but it had come to depend on how late cheerleading practice ran for Katie.

Jana heard her parents not long ago talk about how they knew pizza nights– something they'd done for years with the girls weekly as often as they could– were coming to an end. Katie would surely make the varsity cheerleading squad and be busy with football and basketball on Friday nights. And with Jana heading into high school, they waited to hear what activity she might select to do. Outside of the obvious: the school newspaper.

She never told anyone but she kind of enjoyed the banter Katie created in their family. It made their parents think and she often liked to see how they would respond. Or how often they simply ignored her sister. She learned a lot by watching how everyone interacted, not realizing how much she was setting herself up for her writing career. She simply found it interesting at the time.

But in the days leading up to the trip, there had been a caveat on Katie's end at the neighborhood swimming pool where they spent their summers.

His name was Bruce.

It started with one line at dinner. "If I get a job, can I really stay home?" She asked.

Mike was scanning the *Chicago Tribune*– looking more tired than usual, probably because he had been driving to various hospitals and doctor offices all day, getting ready to be gone for two weeks.

"Yes," he said.

"Okay," Katie said. "Can I stay with the Browns?"

"No," Donna said.

And that's when the argument began.

"Why not?" Katie asked, looking confused. "You said if I got a job and worked while you were gone, I could stay home. But you won't let me stay here by myself and you won't let me stay at the Browns. So where do I stay?"

"It's too late," Donna told her. "Yes, we told you that you could stay home if you got a job but we needed several weeks notice so your cousin Josie could stay here but she got a job in Michigan on Mackinac Island and she's leaving tomorrow."

"That's not fair," Katie said.

"Yes it is," Mike told her, making a long sigh before he spoke, Jana knowing whatever he said was going to go. "You told us Dairy Queen didn't need you until we got back."

Katie sulked the rest of dinner and Jana wondered why her sister had suddenly changed her mind. While she personally wasn't looking forward to all that togetherness in the car, what Jana was looking forward to was Los Angeles and she thought Katie was, too.

A place she'd never been, a place she'd always wondered about. And a place few of her friends had been because most of them– like her– usually went to Florida for their vacations. Or to visit family at cabins in Minnesota or Wisconsin. Her friends had told her how envious they were of her, the first time Jana had thought it possible that she had something others didn't.

Katie continued her sulk as dinner ended, Donna reminding her that it was her night to load the dishwasher. After she did that noisily, she stomped up to her room and slammed the door, Jana feeling a jump from the noise that shook the two-story house. Her parents seemed to have gotten good at ignoring Katie's moods.

But an hour later, as Jana sat on the floor of her room, leaning against the side of her bed like she usually did, writing in her journal for the day about junior high ending and the building excitement of the trip, Katie slipped into her room and flopped herself across Jana's empty twin bed.

"Bruce."

That was all she said.

Jana finished writing and looked up at her sister from where she sat on the floor. "Springsteen?"

Who else was named Bruce? She wondered.

"I met a guy named Bruce," Katie said, looking like her usual dramatically sad self. "And now we're leaving for two weeks."

"Won't he be here when we get back?" Jana asked.

That's when Katie rolled over so she was looking over Jana's shoulder, making Jana feel self-conscious about what she was writing. Her journal wasn't something she shared with anyone. Ever.

But it was obvious Katie– if she was even looking at what Jana was writing– wasn't paying any attention.

"If I leave then Beth Matthews will dig her blood-red claws into him and my chance will be long gone by the time we get home."

Jana closed the royal blue spiral notebook– that didn't close so well now that she had used it for a full semester science class and the spiral had flattened in spots– and set it on the floor, tapping her pen on the notebook's cover. She had no idea what the words on the pen meant– it was some pharmaceutical drug, like all the others.

"Don't worry about what they are," her dad sometimes said when she would ask. "They keep this roof over your head and dinner on the table."

"That means he's peddling cocaine on the side," Katie might whisper later when their father was out of earshot– usually on his way to the golf course.

Jana never believed her sister but she always laughed at the absurdity of the things she said, wondering where they came from because she didn't think them herself. She simply really wanted to know what drugs her dad sold; she wanted to know if they truly helped people get well or live better lives. Although her father wasn't a doctor, maybe he had a hand in helping people heal their bodies from some sort of illness. But he never shared any of that and she found it hard to ask.

That evening it was about Bruce though and Jana didn't understand it. "But," Jana said, looking at the big green rug in her room that she was sitting on the edge of, "if he really likes you, then won't he ignore Beth and be there when you get back? Surely you told him that you're going on a family vacation and you have to go."

"Oh, you're so logical," Katie said, shaking her head so much that her thick blonde hair flew everywhere even though it was stiff from the mousse job earlier that day. "I don't trust Beth. And how can I trust Bruce? I don't know him. Two weeks is a long time."

"Maybe you'll meet someone on our trip," Jana said hopefully, always trying to counteract what her sister thought was impossible.

"A movie star maybe," Katie said, sitting up, her legs dangling off the side of the bed on top of the green and blue plaid comforter. "Then I can come home and show both Bruce and Beth that I really am better than both of them." She started to giggle at the idea of the scene and got up to leave the room.

Jana hoped her sister would forget about Bruce– and quickly. The drama around her breakups was always much worse than when she met a boy and wasn't able to even get anything going with him. The days of sulking that the entire family endured; Lisa getting snapped at by Katie, even though Katie usually loved to banter with their younger sister.

Jana had learned to steer clear of her older sister unless she came to her for something. And that's usually what happened.

"I feel so awful," Katie would say, practically stumbling into Jana's room, her face red from crying. "Why didn't he like me?"

The boys always seemed to break up with Katie at some point– or they cheated on her. Jana never had any answers for her sister but she would listen to Katie talking endlessly until Katie would sit up and say, "I feel better. Thanks, sis," and she would leave the room.

"What do you say to your sister?" Donna would always ask because Katie always returned to her usual sarcastic self after a "talk" with Jana.

"Nothing," Jana said, shrugging her shoulders. "I just listen."

Donna– her hands on her hips– would shake her head. "You're in tune with people better than I ever could be. I hope you know what a gift that is."

Jana knew people told her things she usually didn't get and when she asked, they usually said, "One day you'll understand."

After Katie began to walk through the doorway this time, however, she stopped and looked back, saying, "You know. You'll probably meet someone on this trip. I can totally see that happening."

Jana shook her head and picked her journal back up to continue where she left off.

Fat chance, she thought.

Jana didn't feel like she and boys had a good connection. Despite the seemingly million times her mother reminded her that it would eventually all fall into place, Jana found the boys at school to not be so interesting. And the ones she did feel any sort of connection with, she always found they said– shuffling their feet– "I just think of you as a friend."

Mrs. Gallagher had always laughed, too. "Jana, you're an old soul. One day the new souls will catch up with you."

And in the meantime?

Focus on my writing, Jana told herself. Then they all can be sorry they aren't with me.

It was the same idea she told her sister just a few moments before. While Jana wasn't happy about the fact that she couldn't seem to find a boy in the same feeling place as her when it came to this "like" gig– there were boys who she knew liked her but ones she didn't have any attraction to– she reminded herself that one day it would change. She just had to focus on what she wanted to do.

But she was also envious of those who attraction, love, whatever it was, seem to come easily. Jana always felt as if Katie simply batted her eyes at a boy and that boy came running. Jana remembered the woman who cut her hair and her mother's hair, Janie, who one day had a spring in her step and a smile on her face that Jana hadn't seen before.

"You know," she said, surveying Jana's hair that had turned dark blonde during the gray of winter, "I think you need some highlights. On me."

Janie ran her fingers through Jana's wet messy hair and then zipped off to get the supplies she needed for a few summer highlights– the same ones Jana would have in her hair after a few weeks at the swimming pool– only this time a few months earlier.

All because Janie was in love.

Jana dismissed all thoughts of love, turned on the radio, and kept writing.

Chapter 2

$\mathcal{T}$he next morning, they were on to St. Louis and the famous arch before continuing their trek across tree-lined Missouri and then the grasslands of Oklahoma where they stopped at the Blue Whale.

"In the sixties, these roadside attractions were starting to fall into disrepair because the interstates were almost finished being built," Mike told his family as he pulled off the interstate near the town of Catoosa to take them to see a big metal whale that hung partly into a big pond. "But this one wasn't created until the seventies. Danny came this way once after me and sent me a postcard."

"This one looks like it's a dump," Katie said under her breath at the sight of the blue paint peeling off the metal wale. Lisa immediately went running through the whale, reminding Jana of a children's book she couldn't remember the title of where a cartoon child did the very same thing. The inside of that cartoon whale was just as empty as this one.

"Be careful!" Donna called, not seeing many other people at the site. Jana stood at the edge of the entrance of the whale, then looked back, and hoped her mom didn't see how rickety the wood pier had become. She might then call Lisa back from the edge where she hung over the ladder that people obviously used to climb out of the pond.

Katie was behind Jana. "I'm letting you two fall in before me," she said, looking at the murky pond water. "It's like a swimming pool that hasn't been cleaned in years."

"And like that lake we swam in on our trip to Minnesota," she reminded her sister.

"We weren't as smart then as we are now," Katie laughed, and then looked out a hole in the whale to see a slide into the water.

When the girls walked back to their parents– sitting at a picnic table, Donna looking relieved that they were back on solid ground, Mike said, "Well, it used to be a popular place." He said sound sarcastic like Katie.

"Not now," Katie said stating the obvious– which felt redundant to Jana so she stayed quiet.

Back on the road, Jana slipped her headphones back over her ears and hit play on the Heart tape she'd been listening to since they left St. Louis, unable to get enough of the same songs she'd been repeating since the day before.

*****

Lisa complained she had to go to the bathroom, everyone sighing because she hadn't gone at the Blue Whale. Mike pulled off into the next rest area and before they climbed back into the car, Mike suddenly handed the car keys to Katie, whose face lit up like the sun.

"Seriously???" She asked, jumping up and down.

Donna smiled although Jana could see it was somewhat tentative; Mike looked more excited. "Don't get in an accident and you'll get to do it again," he said as he walked by her to the passenger side of the front seat, Donna climbing into the backseat with Jana and Lisa who watched their sister closely as she took the wheel, Mike giving her a slew of directions.

Katie had her learner's permit and this was to be the other part of her summer vacation– taking driver's education class.

"We might as well let you learn the interstate," Mike said as Katie joltingly backed the car out of the parking lot and eased it onto the interstate.

Jana looked over and saw her mother holding her breath, her hands clasped together tightly, her knuckles around her gold and diamond wedding ring turning white. Mike looked more relaxed in the front seat, Jana knowing he was the one who did better teaching them any sort of skill, probably realizing that he had to make a choice when they didn't have any boys: enjoy teaching the girls or there won't be anyone to teach at all.

Except golf. He'd tried that with Katie but she'd been too interested in checking out the boys at the driving range so he'd never taken her again. Jana worried he might never take her because of that experience with Katie but now he was letting Katie drive, that might change. Jana kept her fingers crossed for her sister.

If she does well, it'll benefit me, she thought.

It wasn't perfect, but they all survived and by the time they reached the outskirts of Tulsa, Mike was ready to take the reins of the car again.

*****

Following the humid air and grasslands of Oklahoma, the landscape began to give way to miles of rolling dirt hills dotted with green plants. Amarillo (where they spent their second night) brought the smell of cattle in the morning when they opened the doors of their adjoining motel rooms.

"Oh God," Katie said, looking like she might faint from the smell. "You'd think we slept at the county fair."

Jana bit her tongue, not liking the smell, but wanting to laugh out loud at her sister's comment.

"The cattle haven't been moved from the stockyards," Mike said, packing up the car for the next leg of the trip.

The night had started out uneventfully, Mike once again choosing a small motel– this one with no swimming pool.

"Who builds a motel with no swimming pool?" Katie had asked, her hands on her hips as she stood in front of the small, one-story, L-shaped building with the motel office at end of it.

It had been hot when they arrived and the girls felt ready for a swim to cool off before they went to bed. Now they just felt bored.

"What's this?" Lisa had asked, her hands holding a mysterious looking metal object with a cord attached on the nightstand between the beds. Jana and Katie walked over to where Lisa was and Katie started to laugh first, Jana following.

"A bed jiggler!" Katie laughed, finding her purse and looking for a quarter. "I've only heard about these."

"What is it?" Lisa asked again, watching Katie slip the quarter into the slot. She started to read from it. "What is a magic fingers massaging bed?"

"Sit on the bed and you'll find out," Katie told her.

It didn't take long for the bed to start moving, all three girls sitting on it and laughing.

"The bed's moving!" Lisa laughed, her face smiling but looking surprised.

"Exactly!" Katie said. "And there's no one below us to complain."

Jana looked over at it– the brown metal box also functioned as a clock– and below the name was printed "home models available."

Suddenly Jana started to laugh. She wasn't sure why but the idea of having one of those at home– especially if someone had to always put a quarter in it– made her laugh. And while her sisters had no idea why she was laughing, they started to laugh as well.

The jiggling bed stopped– the time having run out– but the girls didn't seem to notice. They lay on top of the red bedspread and laughed until they were crying.

Then they heard a knock at the door.

"Girls!" They heard their father call from outside the door. "Girls!"

Jana was closest to the door and got up to open it, Mike stood there not looking angry but perplexed.

"We're not the only people staying in the motel," he said, pointing at other cars in front of it. "We can hear you laughing loud and clear next door."

"Sorry, Dad," Jana said, starting to laugh again and falling back on the bed.

"What's so funny?" He asked.

Katie looked up and pointed at the magic fingers box.

"Oh," he said, a smile coming across his face. "You discovered the bed jiggler."

"Do you have one in your room, too?" Lisa asked, looking serious.

"I guess we do," Mike said, grabbing the door knob. "Keep it down girls. And don't use all your quarters on it. You might want to save them for something else."

Jana knew one thing she and her sisters always did well– laugh.

*****

As she stood in the parking lot the next morning, watching her father load up the car with complete organization, she suddenly remembered it was Sunday– feeling so far out of any routine that she had forgotten what day of the week it was.

"It's Father's Day," she whispered to Katie who looked as surprised as Jana felt.

"Crap," Katie said, just as Mike closed the back of station wagon. "Uh, Daddy Dear," she said in her most pleasantly annoying voice, Jana cringing, knowing how irritated he was about to get. "I need something from my bag."

Jana kept her eyes– although painfully– on her father who tapped his fingers on the back window the station wagon, Jana knowing he was counting to ten.

"You're kidding?" He asked.

"No," Katie said confidently.

"And how did yours end up in the car first?"

Jana turned to their mother who looked like she was about to step in and tell Katie she didn't need anything until they reached Albuquerque.

"Mom," Jana hissed, not wanting to get her sister in trouble, but also knowing this was important.

Donna gave Jana a surprised look and Mike opened the back up again and started to remove the bags until he found Katie's. With everyone watching, Jana feeling relieved that in a moment the tense bubble around them would pop and be suddenly forgotten, Katie reached into her bag, fumbled around and pulled out a folded up a piece of paper. And a small box.

"Happy Father's Day, Dad," Katie said proudly, looking at Jana and Lisa–who had been too busy running around the parking lot with Chuck– her worn stuffed monkey– tucked into her arm to care what was happening. "From all three of us."

Jana thought she heard their mother let out a big sigh, Mike suddenly started to laugh, shaking his head while he unfolded the card that Jana had drawn of him swinging a golf club and the three girls had signed.

"Well, I guess it's Sunday isn't it" he asked, looking at Donna and handing her the card.

Jana looked around at her family and what had just happened made her happy. She didn't feel like she knew her dad that well– or did she?– because he seemed to orbit around her world of school and her friends. She saw much more of her mother because she was the one who carted them around to activities, the movies, and whomever's house they wanted to go to spend the night.

She and Katie had thought for days about what to get him for a gift with the two of them blurting it out at the same time when they'd been at the mall just a few days before their trip. Katie now looked over at Jana while Mike unwrapped the package Katie had covered in royal blue tissue paper.

"'The Greatest Hits of The Beach Boys,'" Mike said, starting to smile but letting out a laugh that definitely shook the tension bubble, shattering it into a million pieces.

"Oh dear," Donna said, putting her hand over her mouth.

"Donna! Guess what? We're going to listen to 'Good Vibrations' all the way to Los Angeles!" He called out to his wife, motioning Katie and Jana to either side of him for a hug. "Girls, that's the most perfect gift I've ever gotten." He kissed each one on the top of her head and then Lisa came running.

"Wait! What about me! What happened? What did I miss?" She wrapped her arms around his waist and the four of them stood there in the motel parking lot in Amarillo in a hug, everyone forgetting about the smell of cattle down the road.

Back at the music store at the mall a week ago, Katie and Jana had gone over what felt like a million ideas but none of them seemed right for their dad. They thought about getting him a new golf shirt, golf balls... and then suddenly their idea well went dry.

They were sitting outside Musicland on a bench, Katie swatting the fake plant that kept trying to touch her, Jana not able to believe they couldn't figure it out.

"What would be good for the trip?" Katie had asked.

"We don't need a map," Jana had answered, though they weren't really asking and answering each other so much as they were continuing to throw ideas into the air. "Something about Route 66 maybe...."

"The Beach Boys!" They suddenly called out in unison, high fiving each other and making a beeline for the store.

Katie called Donna from the pay phone in the food court after they had found exactly what they wanted and they waited for Donna to pick them up outside of the Marshall Field's entrance, their designated spot.

"Total Route 66 Los Angeles stuff," Katie laughed as they looked at the tape.

"And with a tape player in the new station wagon," Jana added.

They didn't tell Donna what they had done but they could see– despite the fact that it seemed clear she wasn't a fan of one song– that she was proud of the girls. Once Mike pulled the car onto the interstate and they reached the outskirts of Amarillo, he slipped the cassette into the tape deck and "Surfin' USA" came on, everyone in the car singing along.

"Now I can play it over and over and over," Mike said, giving Donna a quick look.

"Don't get carried away, Dad," Katie told him, returning to her sarcasm.

After a few songs, he turned the music down and Jana found herself looking out the window at the changed landscape. Long gone were the grasslands of Oklahoma, now she saw cattle roaming a vastness of brown soil– not like the black nutrient rich soil back home in Illinois– that looked parched. Bushy plants dotted the landscape, filling the scene perfectly because nothing took over like a cornfield where you couldn't see where you were going– or where you'd been.

Jana played her mix tape that had taken her several hours over Casey Kasem's Top 40 radio show the previous Sunday morning to record all her new favorite songs off the radio just to have them for the long hours Mike had warned they'd be in the car.

"I'm bringing my headphones," Katie had stated at Oodles, the same night he told them details about the trip that only he seemed excited about. Diners, motels, two-lane roads. Jana didn't think it mattered to her and looking around at the others– especially Lisa who was watching a little girl her age celebrate her birthday several tables away– they didn't care either.

"That's good," Mike had said. "Keep yourself quiet in the car."

Jana had too many favorite songs to remember them all although they were now playing on the tape as they had been counted down by Casey Kasem. "Secret Separation" by The Fixx, "Glory of Love" by Peter Cetera, "If You Leave" by OMD, and "Out of Mind, Out of Sight" by The Models were just a sampling of the pop hits that inspired her in some way.

The songs made her think of her writing, maybe not consciously, but that they had something to say, or maybe it was just the sound of something she liked although the lyrics didn't mean much in her life. After all, the songs about love and break ups didn't really resonate with her although she loved "I Miss You" by Klymaxx. She couldn't relate to the love lost in the song and yet she did. She knew it was something she couldn't explain to anyone.

Jana was constantly creating stories in her head although in her "real" life, she'd never experienced so much of what she thought about. Love found, love lost, love found again, love rekindled. It went on and on. What would her life hold for her? She wondered. Would she write about all of that?

Jana looked over at Katie who also wore her headphones and was watching the scenery outside pass them by, not that it was changing much. Katie had experienced so much more than Jana.

And even without taking her long-term future into consideration, Jana thought about what would be a little bit of weird summer ahead of her, she knew. No longer was she in junior high, yet she wasn't really a high school student.

Who am I? Then she added. Who do I want to be? How do I get there? Who will travel this road of life with me?

She wanted to be writer, she knew that. And for whatever reason– because she saw everyone paired up around her? because it was constantly talked about that "the day she got married"– she saw someone traveling the road of what she hoped was a successful career with her. Right now though when she pictured that, it was as if someone had cut him out of the photo and all that was left was the white area and his outline.

24

But it wasn't because he'd been cut out, it was because he hadn't arrived into her life yet. He was unknown. Jana had no idea how much life she would need to experience before it was his turn to join the journey, as if being egged on by the director offstage who was looking at a script of Jana's life.

Several hours later, they found themselves crossing into New Mexico, the landscape not having changed much from Texas.

"But it doesn't look like another state," Lisa said, frowning as she looked at the scrub land they cruised by.

"It's invisible," Katie told her. "Invisible lines divide states."

"That's weird," Lisa said, looking bored by the idea.

"Land of Enchantment!" Mike called from the front seat. "And breakfast just ahead in Tucumcari!"

Jana looked toward the front of the car from behind her mother's seat, taking her eyes off the alien landscape for a moment. Her parents were discussing everything they had planned for Albuquerque, their next stop, and where they would spend several days.

As Mike pulled the station wagon into a Denny's in Tucumcari, Jana looked around.

What a sad little town, she thought.

"This is old sixty-six," Mike said proudly as he always announced each time they were able to travel on the old road.

"Did you eat here?" Lisa asked, oblivious to what Jana and Katie saw— depression and desolation.

Jana stretched her legs in the parking lot for a moment while she waited for her parents to climb out of the car. She looked around her and could see for miles behind the Denny's and a freight train running through town.

"I bet it doesn't even stop here," Katie whispered. "This place is awful. Can you imagine living here?"

Jana shook her head and wondered if Albuquerque would be any better. No, she worried that Albuquerque wouldn't be better. Especially since they arrived in Amarillo, Mike had talked up Albuquerque as if it were the best place ever.

"What if it's not as you remember it?" Donna had asked her husband at dinner at a steakhouse the evening before. "That wasn't exactly yesterday."

"I'm not worried," Mike had waved her off. "I'm sure it'll still be great."

"What's so great about it?" Lisa asked, ignoring her mother's prodding to eat her steak and instead focusing on her baked potato and the sour cream she kept dropping on top of it.

Jana watched her little sister for a moment, appreciating the questions she asked. No one thought Lisa asked too many questions and often they were things Jana wanted to know but was afraid to ask herself. Lisa hadn't developed any fear of that. Yet.

"It's this city that sprang up in the middle of the desert."

"Thanks to the atomic bomb," Donna reminded him, placing her fork on her plate. "They did build that nearby."

Mike ignored his wife. "The culture." He paused. "The sunshine."

"Does our motel have a swimming pool?" Katie asked. "If there's sunshine, I want to swim."

"Yes yes yes," Mike reassured her.

But now they were in depressing Tucumcari and Jana worried there was more of the same ahead.

Several hours later, they entered Tijeras Canyon of the Sandia Mountains via their continued journey on Interstate 40– and what was originally Route 66. Jana kept her eyes on the landscape, on the mountain range as it came closer into view, anticipating what was ahead.

"There she is!" Mike called out from the front seat where suddenly the city of Albuquerque was laid out in front of them, as if someone had opened the door and the city was on the other side of it.

Jana looked ahead and was surprised to see such a large city– not that she had bothered to look at the population anywhere. This definitely wasn't Tucumcari. Katie was glued to her window, too, the whole family taking in this new place. And one they'd been hearing so much about.

"I believe we take this first exit, is that right?" Mike asked Donna, who had both the road atlas and the Trip Tik from AAA on her lap.

"Yes," Donna said, checking both and then looking up as they made their way to Route 66. "And we can take it all the way to the motel."

"Central Avenue they call it here," Mike said, making a right at Tramway onto Route 66 and heading west.

Jana continued to watch out the window at the little motels surrounded by car dealers and other businesses. She felt as if she were taking a trip back in time. The only motel in their town that came close to this was the Lamplighter on Ogden Avenue, often a joke about prostitution.

"They have hourly rates," people always said.

But it didn't have the character or the age of any of these places that they passed in Albuquerque. Jana loved the names– Bow and Arrow Lodge, Desert Sands, Frontier Lodge, La Puerta Motor Lodge, Tewa Lodge, Sundowner– it was like a trip back in time.

"Our motel should be coming up on the right," Mike said, craning his neck toward the windshield, Jana thinking he wanted to be the first to spot it.

We don't even know the name of it, Jana wanted to remind him, biting her tongue.

They passed the state fairgrounds on the right and came into an area that looked like an old shopping section with various businesses and a gas station.

"There it is!" Mike called out, pointing his finger to the right at a sign which said, "The Twilight Sands Motel."

The sign stood tall and proud, the neon would show it off brightly that night. But for now they could see the name and what looked like some kind of plant that grew in the desert. And a series of stars that Jana thought must flutter around the words and the plant– she would learn it was a yucca– when it was lit up at night.

He pulled into the car port under the lobby sign and turned the car off, taking the keys with him.

"Ugh," Katie said. "Why does he do that?" She waved her magazine in front of her. "It's hot out."

"Bad habit," Donna said, digging in her purse for her set of keys. "He's used to being in the car without us."

"But you never do that to us, Mommy," Lisa pointed out, crawling from the very back of the station wagon, where she had a small space by herself, to the middle of the car to sit between her sisters.

"Because Mom is smarter than Dad," Katie said looking at Lisa and then they burst into laughter.

"Can we get out, Mom?" Jana asked. "Surely it's not a long walk to wherever our room is."

"Yes, that's a good idea," Donna said, looking relieved she didn't have to look more for her keys in what looked like a packed purse.

Jana was the first to exit the car, glad to feel the pavement under her, even if the sun was hot when she left the carport. She slipped her sunglasses on and stretched a moment before walking toward the swimming pool, a chain link fence around it and no one swimming in it. Jana stood for a moment, staring at the odd shaped pool, then took a good look at the surroundings. The two-story motel was dated and she tried to picture her dad there in the early sixties. He'd shown them photos, but now she wanted to see them again, now that she was actually there. Is this what it looked like then? She wondered.

She stared at the sign placed right at the sidewalk and noticed the "Free HBO" on the marquee for the first time.

Just like everyone else, Jana thought, turning back to the pool with its diving board and curved edges. It was like all the other motels they'd stayed in– or passed– on their trip. This one did have two floors, but the rooms all opened to the parking lot with colored doors in orange, yellow, and green.

Jana craned her neck to see that beyond the lobby sign, there was a sign for the restaurant and a night club. She giggled to herself, wondering if her parents would go there. She pictured her dad saying to her mom, "I went there in 1964! Come on!" But she knew her mom would wonder with whom he went there.

"Jana!" she heard her mother call and interrupt her thoughts, and looked to see her waving. "Room 106!"

Jana followed the station wagon across the nearly empty parking lot where everyone piled out and began to unload it.

The motel wasn't new, nor had it been painted in a while. But there was something Jana liked about it even though she couldn't put her finger on it. She reached into the middle seat to grab her tote bag and then to the back of the car for the duffel bag she used for a suitcase.

"Do we have time to swim?" Lisa asked, beating Jana to the question.

"Sure," Mike said, carrying three bags and directing Donna to their room, 105, the doors next to each other. Jana liked the orange door of their room, 106. Their parents had a yellow door.

"Sunny," Lisa said, pointing at it.

As Katie opened the door, she let out a "Yew!" and Jana– who was standing behind her– felt a burst of musty air flow out of the room and into the parking lot behind them.

"When was the last time someone stayed in this room?" Katie screeched.

"Oh girls," their mother said, opening the door of their room and then letting out a "Yew!" herself.

"Come on," Mike said, taking the luggage inside their room. "Leave the door open for a bit and it'll be fine."

The room was dark.

More dated, Jana thought, dropping her duffel bag on the brown and orange patterned bedspread.

"I'm sleeping with Katie," Lisa announced, putting her bag on the other bed and sitting down next to it.

"Does it ever occur to you that I might want to sleep alone?" Katie asked her sister, her arms on her hips.

Lisa pointed her head at Jana. "She tosses and turns a lot."

Katie rolled her eyes at Jana and Jana shrugged her shoulders.

"Let's go swimming!" Lisa announced, looking for her light blue swimsuit.

Their parents still in their room, the door open and having a conversation that the girls didn't care to know anything about, the three girls headed to the pool with their towels and sunglasses.

"The sun is much brighter here!" Donna called across the parking lot when she spotted them. "Be sure to put suntan lotion on first! At least the eight."

"I think all I have is two," Katie said with a smile. "And baby oil."

As Katie slathered the messy oil onto her body, Jana used the suntan lotion, knowing she would turn red– not a golden bronze like her sister who inherited a different skin tone than she although no one in the family knew where it came from– if she didn't use it. Jana could brown but not without some protection. She felt like the loaf of bread that was brushed with butter before it was placed into the oven for a deep brown sheen. She took a deep breath of the familiar lotion, the same lotion their mom had used on them for as long as they could remember. She called Lisa over to do the same for her, Lisa itching to get into the pool.

"I want to go off the diving board," she said, looking uncomfortable in the hot desert sun.

"You're at altitude," their dad had reminded them as they drove into town. "The air is thinner, the sun is hotter."

"So we won't be able to breathe?" Lisa had asked, confused. "Do we need space suits like astronauts?"

"No, not like that," he had said.

Katie didn't get in– "I need to get some rays," she had said– but Jana watched Lisa jump in off the diving board and then took a shallow dive herself, her hand skimming the surface of the eight-foot deep pool and feeling refreshed by the cool water.

When she came up for air, she held onto the concrete coping, resting her folded arms under her chin, feeling a chill in the air at first from the lack of humidity– "The humidity doesn't make it feel cold when you get out of the pool," Mike would explain to the girls later, "the moisture in the air is matched by the moisture in the water." So much of what he had said was starting to make sense now.

The familiar scent of chlorine permeated her skin and Jana took a deep breath. Another smell of summer, she thought.

"Jana! Come see me jump off the diving board!" Lisa called, having gotten out of the pool and was now walking quickly back to it.

"Don't walk too fast," Jana called to her, only saying it so she didn't have to hear it from Donna if something happened to Lisa.

Jana watched her sister, Katie opening her eyes, too, and they cheered Lisa on as she took a big leap off the board and right into the deep end.

It feels good just to sit here, Jana thought, swimming lazily over to the steps in the shallow end and sitting on the lowest one, her body submerged up to her neck.

Because it was getting late, the sun had started to set in the west and now it was quickly disappearing behind the two-story motel, the shadows growing long as it did because of the building hiding it.

"Hey," Katie called out to no one in particular. "I want to get some tan here."

"You'll have to wait until tomorrow," Jana teased her sister from across the pool.

"I hope we're lounging tomorrow. I need a break from playing sardines in the car."

The drive hadn't bothered Jana, but she also was looking forward to pool time. She found the changing landscape interesting, even inspiring, although she wasn't sure if that was the term she would use to describe it at that time in her life. She just knew it made her feel good and that it gave her hope and motivation in some way. And yet she still had no idea what she was going to write about.

Several days later when they drove north to Taos and then to see the Rio Grande Gorge, Jana would stand at the edge of it– not close enough to scare her mother– but close enough that she could clearly see there was a gap in the earth. And that gap was how she felt about her writing. She could look down at the river running through the bottom of the gorge and then ahead to the other side where the earth had separated.

That's my writing, she thought. It's over there and I feel like I can grasp it but I don't know how to get to it. There was a bridge, the bridge they had driven over to get there, but how was that in writing? Jana wondered, looking ahead. I know I'm supposed to do something, but how do I figure out what it is?

"Mom says to back up a bit," Katie said, coming up to Jana. "You know I would never tell you that."

Jana turned back with her sister and asked, "Do you think we'll end up like her?"

Katie laughed, her mouth opening wide so her face looked like it was all sunglasses and mouth, and said, "I hope not! I hope I never worry as much as she does."

"But how much does she really worry?" Jana asked her sister, there still physical space before they reached the rest of the family waiting for them. "She tells us not to do stuff and then she disappears with those romance books."

"Maybe it's a façade," Katie suggested.

"Or maybe she reads them so she doesn't worry," Jana wondered. "She tells us what not to do and then she goes off and reads and forgets about us."

"Until we show up looking like we were playing in a swamp," Katie laughed about the one time when they were younger they had gone to play in a field after the rain and found the mud more interesting than Donna did. They had arrived home covered in wet, messy mud, and she threatened to ground them for life.

Until Mike came home and laughed so hard, he had doubled over in the kitchen.

"Donna," Mike had said between breaths of laughter. "It's a good thing we never had any boys. This was a regular happening at my house growing up."

"Come on girls," Donna called back at the motel, walking across the parking lot to the pool and waving at the three of them.

Jana felt jolted out of her thoughts and climbed out of the pool, her body shaking from the hot, dry air. She wrapped her towel around her, sitting down a moment to dry off while Donna dried off Lisa, who shivered with goose bumps.

"Let's get ready for dinner," Donna said, urging them back to their room.

"We all need showers," Katie reminded her, looking sorry she had slathered on so much oil.

"Then hurry up," Donna said, Jana watching the interaction between them.

Katie rolled her eyes as she walked past Jana, her flip flops sounding as if they were sticking to the hot pavement. "Obviously these weren't meant for New Mexico," she said, checking to see if they actually were melting.

Chapter 4

"I think we'll take a break tomorrow," Mike said at dinner that night.

"Thank God," Donna told him, shaking her head. "We're all tired of being in the car."

"Girls, you can stay at the pool and we'll go out and get groceries. And explore."

Jana looked out the large glass windows of the motel restaurant, also looking like it hadn't been updated in some time and making her feel like she had disappeared into the sixties with the orange vinyl chairs and dark brown tables. The dark-skinned waitress placed in front of her a cheeseburger with green chile.

"If you don't like it, I'll eat it," her dad had said when she was hesitant to order it.

"I want to try it," Jana reassured him, her mother giving her a worried look that she wouldn't like it.

Lisa stuck to a grilled cheese and Katie a steak.

She bit into it and instantly liked the heat of the green chile, blending with the meat and cheese of the burger. She nodded at her dad who looked pleased, taking a bite of his green chile enchiladas.

Jana tried that night to get past the weird smell in the room, reminding herself about the history, the stories that the motel could tell. She knew it was true because her father had told them stories for years. He was just one of many people who had traveled through and stayed at The Twilight Sands. How many other stories were there? Jana wondered, turning over for a cool spot on the white pillowcase.

After dinner, Mike had stood in front of their two rooms and held up the newspaper, *The Albuquerque Journal.* "No need to change our Sunday routine," he said with a smile to the four girls who looked at him.

"Can we go back to the pool?" Lisa asked, not caring yet that every Sunday the entire family poured over the fat *Chicago Tribune.*

"I'll make it one better," Mike said. "We'll *all* go to the pool."

The girls changed back into their swimsuits and met their parents at the still empty pool, the sun still descending over the city, leaving the pool and parking lot with larger shadows.

Jana got in for a quick swim to cool off, diving into the deep end and coming up at the shallow end. She dried herself off and joined her parents and Katie at the table under the umbrella, each having taken a section of the paper, while not as thick as the *Chicago Tribune*, sizable enough.

"At least it won't take us all day to read it," Katie joked.

Reading the Sunday newspaper was one of several family rituals that had developed after the girls had learned to read. If someone asked anyone in the family how it started, they would all look at each other and shrug their shoulders. No one could pinpoint a day or time.

On Sundays at home, Mike made the girls pancakes– omelets for Donna and him– and everyone sat down at the kitchen table. Lisa wasn't so into it yet although she had learned from her sisters to start with the comics and then check out the tv section because "That's what we did," Katie would tell her, about their younger years.

"Look at these headlines," Katie said, taking the front page. "Mother Theresa was in Gallup. Where is Gallup? Is that like the Gallup poll that we hear about?" She asked.

Jana looked over her shoulder at an article about a biologist who had gone missing in the mountains. There were no mountains to get lost in at home, she thought. Just cornfields. And yet no one ever seemed to get lost in those.

"And Queen Elizabeth turned sixty!" Katie said. "Happy birthday to her!"

"Do you think she'll be queen forever?" Donna asked Mike who shrugged.

"She's better looking than Charles, that's for sure," Katie reminded them.

"The US Open final was today," Mike said randomly, looking at his watch.

"Golf on tv is so boring, Dad," Katie reminded him. "You fall asleep every time you watch it."

Jana flipped through the sections of the newspaper– there was a farm and ranch section– and then she scanned the color advertising sections, perusing the Columbia House record and tape club. Eleven records or tapes for a penny. She spent a moment looking at ones she would choose if she wanted to join. Maybe one day but not now– she was saving her money for Los Angeles where she and Katie knew they could get some fun clothes their friends and classmates in the Midwest wouldn't have.

When the first section reached her and she read about the apartheid protests in the US, people wanting the people in South Africa to be free, she sat back in her chair and looked around.

How lucky we are, she thought, grateful for her family, not caring for the moment about anything that didn't feel cool in her life.

"There's a coupon for French's steak sauce," Katie said interrupting Jana's thoughts. "This is for you on Father's Day, Dad. How to grill without a grill."

"Ooh, I want the free Reese's Pieces in Cheerios!" Lisa called out, looking over her sister's shoulder.

"We got you a bag of Reese's the other day," Katie reminded Lisa.

"But this one is in a box of Cheerios," Lisa reminded her sister, sticking her finger right onto the ad.

"It's cheaper to buy the bag. Since when you do you eat Cheerios?"

"I've never had Cheerios," Lisa admitted.

"Sizzle! Point!" Katie teased her.

Jana looked up and both parents were shaking their heads. Kate went back to reading out loud that the new Jolt cola had twice as much caffeine as any other soda. And real sugar.

Katie's final comment came from the sale papers. "Hey, we could use some ice cube trays," she said. "They're on sale. It's hot here."

"That's what the ice machine is for," Mike told her.

"Is there one?" Katie asked, looking at Jana and the two of them realized they hadn't completely explored the motel.

"Isn't that the first thing you two used to do when we arrived at a hotel?" Mike asked, checking to see how the Chicago Cubs did the previous day. "Ah, you must be getting older if you forgot."

He tapped Donna who was next to him. "Our girls have forgotten about the ice machine," he teased.

"We never taught Lisa that, did we?" Katie asked.

"What?" Lisa called from the pool, bobbing up and down, in and out the water, attempting to do handstands in the shallow end. "I heard my name."

"But it wouldn't be much fun for her to do it without us," Jana said, kind of not caring anymore.

"Yeah, we'll skip that tradition," Katie said a little sadly. "Moving on…what else is in these sale papers that might be interesting?"

By the time they left the pool because the sun had set so much that there wasn't much daylight left, Jana felt tired and was glad to climb into bed. She picked up her magazine but let it drop to the floor, her eyes drooping shut.

I can read tomorrow, she thought, drifting off to sleep.

The next morning, surprisingly, while Lisa opted to go with their parents to run errands, Katie announced at breakfast that she wanted to catch up on "Days of Our Lives."

"You can do that at home," Mike reminded his daughter. "Isn't the VCR set to tape it for you?"

Katie shrugged her shoulders. "I want to watch."

Jana was more surprised she was willing to sit in a dark room and watch when they were surrounded by clear skies, perfect sunbathing weather.

On the way back to the room from the glass-windowed restaurant, Jana tagged along with her dad to the motel lobby, wanting to see what interesting things they had there that she might take home as souvenirs from their trip. And postcards. She had promised several of her friends she would send postcards.

"At least Los Angeles," they all had said at separate times.

Jana found the free motel ones and picked up a few, planning to draw a stick figure of herself on a lounge chair at the pool in the photo card. Mike fished for some coins in his pocket and handed them to the moustached man across the counter. She took a look at the headlines, something about the "Gettysburg of the West"– the reenacted battle at Glorieta Pass of which she had heard nothing about in history class– but knowing that her dad wanted to read about Ray Floyd winning the US Open.

"He's forty-three," Mike said with a grin pointing at the paper. "He's the oldest US Open champ. Maybe there's hope for me yet."

Shortly after 10:00, Jana settled into the same fiberglass lounge chair as the day before, the pool to herself, and pulled out her pink notebook and a pen. She set that down and wrote in her journal– the other notebook– and caught up on all that happened– before opening to a blank page in the pink notebook again.

She looked around at the pool area, feeling some loose sense of being on her own. As if this was what adulthood felt like, to be alone, to be on one's own. From where she sat, she could see the Route 66 traffic going by, a regular day for most people. Of course, she had no idea what life in Albuquerque was like.

What should I write? What story should I tell? she asked herself, looking to the pool water as if the inspiration were there waiting for her to grab it and start writing. Had she missed it in the pool water of that first night in Southern Illinois? This time all she could see was the mirror image of the Twilight Sands sign staring back at her.

Jana sat back on her lounge chair and stared at the water, thinking about the history of the very place where she sat.

How many people visited here? She wondered. And how many swam in this pool?

"I can't believe I've had to miss two episodes," Katie said, flopping down on the lounge chair next to Jana and interrupting Jana's thoughts. "It's like I missed a year."

"You better put suntan lotion on," Jana said, handing her sister the brown plastic bottle.

"Why?" Katie laughed, standing up to rearrange her red towel. "I've got my baby oil."

"The sun's a lot stronger here," she told her sister.

"Are you Mom?" Katie laid back down, readjusting the small ponytail of hair she'd pulled her curly bob into on top of her head. Then she retied her pastel pink bikini top.

Jana shrugged her shoulders and let the bottle drop from her hand into her tote bag. When she looked down to make sure it had landed in the bag– and not on the concrete pool deck– she saw the pink notebook where she had dropped it a bit ago, still not feeling it. She felt inspired, but not more than that. At least not yet.

What could I write? she wondered, laying back and shutting her eyes. What story could I tell?

Jana had stories she wanted to tell, that she knew. The pieces came to her all the time. The challenge she felt– although she didn't understand it– was that she wasn't sure how she was supposed to tie it all together. It was as if she were collecting details, but she didn't have the big story that was the thread to make it one complete novel.

She drifted off, although she wasn't sure for how long, and woke when she heard the squeaking of the chain link fence and Lisa running to her sisters.

"Don't run across the pool deck!" Jana heard her mom call, probably from the car in the parking lot.

"She never stops, does she?" Katie asked Lisa, who excitedly shared her adventures of driving around Albuquerque that morning.

"That doesn't sound like fun to have spent the morning with Mom and Dad," Katie said.

"Why do they bother you so much?" Lisa asked Katie, staring at her until she answered.

Katie shrugged her shoulders and readjusted her bikini. "You'll understand when you get older. They won't seem so cool to you."

"They'll always be cool to me," Lisa informed her sister, Jana staying out of the discussion, thinking about how hot the sun was.

When Lisa left to put on her swimsuit, Jana took a dive into the pool and then swam a few laps, feeling not a sense of freedom, but a word she remembered from vocabulary somewhere along the way– unencumbered. It was as if she didn't have a worry in the world, her mind felt free with no school to think about, no worries about the babysitting ahead of her that summer. She felt as if her mind could rest. As it rested, she finally felt the freedom– that's where the freedom came in– to pursue her writing, her story telling.

Lisa returned to the pool, their father following, Jana watching him almost skip across the parking lot. There was something in his step she hadn't seen before. A happiness. He was feeling free, too, she thought. No work to worry about. No leaks in the roof to think about. And she noticed her parents didn't seem to be picking at each other like usual at home.

Maybe this vacation was a good idea, she thought.

Katie was playing with Lisa in the pool, a game of volleyball with the big yellow and white striped blow up ball they had brought with them.

Mike sat down in the lounge chair on the other side of Jana, where Lisa had dropped her towel before she jumped into the pool with the ball.

"Isn't this great?" he asked, adjusting his sunglasses and getting comfortable in his khaki shorts and blue and white striped polo shirt.

Suddenly– and Jana wasn't sure where it came from– Jana had confidence enough to ask her father about love. Maybe it was her own feeling of freedom to write, to tell a story. Or maybe it was because her dad didn't look so preoccupied as he always was at home.

"Dad," she said, quietly, feeling tentative.

"Hmm," he said, laying back in the lounge chair and letting out a yawn, the kind that made him seem as if he were relaxed to be at the pool. And happy.

"How do you know you're in love?"

Mike immediately turned to Jana and lifted his sunglasses to his forehead. "Do you think you're in love?"

Jana realized he looked slightly panicked and laughed. "Oh no, Dad. I'm not in love. Boys and I don't seem to be on the same wavelength." She shrugged her shoulders. "I'm just wondering."

He looked relieved and slid his sunglasses back on his face, laying back on the lounge chair again. "Hmmm. How do I describe it?"

She watched him for a moment, realizing it might take him a while to answer, so she turned back to watching her sisters in the pool, and tried to forget that she had asked, worried maybe she had asked the wrong thing. Maybe she didn't want his response.

"I'm not sure there's one answer to your question," Mike finally said. "There are so many ways that you can love a person. But love also morphs and changes in your life. I'm not sure Katie has ever been in love. What she experiences is infatuation, nothing long term." He stopped and shook his head. "I'm not ignoring your question. I guess I haven't thought about it for a long time."

Without moving toward her, he reached over and touched Jana's arm, "Let me think about this. Is that okay?"

Jana shrugged her shoulders. "I don't need an answer today," she said. "It's just something I've been thinking about."

"Good. I'll get back to you on that."

They sat quietly for a few moments and then Mike started to speak again.

"It is sad– the Twilight Sands isn't as great as I remember it," Mike admitted. "I'm not so sure your mom is happy about us staying in this area of town. It's not as nice as it used to be. I still like it, but I can see that it's changed."

"Why is that?"

Mike shrugged his shoulders. "People use the interstate now. They prefer quick meals in the car or the drive through. They want all their motel rooms to look the same so they know what to expect."

"That sounds boring," Jana said.

"That's why we're taking as much of Route 66 as we can."

"Why did you like it so much here?" Jana asked him, realizing she hadn't seen much yet beyond the drive to the motel from the interstate.

"It's very different from Chicago," he admitted. "How can you beat this sunshine?" He held up his arms around them. "Doesn't it make you feel good?"

Jana nodded. "I guess."

"Wait until you see the views." He shook his head. "Hey! Only dive off the diving board!" he called to Lisa and then to Katie, "You're watching your sister, remember?"

Jana knew Katie rolled her eyes once she turned away. She looked at their dad and thought about how he probably didn't want to be the adult all the time. It seemed easier for their mom, but then relaxing didn't appear to be in her vocabulary unless she had a book or magazine in her hand. She loved to read her romance novels, that the entire family knew.

Each Christmas Katie snuck into her "stash" and made a list of what she had so they could find the new ones she hadn't bought yet. They painstakingly wrapped them up individually for her to open on Christmas morning. And no one looked happier than Donna with a new stack of romances to read.

"So it was the weather and the views?" Jana asked, trying to understand.

Mike turned to Jana. "Haven't you ever felt connected to a place? Maybe you haven't experienced that yet," he realized. "When you do, you'll understand."

"So why didn't you move here?"

Mike laughed.

"You weren't married yet, right? You didn't even know Mom."

"Are you trying to change the course of your life?" he asked her.

It was Jana's turn to shrug her shoulders, then she felt a little embarrassed that maybe she shouldn't have asked the question. She watched her sisters in the pool, now playing a game of tag with each other, Katie finally having given up on not getting her hair wet.

"Jana," Mike said. "I met a woman when I was here."

She turned to her dad, who watched Katie and Lisa play…but not really. He was lost in another time.

That explains a lot, she thought, then wondering what her mom thought.

"Mom knows, doesn't she?"

Mike nodded and Jana knew he couldn't look at her now. He'd just shared something she'd never known anything about. Not even when he'd shown the slide show. There had never been any women in them.

"Could you have moved here?"

He shrugged his shoulders. "You always look back and wonder," he said. "But we went on to Los Angeles. And then we headed home. I met your mom two years later."

"But we're here. You must be wondering what she's like now."

"I do," he said. "It might be why it took me so long to come back. Why we always went to Florida when we could have easily come this way to the Southwest and the West Coast for our vacations."

It began to make sense to Jana, why he had never taken them to a place he always talked so much about. Because he was afraid to revisit it. He was afraid his love for the memory might not ring true.

They went quiet and a minute later the squeak of the chain link fence gate signaled the arrival of Donna. After she finished lecturing everyone about suntan lotion, she walked over to the patio table with a dated orange umbrella– the kind with fringe on the ends and a flower print underneath– where she sat down in the shade with one of her Harlequin romances. Mike stood up and walked over to the table and sat with her.

Jana watched her parents from behind her sunglasses, hoping they weren't watching her. Her dad sat down in the lounge chair that was next to the patio table, looking content even without swim trunks on. Jana figured he was itching to golf– his clubs somewhere buried in the car despite her mother's unhappiness that he brought them– "You're the only one who golfs," she reminded him, clucking her tongue not so much about the space it would take up in the car but the time it would take from the rest of the family.

"I'm sure he's hoping for some time away from the rest of us girls," Katie had whispered to Jana after the scene in the driveway of their house the day before they left, Jana almost bursting out from laughter, knowing that was probably the truth.

She shut her eyes, not wanting to go back to the stuffy motel room. She knew the next day her dad had promised– his word– that they would begin touring Albuquerque and the surrounding areas. That meant they should enjoy a day of doing nothing. Enjoy the sun, she reminded herself. We'll be back in the car tomorrow.

The sun didn't last though. While they were enjoying it, no one bothered to look up and see a storm forming over the mountains.

"Look at that," Mike said pointing at the dark clouds making their way over the top of the Sandias. "That's quite a storm coming."

And with that, the lightening cracked, sending Donna up off her chair, higher than the others. "Let's go!" She called out, quickly gathering up the family.

"But it's not raining yet?" Katie called, still in the center of the pool and pointing at the dark sky that hadn't reached them yet.

"It's coming fast!" Donna called, her hands on her hips. "Get out of the pool NOW!"

Katie didn't move that fast, but she did get out of the pool. And because Katie had the room key, Jana waited for her sister. "My God," Katie said when she reached the lounge chair and wrapped her big towel around herself. "You'd think there was a shark in the pool."

Donna had long left the pool, taking Lisa– and her beach ball– by the hand to their room while Mike waited for Jana and Katie.

Jana didn't tell anyone, but she dreaded sitting in the stinky and dark motel room. Katie turned on the television and found MTV. "Or we could watch some R-rated movie on HBO," she teased. "I guess those aren't on this early though." She looked at Lisa who was sitting on the bed looking bored, her arms wrapped around Chuck.

"He has a hole in his arm," she said.

"Then he should eat more bananas and he might heal faster," Katie said, settling into the "Papa Don't Preach" video that was playing.

Jana reached into the desk drawer where she thought she had seen a sewing kit. "Aha," She said pulling it out, everything she needed to fix Chuck.

"See," Katie said. "Who's the better sister today?" She asked, not really expecting an answer.

"Jana," Lisa said anyway, watching Jana sew up Chuck.

The stuffed monkey had seen better days– his brown fur was fraying in spots, but from the moment Lisa had opened him the Christmas she turned three, she'd been attached to him. So much so that the day he disappeared in the house, Lisa crying while everyone else turned it upside down frantically searching for him, Donna and Mike chastised themselves for not having bought several and kept the spare Chucks packed away in a closet.

However, all turned out well when Jana found Chuck in the twisted sheets from Lisa's bed crammed in a white plastic laundry basket where they were waiting their turn in the washing machine.

"He should eat more bananas anyway," Jana said as she handed him back to her sister when she was finished sewing up the hole in his arm. "He's not getting enough potassium."

"Um, whatever that is," Lisa said.

"Just one of those things you'll understand when you're old like us," Katie said.

The next day they traveled north to Santa Fe and Taos, walking around both plazas, all five of them seemingly with their necks craned toward the windows to drink in what looked like an endless landscape of brown dotted with green plants. Cactus, sage, tumbleweed. Mountains jutted out of the ground, not in the gentle sloping grassy way they did in other parts of the country.

*****

"Go golfing today," Katie begged, pushing her pancakes around her plate at the Twilight Sands restaurant the following morning after they had spent the previous day exploring Northern New Mexico. "I can't stand the idea of being in the car again. Or seeing one more cactus." She slouched back into the orange vinyl booth and sighed.

They were seated in the corner of the restaurant, the light filling the entire place with its glass windows that ran floor to ceiling. Jana liked the restaurant. While she could definitely tell people sometimes smoked in there– the smoking section was off in a corner now– she felt like she was in a time warp each time they walked in there for breakfast. There seemed to be a few regulars who the waitresses immediately filled coffee cups for while the patrons opened their newspapers.

"That's a good idea," Donna said, her face brightening up. "I need to do laundry. You can golf, the girls can swim, and we can meet back up for dinner."

Jana watched everyone at the table converse, once again feeling as if she were on the outside of the conversation. She had learned early– especially with Katie around– that she didn't always need to add her opinion. While Katie was definitely the most vocal family member– and the most dramatic– there were times when she did make sense. Because Donna agreed with her, Jana knew this was one of those times.

Donna's face suddenly looked relaxed, a look that Jana didn't think she wore too often.

"You're choosing laundry over me?" Mike asked, raising his eyebrows at his wife.

Donna smiled, laughed, and said, "I am."

"And telling me to go golfing?"

"Yes," she said, smiling more.

He shook his head. "The altitude must be getting to you. But I'll go."

"She's not choosing any of that over you," Katie reminded him, sitting up again and gathering up several bites of pancake to eat. "She's choosing to be out of the car today. Especially because we know we're in the car all day again soon."

Donna and Mike shared a smile and Mike said, "Fine."

Jana hadn't minded the car as much as Katie and her mom did, but she was glad for a day to relax by the pool. It felt like such a luxury to walk across the parking lot to the pool. And because so few people used it, she sometimes could pretend– in her mind at least– that it was her own.

As she made herself at home in the late morning desert sunshine, she did just that.

What is the life that I want? she wondered, also wondering what it might be like to have her own swimming pool. She remembered a girl named Lucy from fifth grade whose family had a pool and her birthday fell in the summer so there was always a pool party. But the fun ended when Lucy's dad was transferred to New York that August and Lucy moved away.

The motel was quiet, the few other people who stayed having left early that morning as Jana and her family walked over to the Twilight Sands restaurant for breakfast.

This is the closest I've ever felt to us having our own pool, she thought, using her imagination to take away the parking lot that created a divide between them and their rooms. One day I'll have my own pool in my backyard.

As she lay there, listening to her sisters still splashing around in the pool– probably the only time that Katie acted like she wasn't too cool for the rest of them– and the cars traveling by on Central– Jana's thoughts took her back in time.

She imagined that it wasn't 1986, but instead 1964, the year that her dad and his buddy Danny took their trip across the country on Route 66. She was an onlooker to the scene, as she would be as the one telling the story.

And what story was that? She wondered, picturing her dad– based on the photos she had seen of him on the trip and now wishing she had paid more attention to each time he made them watch the slide show. He had a crew cut and he always wore some sort of short-sleeved button down shirt, the kind that needed to be pressed, and khaki pants or long blue plaid shorts.

Jana wasn't thinking about how this woman her dad met might have altered the history with her parents because she knew she couldn't change the past. But she could think about the story around it and how it might have played out differently.

Still, it was hard to think of her dad as a man she found interesting in a romantic way.

He's my dad, she thought, knowing Katie especially would be repulsed by the thought.

But when he was in his early twenties, he had dreams and hopes.

Did those dreams and hopes come true? Jana wondered. Would he answer that question if she asked him?

She pictured a woman with jet black hair, curly from rollers, in a printed shift dress with a big straw hat and cat eye sunglasses. Why might she be at the motel? Jana thought. A woman who had to look vastly different from her own mother who had long straight brown hair in the photos Jana had seen of her in the 1960s.

And then she remembered the old night club that was around the corner from the restaurant. It looked like it had been turned into storage but if one looked past all the boxes and extra beds and dressers, the red carpet and small tables were still there, as if one day they had decided not to use it, but left everything as it was in case they changed their minds.

That was probably where they met, the woman now wearing a printed dress that spun around her on the dance floor, her dad in a tie. Then they would sit at one of the little tables and enjoy some sort of mixed drink– didn't they drink a lot of daiquiris in that time?– those mixed drinks she knew nothing about but sounded so sophisticated. She wondered– would they talk about who they were? And the life they wanted to have?

Maybe it ended there, Jana thought, when she found out he was from Chicago, bound for Los Angeles, then back home to Chicago to a sales job that he would start right after the trip ended.

Or maybe not. Maybe they didn't think that far ahead. Maybe she showed him all around town and her life in Albuquerque, a bustling town at the time, her father had told them, growth everywhere between the Rio Grande River and the Sandia Mountains.

That's when Jana remembered the box.

Once when they had been left home alone when Lisa was three and they were bored, she and Katie had decided to snoop through their parents' belongings in their bedroom. Really, they just wanted to look at Donna's jewelry, which always seemed sacred to them.

Donna had a drawer filled with jewelry in her dresser and she always wore a necklace, bracelet, and earrings– as well as her wedding ring. Katie and Jana often thought she slept in her big hoop earrings because they hardly remembered a time when she didn't have any earrings in her ears, especially those.

They looked through her jewelry, admiring all the gold, the shiny stones, and the hoop earrings that she loved, all laid out so she could find everything easily. Katie closed the drawer slowly to keep everything from moving, a dead giveaway that they had been snooping.

But that day they knew they had a lot of time, Lisa was sleeping and Mike and Donna were at a wedding, so they moved onto the closet, pulling out her dresses and admiring the patterns and styles.

They both loved the way Donna had dressed from a young age, always making sure she looked put together. Her organization of her dresser and closet reflected that as well. Katie and Jana both knew they wanted always to be that way themselves although it wasn't something they ever said out loud as if they had to keep it secret.

While Katie was running her hands over Donna's long white taffeta wedding dress that hung in the back of the walk-in closet, Jana had turned around to their father's often neglected side. The girls never found his things as interesting but on this day, Jana saw a box marked "Trip" and ignored what Katie was doing and pulled the box out from where it sat under his pressed slacks.

"Dad's stuff is never as interesting," Katie said, waving it off.

Jana ignored her and opened the box. Quickly she forgot she was a ten year old rummaging through her father's things. There were postcards and matchbooks– plus plastic swizzle sticks– in pink, black, and mint green. The postcards had no writing on the back, probably ones he had picked up along the way.

"Boring," Katie said, taking a peek over Jana's shoulder and then standing with her hands on her hips. "I think I'm about done."

She walked out of the closet and back into the master bedroom– Jana figuring she went to the bathroom to check for any new makeup Donna had bought. That was Katie's true love, even more than the jewelry. Katie devoured the Avon catalog each time the Avon lady left it in the plastic bag on their front door.

Jana stayed right where she was and continued looking at postcards of small motels with swimming pools in their parking lots and funky neon signs. There were other assorted items, like printed paper napkins– although she wondered why people saved them because they ripped and crushed easily– and a few maps. But at the bottom of the box, practically stuck to the cardboard as if it had been wet at some point, there was an envelope. There was even a motel ash tray. None of the names of the places would resonate with Jana until the years later on the trip though.

She tried to lift out the contents of the yellowed paper envelope and found several photos, the kind from the 1960s, filled with bright and bold colors and a white border. Her dad at various points along the way, including his parent's house where he and Danny started the trip, standing in front of Danny's red convertible. Then he and Danny in Los Angeles by the ocean. And other places that Jana didn't recognize, nor marked on the back.

It didn't mean much to Jana and she continued to leaf through the pile, thinking Katie was right, it was boring even though she kind of liked looking at the motel postcards.

When she reached the bottom of the stack there was her father standing with a woman in what Jana would realize in Albuquerque was the Twilight Sands lobby. She could see the sign in the large glass windows in the background.

Mike was smiling as she had never seen him smile before, wearing a white pressed short-sleeved shirt with khaki pants, his favorite uniform, Donna always teased him. His arm was around a woman in a white dress with a green floral print. She held a small black patent leather purse and her short hair was curled all around her head. Was that her?

Jana turned the photo over and read her father's neat handwriting where it said, "Gloria and me, Albuquerque."

Gloria. That must be her.

Katie had come looking for Jana at that moment and Jana had quickly shoved everything back in the box, hoping she did it so it didn't look like she ever touched it. Not that she knew if her father would notice. Or if he ever looked at the contents of the box.

"Are you still looking at that boring stuff?" Katie asked, holding Lisa's hand, Lisa holding a fairly new Chuck under her arm and looking sleepy from her nap. "Let's go outside or something. I'm bored looking at their stuff."

Jana knew then she couldn't ask her dad about the woman in the photo, and yet she also knew– because he told them when he started making them watch the slides– that the trip had taken place long before he'd met Donna in a hospital one day where she worked as a nurse.

She quickly forgot about the box. And her father's past. Until she was laying on a lounge chair at the Twilight Sands pool and somehow– she wasn't sure how– it all came flooding back. The hard part, Jana knew, was that she couldn't say anything to anyone. How could she bring it up when she and Katie had been doing something they weren't supposed to be doing?

And yet at the same time, she wasn't really sure all that she remembered. She so badly wanted to go back in time to that box and go through everything again now that they were on the trip. And she wondered why her dad didn't share everything in the box except the photos? He could have done that.

None of that made sense to her now, although she could picture this woman, who looked almost like she thought she would, not that Jana had any idea where her ideas of the woman's looks came from. It was something she had created in her mind.

What Jana still couldn't wrap her head around, especially as a fourteen year old, was why her dad had left the relationship behind. And while she knew it would have altered the history of her own life, she couldn't help but imagine what would have happened if the love story had played out differently.

It got complicated, wondering how life might have been different for her mother. Jana felt bad for her thoughts and pulled out a magazine to read, wanting to forget about it all for a while. It was feeling too heavy and too challenging for her to understand.

Jana didn't get far into her thoughts when she heard Donna calling to her and Katie, who was on the lounge chair next to Jana.

"Girls!" Donna called, waving, although Katie never opened her eyes to see, walking across the parking lot, her sandals flapping on her feet. "I need one of you to come with me to the laundromat."

"That's you," Katie said, digging into her lounge chair. "I'm not moving until 'Days of Ours Lives' comes on in forty-five minutes."

Jana looked at her sister and knew she wasn't getting out of it. She didn't relish the idea of sitting in the laundromat but she thought she'd make the most of it and grabbed her notebook and pen, leaving her tote bag in the room, and helping Donna carry the laundry two blocks east on Route 66 to the Laundry Basket.

Jana looked up at the top of the one-story brick building and thought about how cool would be if they had a big sign that was fashioned like a plastic laundry basket, replicating the brown and green ones they had at home.

No one would miss it, she thought, proud of her advertising idea.

"I guess this isn't a place you've ever been," Donna laughed as Jana absorbed their surroundings.

"I don't think so," Jana agreed, not having known a day when they didn't have a washer and dryer at home, the laundry room set right off the kitchen where the door to enter from the garage was located.

"You're lucky," Donna said, with a sigh.

With glass windows across the front of the space situated in the middle of a strip mall that included four other businesses, it– like everything in Albuquerque but their rooms at the Twilight Sands– was filled with light. Extra-large washers and dryers lined the walls, carts on wheels sitting in random places where people had left them when they'd finished their laundry. Music played over a speaker system that could barely be heard over the hum and whirring washers and dryers. Jana recognized the song "Cruel Summer" by Bananarama as they walked into the establishment where a man in the back behind a counter doing paperwork barely looked up when they opened the door.

Jana thought about the many times she had seen laundromats on television or the one they passed in Naperville, sandwiched between the Ace Hardware store and the seasonal Dairy Queen where Katie was slated to work the rest of the summer. But in person it was completely different, the oversized avocado green Speed Queen washers and dryers filled every row in the space. Maximizing output, she pictured her father saying, making it a lesson in business economics as he sometimes did.

Donna used two rolling metal carts to sort the clothes, Jana watching her do it, knowing whose underwear was whose by size and shape. Only her and Katie's things seemed to be closely related, mostly because they were so close in age, size, and style. Occasionally Jana found something of Katie's in her clean laundry and vice versa for Katie although Katie would act like she had no idea that it was Jana's.

"Oh? That's yours. Oops," she would say nonchalantly when Jana would see one of her shirts sitting on Katie's dresser with the rest of her clean laundry that she hadn't put away yet.

"You know it's mine," Jana would mumble with a snap in her voice, not caring so much that Donna had messed up the laundry, after all she did do it for the five of them, but that Katie hadn't bothered to bring it back to Jana, as Jana did each time something of Katie's landed in her clean laundry.

And yet inside her, Jana knew the real reason was that Katie wanted to wear it. Still, she never asked. She just waited for their mother to mess it up.

Donna slipped Jana several quarters. "I should have taught you girls to do laundry a long time ago," she sighed, pointing her head toward the washing machine directly in front of Jana. "Quarters go in first, then a cup of the laundry detergent." She placed the zipped plastic bag of powdered detergent in front of Jana on top of the washing machine and then pointed her finger at the basket of colors and darks. "Regular cycle," she said.

It took Jana a moment to figure it out, surveying the machine, and then seeing which item went where.

"I always thought it was better if I took care of the laundry," Donna said, Jana not really sure if her mother was talking to her. "I want you girls to do well in school. I want you to know that you had every opportunity to do well."

Jana tried to listen, but found it somewhat of a challenge as she didn't want to mess up the laundry either. The bell of the door of the laundromat chimed and a Native American lady in a print dress walked in with two big cloth bags of laundry. Jana smiled to herself, the bags were almost as big as the petite woman with dark weathered skin and a long black and gray braid running down her back. She wore a long, chunky turquoise necklace around her neck.

She looks cultural, Jana thought, having had limited exposure to Native Americans.

"But one day when you have kids of your own, you'll understand," Donna was still talking.

Jana knew she should listen to her mother because Donna had never been as open about her life as their father. Mike loved to tell stories of his life while Donna listened with the girls, Jana watching her for reactions, knowing that surely she had heard all of these stories before. Maybe her mother did a good job acting like she was listening even though her mind was a million miles away in a romance novel. Maybe wondering how the most recent one she was reading would end (although Jana knew all the endings were the same– the couple always somehow ended up together).

She watched her mom as she kept talking, listening but not really paying attention to what she was saying. She couldn't snap out of watching her, her mannerisms, her ability to laugh at what she just said, knowing it didn't sound the same when it was verbalized versus what it was in her head. Donna's tight perm had loosened somewhat over the nearly week since they'd left home. Jana knew she liked it to be curly but not that just-from-the-beauty-salon tight look. And she'd spend the next few weeks maintaining just the right curl with a black plastic pick and a bottle of hair spray.

The photos Jana had seen of her parents when they were younger showed a much different couple. Her father sported a crew cut in the days of his Route 66 trip although now he wore his hair somewhat longer on his head but short like most men. And Donna had long brown hair that was always tied back or, when she was working, pulled into a bun behind her white nurse's cap.

She'd cut it not long after Jana was born.

"See, look what you did," Katie would tease Jana when they saw photos after Jana's birth. "You drove Mom to cut her hair."

"Oh Katie," Donna would interrupt. "Don't blame your sister. It was too much work with the two of you to take care of."

"Exactly, Jana was too much work," Katie would tease with her million-dollar smile directed at Jana, who simply ignored her sister although she'd always heard that Katie was the one who was too much work. When their parents discussed having the two girls, they often said how easy Jana was after Katie.

"You came out ready to run the world," Mike would say, letting out a big sigh. "And just thinking about that day wears me out."

But her father had also once told her that Jana had been easier because he wasn't afraid as much as he was with Katie, of dropping her, of doing the wrong thing.

"By then I'd made so many mistakes and Katie didn't seem any different so I didn't worry as much," he joked. "I'd like to think that I'm partly responsible for you being more introspective than your sister." At which time he would pat her on the head and she knew he meant it to be the most positive thing in the world.

"You'll understand when you have your own family," Donna would add. Again.

Just then– in the laundromat– Jana realized that had been one of their mother's key sayings for their entire lives. "You'll understand when you have your own family."

Jana watched her mother, the laundry now spinning around the washing machines with the glass-door windows– Jana wishing they had that at home, thinking it would at least make laundry more interesting to see the colors meshing together like a kaleidoscope. Donna waved Jana to the row of orange plastic molded seats by the window along Central Avenue.

Donna pulled her paperback romance novel out of her purse and started to read. Jana placed her notebook and pen on the empty seat next to her but she didn't open them just yet. She watched the Native American woman sorting her laundry, mostly filled with denim pants, and then craned her head to watch the traffic go by.

She wasn't really watching the traffic though, she was thinking about what her mother said. And then Jana began to wonder, What if I never have a family? Would that disappoint them? And she wondered if it was possible to have a career and a family. How could one person possibly have enough time to do everything?

No, she thought. It's not that. Do I even want a family? she wondered. She couldn't picture herself sitting in the passenger seat of a station wagon, her unknown husband driving, kids in the backseat. The thought reminded her of the game of Life, the little colored cars and the pink and blue sticks that represented the people.

It really was like that, wasn't it?

She didn't know how long she sat there deep in thought until Donna got up, tapping Jana on the shoulder. "Time for the dryer."

With the loads safely tucked into the dryers– also with glass windows– Jana stood watching the clothes spin around, the heat making them wear worthy again, while Donna returned to the seats and her book. The Native American woman sat at the opposite end of the orange chairs, her arms crossed in front of her, her eyes shut.

Maybe she didn't sleep well last night, Jana thought, turning back to the clothes again. But then she looked at Donna who was deep into the book she was reading. This one about an airline pilot and stewardess.

"Isn't the new word flight attendant?" Katie had asked when she picked up the back to read the blurb about the book. "Now that they're letting men do the job, too."

"It's an old book," Donna had said, pointing at the photo on the front that looked at least ten years old.

"How can you read the same ones over and over? It's bad enough they all end the same way," Katie reminded her.

Donna shrugged her shoulders. "They go to interesting places."

"Hmmm," Katie said, flipping through and wondering here this one took them. "I see Paris…Okay, I'll let you have that."

"When was the last time they went to Paris on 'Days of Our Lives'?" Jana teased her sister.

Katie waved Jana off. "That's tv. That's different. Mom likes to use her imagination more than me."

There was something to be said for that comment, too, Jana had thought. TV was someone's interpretation. Someone dictated what everyone looked like, who the actors were. Katie didn't need to think about it when she watched her soap opera whereas Donna actually created in her mind what the people and places looked like from the words on paper.

Jana looked down at her notebook and opened it. She had about a half hour until the clothes would be dry and went back through what she had written, scanning her descriptions and wondering how she could strengthen them. The ideas were flowing even if they weren't flowing in the right order. Jana thought it was better to get it on paper and she could redo it later rather than putting it off and forgetting what she wanted to say.

When the buzzers sounded and Donna closed her book and motioned Jana to help her fold, Jana glanced quickly at her pages and realized she had a mess.

I'll need to re-copy this, she thought, now realizing the pink notebook might be full very quickly.

Donna didn't say much as they folded the clothes. Because the laundromat was still fairly empty, they spread out over the tops of several washing machines– lids shut of course– each washing machine representing one of the five of them. And with the stack of laundry sorted and folded, Donna piled Jana's arms with the still-warm clothes that belonged to her and her sisters.

As their trip to the laundromat came to a close, Jana watched her mother and thought more about her. She was a good mom, Jana knew that. She was organized and took care of the girls in ways their friends envied. The notebook she gave Jana was one mark of that. Donna didn't speak a lot, as if she thought that words were expensive, as a Scrabble game, so she was careful to choose them.

And yet she made sure everything was taken care of. Katie once told Jana what she appreciated most about their mother was that they could have their friends over and Donna would feed their friends – even inviting them out for their Oodles nights if it happened to be on a Friday– and then let them go up to their rooms and hang out. She didn't care how late they stayed up as long as the rest of the family didn't miss out on any sleep.

Jana thought about her friend Marcella's mom who was so different from Donna. Mrs. Lopez was vibrant, the word that always struck Jana about her, remembering it from seventh grade vocabulary. Mrs. Lopez wore bright floral dresses to her job as a secretary in a law firm. You couldn't miss her walking down the street. Ever.

"Mom, black is classic," Marcella would say sometimes as her mom put on a purple dress with red flowers. "You look great in black."

"Black? Please," Mrs. Lopez would say, waving her daughter off as she teased out her curly black hair. "People wear black to funerals, remember? And I am definitely not going to a funeral."

They functioned more like sisters as a family unit, a far cry from the life Jana had with her family. But Jana realized that Mrs. Lopez hadn't been to college, she'd had Marcella soon after she graduated from high school and with Marcella's dad long gone to somewhere like New Jersey– Mrs. Lopez always referring to him as "the dirty rat"– Mrs. Lopez clearly knew she needed to be both parents to Marcella and yet Marcella was too much of a bookworm to need that kind of support and instead Mrs. Lopez had become more like a sister.

"She just wants someone to hang out with," Marcella would sigh.

It was just the opposite for Jana. Donna always seemed relieved that the girls could entertain themselves, probably the entire reason she was happy when their friends came over or they were invited over to their friends' house. However, she also seemed more nervous when they left, as if she worried they might not come back.

"Call me if you're going to be home later than ten tomorrow morning," Donna would say, wringing her hands as Jana waited for her friend Kelly's mom to pick her up and drive her and Kelly to the mall. Then she would pick them up in a few hours and take them back to their house on the other side of town.

"We aren't going too far so you can carry this to your room. Put them in stacks there so each of you know whose is whose," Donna was telling Jana as they found a break in the traffic to cross the street back to the motel.

And I can make sure Katie doesn't steal my clothes, Jana thought wryly.

When they had walked back outside, it felt as if someone had turned the oven on to a hotter temperature. Jana thought about how hot it felt, not the moist air she was used to, but the sun baking down on her.

"It must be over ninety degrees," Donna sighed. "It feels like the pavement is melting."

Katie was watching "Days of Ours Lives"– laying on her stomach with a pillow under her chin when Jana walked into the room. Lisa was watching, too. But looked bored.

"Want to go the pool with me?" Jana whispered, after she had set their clean clothes on the dresser and put hers away before Katie could make an attempt at pretending they were her own.

"Really?" Lisa asked, her eyes growing big.

"Yep," Jana said, pulling out her swimsuit.

Donna didn't re-emerge from the room next door when Jana and Lisa walked across the baking pavement to the pool, Lisa carrying the beach ball when she thought the hot pavement might melt the vinyl and stopped kicking it across the parking lot like a soccer ball.

"It's hot here," Lisa sighed, opening the chainlink gate to the pool.

"It's worse at home," Jana reminded her sister, making sure they both wore suntan lotion. "At least we aren't all sweaty and gross from the humid air."

"People are stinky at home," Lisa said, turning up her nose.

Jana swam a few laps of the pool while Lisa played with her ball, not asking Jana if she wanted to play, Jana knowing it was probably because Katie had told her that morning to make up a game by herself so Katie could take a nap.

When she felt cooled off enough, Jana lay in the sun until her skin felt dry– although not hot yet– and then she moved over to the table nearest them with a striped green and white umbrella where she opened her notebook and set to reading over, again, what she had already written.

As she sat there reading– starting to get hot again, even in the shade– she was reminded of a conversation with Mrs. Gallagher. One morning near the end of school Jana had stopped in to see if Mrs. Gallagher had had time to read the short story that Jana had dropped off to her the week before.

Mrs. Gallagher pulled the story out from her tote bag filled with papers to grade– making Jana more grateful Mrs. Gallagher had read it when she saw how much work Mrs. Gallagher had to do, and also realizing that was probably why Mrs. Gallagher's bun on top of her head always looked like it was about to fall apart. Mrs. Gallagher never seemed to stop work. Or caring about how her students excelled and how much they learned.

"Keep writing and you'll become a better writer," she often said. And, "There is a correlation between how much you read and the better writer you become. So read more and become a better writer, too."

She handed the paper-clipped papers filled with Jana's loopy cursive back to her and before she gave her any feedback about the story, she said, "I was thinking about you the other day. I read somewhere that Ernest Hemingway used to read his entire story from the start each day before he began writing."

Jana smiled at the idea that Mrs. Gallagher had thought of her in such an adult way– as the writer she wanted to be– and waited for her feedback on the story she had written.

She sat back and watched her sister in the pool, Lisa having a conversation with herself as she played with the beach ball.

Probably a game she would be playing with Katie or me, Jana thought, feeling a little guilty she wasn't in the pool with her sister. She wished Katie could would come back out, but for now Jana set to reading the few pages she had written and seeing how confused she was by her own changes, she tore them out and set to recopying them.

"Hmmm," a familiar voice over her said– Jana having been so engrossed in her writing that she didn't hear her father walk into the pool area or have a conversation with Lisa. "Maybe we need to get you a typewriter. That looks like a mess."

Jana looked up and saw her father with a smile on his face, his skin looking tanned from not just the trip but the eighteen holes of golf that he had just completed.

"I don't know how to type," she reminded him, looking skeptical.

"I'm sure you'll be learning soon," he laughed. "Did you sign up for typing class this fall?"

Jana shook her head, realizing she hadn't. And that she hadn't thought about it.

When Jana woke up the next morning, her sisters were still sound asleep. She lay in the darkened room, grateful that when Katie had closed the curtains the night before she, not realizing it, had left a sliver of light filtering in. Jana figured her sister must have been tired and not paying attention if she did that because she usually pulled them tightly closed, like at home.

Jana could see that Katie was curled up in a ball on the far side of the bed– not where she had started the night before. After all, it was Katie who had turned out the light on the nightstand between the two beds. But now it was Lisa who was nearest to Jana in the other bed, still clutching Chuck.

She smiled and wondered what would happen if she freed Chuck who looked like he wanted to escape the tight arms of Lisa's zoo. But she sat up and decided to leave him alone, not wanting to wake her sisters.

Mike hadn't told them what they had planned for the day so Jana pulled on the t-shirt dress she had brought, something casual, with the idea that she could change for the pool if it turned out they were going to hang out. While she wanted to see more of Albuquerque, she found she was quite content to swim, then write, swim, then write all day.

However, she did remember that Mike said it might rain and he heard that the monsoons were coming early this year, like the afternoon storm earlier that week.

"I think they say that every year though," he laughed. "It's just a way of hoping for more rain in the desert."

"What's a monsoon?" Lisa asked, scratching her head.

"Don't do that at the dinner table," Donna had corrected her with a light swat to remove Lisa's hand from her scalp

"Lots and lots of rain," Katie said. "You'll learn all about it in science class one day."

For now though, the skies were clear and Jana slipped out the door, placing her flip flops on her feet when she had stepped onto the cool, shaded concrete walkway in front of the rooms, using the front of the station wagon as a way to steady herself.

She loved her new t-shirt dress that she'd gotten at the mall before their trip, her one splurge before they left, Donna suggesting she get one new thing.

"I know you two want to shop in California but you could use a sundress," she had suggested.

It wasn't a sundress but Jana loved the beach scene on it, looking as California as possible without being in California. The bold, colorful lettering and simple scene that included an umbrella, a beach chair, and a beach ball, all with the water in the background. And a sun of course. A belt had been sewn in around the waist making it cinch and giving it a dressier look than wearing a t-shirt. It came to Jana's knees which made her mother happy.

The door next to their room opened and Mike stepped out, looking like he'd just woken up, wearing a Chicago Bears t-shirt and a pair of navy shorts, the kind of thing he wore on weekends at home working around the house.

"Good morning," he said, running his hand through his hair and adjusting his eyes to the light. He left the door to the motel room slightly ajar so it didn't shut and lock him out. Jana could see it was dark in the room. Her mother must have still been sleeping. He held out his closed hand to Jana and waited for her to place hers underneath his. When he did, he dropped a quarter into it.

"Would you please get a newspaper?" He asked. "You don't need to bring it back here. You can hang onto it for now. I'm going back to bed."

"What? Did you have a big night?" Jana asked, feeling like she had stepped into Katie's shoes for the moment, then regretting what she had said.

Mike laughed. "I wish I could tell you that we were drinking all night in the cocktail lounge but I think all this travel has caught up with me. And the altitude."

Then he looked at Jana for a moment. "Hold on," he said propping his running shoe into the door to keep it from shutting. He returned with several dollars and gave them to Jana. "Get yourself a breakfast burrito because it doesn't appear anyone else is getting up any time soon."

"What's a breakfast burrito?" Jana asked, feeling slightly confused.

"Breakfast wrapped in a tortilla," he said waving her off. "They have them in the restaurant to go."

Jana walked across the paved parking lot noticing license plates from New York– her mother would say they had come a long way– and Ohio, not walking to the back of the property to look at the ones there. She passed the empty pool, the water looking like glass in the quiet morning, and opened the doors to the light-filled lobby.

Inside, she walked right across the lobby to where the newspapers were piled on the counter and pulled the top one off the stack, noticing the headline that William Rehnquist had been picked for Chief Justice of the Supreme Court.

Current events, Jana thought, telling herself not to forget that detail because surely it would come up somewhere in school.

An older man walked out from an open doorway behind the desk.

"Good morning," he said, his hair mostly gray, his smile warm and friendly. He wore a button-down shirt with a tie.

"A newspaper," Jana said, handing him the quarter.

"Very good," he said.

Although she felt shy, she also felt for some reason like she should start a conversation with him. Maybe it was the friendly face. "My dad said I can get a breakfast burrito in the restaurant?"

"You sure can," the man said pointing. "And you can get a cup of coffee right over there." He pointed to the coffee machine in the lobby with a stack of white styrofoam cups next to it with the Twilight Sands logo on them. "The decaf is the one with the orange rim." The man chuckled. "I'm sure your parents wouldn't appreciate your drinking any caffeine."

Jana nodded but before she looked away she noticed his name tag said, "Nick."

Hmm, that's a good name, she thought, thinking of character names for her novel. She started to walk away, thinking it might be nice to get a cup of coffee. Why not? She thought, feeling in that moment like she was an adult traveling on her own.

The restaurant was quiet, just a few older people dining. Jana forgot that it was only 8:00 am. There were several men in suits looking like they were having a business meeting, giving the impression that they came to the Twilight Sands frequently.

Jana waited quietly by the cash register next to the "Wait to be seated" sign but no one came. She was about ready to leave when an older man peeked out from behind the door to the kitchen and asked, "Good morning. Has anyone helped you, dear?"

Jana shook her head.

"Good grief." He turned to walk back into the kitchen throwing a white towel spotted with food and water from his hands over his shoulders. "Cheryl! Cheryl! Where is that woman? We have customers."

She heard another language spoken in the back– was it Spanish?– and then the man returned, grabbing a menu.

"I don't know what I pay her for," he said shaking his head. "Let me tell you, if you work hard, you can do anything. Just don't be lazy."

"Um, I wanted a breakfast burrito," she said, holding up the dollars. "My dad said I could get them here."

"Sure!" The man said. "The best in town. Red or green?"

Jana made a face, not knowing what red or green meant.

"Oh, you aren't from here. Hmm. Where are you from?" He asked, looking entertained.

"Illinois. Chicago."

"Not so much hot food there. Green, for sure."

He held up his finger, went around the corner, and returned with something wrapped in foil. "Two dollars. Enjoy."

And with that Jana walked back to the lobby and poured herself a cup of coffee in the styrofoam cup– careful to pick the orange rim, not really wanting any caffeine anyway– trying to act adult and not spill anything.

Jana held the foiled-wrapped burrito in one hand and the coffee in the other, the newspaper under her right arm, seeing there were oversized black and white photos hung on the walls of the lobby seating area. They'd been in there several times to eat at the restaurant and she hadn't noticed them. Before going back outside this time she walked over to check them out.

They looked like a history of the Twilight Sands, Route 66 looking almost rural compared to how it looked now, Jana now seeing the year it opened was 1960.

In the photos of the property– most with people having a good time at the pool, chatting outside their rooms, or eating in the restaurant– it looked modern and new. Of course, she knew that black and white could do that, deceive one into thinking something was much different without color. Shading versus color often accomplished that well.

Nick, the man behind the counter walked up behind her. "Ah," he said, "I started building this place in 1958."

Jana went between looking at him– as he gazed at the photo with his own history in his mind attached– and the photo in front of them. It was a longer shot showing the entire view of the motel from Route 66. That meant the sign, the pool, the lobby, and the rooms, with the parking between the U-shape.

"You did?" Jana asked, not sure why she felt so surprised.

She didn't think much about who owned these places. It didn't occur to her that they might the ones behind the desk.

"Yes, and I had a great run," he admitted. "People thought I was crazy because Albuquerque was growing so fast, so far out of what then was the actual town part." He shrugged his shoulders, a wistful look on his face. "And they were building the interstate. They thought that no one would travel Route 66 after that." He laughed lightly, seemingly mostly to himself. "It did last but now it's definitely changed."

"Why do you think it's changed?" Jana felt her mind start forming questions and she tried not to ask them all at once, to give him time to respond. She wasn't sure where they were coming from either, they just seemed to be forming quickly in her mind.

"Hmmm," he said, looking at Jana with that same kind smile. "When I built the Twilight Sands, it was a unique place and we had so much to offer." He shrugged his shoulders. "But with time new places come along. And people wanted something the same in each city."

Just like Dad said, Jana thought. And how her mom wanted it.

"I thought about branching out but I…." He shrugged his shoulders, "well, I decided it wasn't going to be the same. I couldn't recreate what I have here without losing something. Being on Route 66 is part of what made the Twilight Sands so unique." He sighed. "So I've invested in real estate instead. I'm not sure how much longer I'll own this place. It's probably best to get out sooner than later." He looked around, as if inspecting all that he had created.

Jana felt a sadness permeating from Nick, one of having to let go of something that she could see he cared so much about.

"Oh," she said softly.

"Well, we'll see. It'll have to be the right buyer. I would hate for someone to come in and tear it down. I've kept it up pretty well. Not perfectly but pretty well considering how old it is. The Western Skies up Central," he pointed east toward the mountains, "was my competition and it's closing and it'll be torn down." He chuckled. "And it has a new name. Mountain View Inn, I believe."

Jana wanted to hear more but she was getting a little uncomfortable holding both her burrito and the coffee. And she was hungry.

"You better eat your breakfast," Nick said with a smile, coming out of his trance. He shook his head at the coffee. "That will be an ice coffee by the time you drink it."

He reached out to take it and said, "In fact, I'll pour this one out. Go get yourself another one." Before she walked away, he said, "I hope that young people like you don't lose sight of all the history that's come before you."

Jana nodded and then thanked him before walking back over to the coffee pot and making her way back outside. She found a spot at what had become their usual table by the pool– the one to the side of the middle of the pool where it started the incline to the deep end but facing the mountains rather than the lobby behind them– and settled in to eat the burrito and drink the coffee while she read the newspaper.

She unrolled the wrapping around the burrito, thinking about Nick and his motel and then looked around at the property that surrounded her. Jana wondered about all the people who had stayed there. How many stories were there to tell? This thought had come to her several times now.

Then she looked down at the newspaper and got distracted by the Albuquerque headlines.

"Any good news?" Mike asked appearing out of nowhere, although Jana had no idea how long she'd been at the pool by then. The sun was starting to cross the pool and soon the umbrella she sat under would be the only shade on the pool deck.

Mike pulled back one of the chairs and reached for the first section of the newspaper.

"Arthur Frommer said New Mexico is a good place to travel to," Jana told him. "But I have no idea who Arthur Frommer is."

"He's a travel writer," Mike said with a chuckle. "I guess we made the right choice to come through here this year." Then he added, "Look at you drinking coffee with your burrito."

Jana laughed and shrugged her shoulders. "The man in the lobby said I could have some."

Mike laughed and got up. "I'm going to get some for myself," he said. "I'll be right back. How was the burrito?"

"Yummy," she told him.

"I think I'll get one of those, too," he called.

Jana then called back to him, "It might take a while. The waitress named Cheryl seems to have disappeared so the cook helped me."

Together the two of them sat and read the newspaper over breakfast, the rest of the family still sleeping. It wasn't much unlike Sundays at home except that it was usually the entire family– sans any of the girls who might have spent the night at a friend's house.

"These are great burritos," Mike said. "Did you get red or green?" He peeked over at Jana's empty foil wrapper as if for a clue.

"Green," she said, admitting she had forgotten what it all meant.

"He steered you in the right direction," Mike told her. "Green is usually more mild. But the red is tasty, too. And I heard that you and Nick the hotel owner had a nice chat." He smiled at her and Jana smiled back, shrugging her shoulders.

"I guess. He told me some history. It's interesting," she said.

But there was much she didn't say because she wasn't sure how to put it into words. She felt something although she wasn't sure what it was. She knew she was drawn to these places– she at first thought much like her dad but she was starting to realize it was something different. She felt stories to tell but she wasn't sure what they were. It was as if each experience she had added to that feeling inside her, one inside her that was turning, like cookie dough in a mixing bowl, and yet she wasn't sure what the final product would look like. Or be. Or anything.

"Jana," Mike said unexpectedly, after swallowing a sip of coffee. "I believe you know exactly what you're supposed to do in life. You just aren't sure how you're going to get there."

She looked at him, surprised, especially because of what she had just been thinking. How could he know that much about me? She wondered, opening her mouth and then shutting it, not sure how to respond. She watched his hand gripping the styrofoam cup, covering the Twilight Sands sign logo and watching her.

What does he know about me that I don't? She wondered, not sure if she should ask.

"I know that I appear as an aloof dad at times, probably because I have three girls," Mike said, leaning back in his chair and letting out a slight laugh. "I really thought Lisa was going to be a boy. But I'm here, Jana. And I always have been."

Jana didn't know what to say. She fidgeted a little in her chair, knowing full well it wasn't the coffee– after all, she had selected the decaf, but instead was it discomfort about having this conversation with her dad?

She looked at him as he talked. Jana knew he wanted the best for all of them and that's why he worked so hard. But she didn't comprehend how much he knew about *her*. And what did he know about her that she didn't realize about her herself?

"Daddy! Daddy!" Lisa called, running across the parking lot, her hair flying everywhere, looking like she had seen a monster under the bed. She held her beach towel in one hand while wearing her swimsuit. "Mommy said you'll watch me so I can swim."

"Sure," Mike said, letting Lisa run up to him for a hug.

Jana watched them, seeing the smile on his face when Lisa came running, knowing that he probably had the same smile when she and Katie had done the same. While they interacted for a moment, Jana thought back on her childhood and wondered when things had changed with her parents. They had been so engaged with both her and Katie.

Had she and Katie been the ones to instigate the change? Was it when Katie became boy crazy that her sarcasm blossomed and Jana lost what she felt was her partner in crime?

Lisa jumped off the diving board and Donna walked out next, calling to Mike, "Don't forget the suntan lotion on her!"

Most of the cars were gone from the parking lot, except one from North Dakota, and Jana realized it was also past 10:00 am. Hopefully, her mother hadn't woken anyone up in the motel.

"Are we going anywhere today?" Jana asked, watching Lisa in the pool and thinking it looked refreshing. Lisa was practicing her handstands, only her feet coming above the waterline. The coolness of the early morning had changed as the sun was now sky high and beating down on the pavement that surrounded the pool, just a few trees and very little grass nearby to keep anything shady and cool like at home.

Donna and Mike– who were sitting next to each other under the umbrella, looked at each other.

"What do we have left on the list we made?" Mike asked Donna, who thought for a moment before she spoke.

"Not too much," she said. "Old Town."

It was Mike's turn to think, neither one paying attention to Jana, who was watching them, her sunglasses perched on top of her head because her parents were sitting under the shady umbrella. Jana watched them and waited, wondering what took so long for them to decide.

Just then Katie walked across the parking lot with her bikini on and a pair of shorts covering up her lower half.

"Good morning, mi familia," she said as she dropped her things onto one of the lounge chairs. "I should be speaking more Espanol while we're here."

63

She started to pull off the shorts when Donna interrupted her. "We're going to go to Old Town," Donna said and then turned to Lisa. "Time for you to get out of the pool and dry off."

Lisa, who had been practicing her kicking while holding onto the rounded edge of the pool coping, looked disappointed but swam to the stairs of the pool and stepped onto the concrete pool deck.

"Really? You couldn't have told me this before?" Katie asked, looking annoyed.

Jana didn't say anything but she was disappointed, too. She had been hoping they would just hang out at the pool.

"What is Old Town anyway?" Katie asked, picking her stuff back up.

"Shopping," Mike said. "Trust me, it's not for me."

But he went along for the ride anyway, driving the car past the University of New Mexico campus, through downtown Albuquerque, and then into an area of older buildings where they came upon a small square, Mexican dancers in colorful costumes moving around to mariachi music several men dressed in tight– and most likely hot– costumes as they played their instruments.

"I'd hate to see how those guys looked if they were fat," Katie said under her breath as Mike looked for parking.

Setting the girls free for an hour of shopping, Katie and Jana stood in the middle of the square. "Why can't we just go to the mall?" Katie asked, thinking for a moment, then adding. "But we want to save that for California. Ugh. I don't want to spend any money, yet," she sighed.

"I should get some postcards," Jana said. "That will kill some time."

The girls easily found what Jana wanted and once again walked back outside. "Let's go into the church," Jana suggested, pointing at the old adobe church on the north side of the plaza.

"Church? Since when do you want to go into a church?" Katie asked, surprised.

Jana shrugged her shoulders. "It's probably nice and cool in there."

"Good point," Katie said and together they walked across the street, through the little courtyard and into the small church, acting like they knew what they were doing, mimicking their mother– the only religious one in the family- and then taking a seat in the dim sanctuary.

Katie shut her eyes. "Wake me up in twenty minutes. It's definitely nice in here."

Jana looked at her watch and then ahead to the altar.

Church wasn't her thing. She knew her dad tried to get out of going every week, especially in the summer, feigning that he needed to be at a golf tournament for work. Donna would stare him down with her hands crossed her chest and wait.

"Fine," he would say, finally shaking his head.

Maybe that's why I don't like church, Jana thought, it's never something we all go to happily. A short balding Hispanic priest walked out and greeted people. Jana watched him and wished she could hear what he was saying. Two older women looked excited to meet him, almost bowing to him and holding out rosaries for him to bless.

I don't get it, Jana thought, and she shut her eyes, too.

It didn't last long before a little boy ran into the church, his mother running after him and shushing him.

"Kids these days," Katie said, opening her eyes. "I believe that's our sign to leave."

They started to walk again and came across Lisa, who was carrying a stuffed horse.

"Meet my new horse," she said, holding him up for Jana and Katie to inspect.

"What's his name? Are you sure Chuck will be okay with him?" Katie inspected the horse. "He looks like race horse quality. Are you going to enter him into the Kentucky Derby?"

"Katie, he's just a horse. Not a race horse. Just a horse. Besides, Chuck likes everyone."

The three girls were oblivious to the people– the other turistas- walking around them. "Mom and Dad are this way," Lisa pointed toward a little walkway that led to more stores. "They're wrapping up a bunch of breakable stuff for Mom."

Jana and Katie looked at each other. "Yikes," Katie said. "That can't be good for Dad's wallet."

When the three girls arrived into the local pottery store, Lisa said quietly, "They sent me to find you two so I wouldn't knock anything over."

"At least she didn't say 'anything else,'" Jana whispered to Katie, avoiding the stacked up earthenware everywhere.

At the little checkout stand in the back of the store, a woman with glasses and her hair tied up in a bun was talking endlessly to Donna and Mike as she wrapped up a bunch of pottery. Donna was smiling but Mike looked bored and Jana walked up to him and waited for him to speak.

"You're an accident waiting to happen," Katie said, using Lisa as an excuse to leave the store. "Let's go name your horse."

They went out the front door and Jana looked over to see what was being wrapped. "Your mother just bought an entire new set of dishes. Apparently our wedding dishes are old and not good anymore," he added.

There was a stack of dinner plates that the woman was wrapping in newspaper and bubble wrap. "These will look great in your Midwestern home," the saleswoman was saying as Donna looked on eagerly.

Jana craned her head to see what they would be eating off– the dishes were brown with purple swirls in them. They are nice, she thought, watching that smile on her mom's face that she didn't often see.

"Sending all of you to the mall would have been cheaper," Mike said quietly, Donna shooting him a glare before turning back to the saleswoman.

What struck Jana was that her mother didn't spend a lot of money. She always looked manicured– the word that came to mind when Jana would see her mom at an event– but she didn't run out shopping all the time. Most of her shopping was for the girls and she seemed more content to do that than for herself.

And what Jana thought, looking up at her dad, who looked bored but knew he had to stay there to carry the boxes of dishes to the car, was that her mom wanted to take a piece of Albuquerque home with them. That alone said something.

"Maybe Mom really likes the Southwest," Jana said, as she and her dad wandered around the store (and she knew it was probably the tenth time that he had done that).

"Maybe," he said, looking out the front window of the little shop that had once been a home, creaking wood floors below them. He looked at Jana with his hands clasped behind his back and added, "I guess I'll be drinking my coffee out of 'Desert Sunset' and eating my dinner off it, too."

Jana giggled and Donna called Mike over, everything packed and ready to go. Donna handed Jana a small box, Mike took the big one, and Donna carried the brown paper shopping bag that later Jana would learn held the mugs.

"Come back any time!" the woman called as they left.

"Of course she wants us to come back," Mike snickered to Jana. "Your mother just gave her her biggest deal of the summer."

"Everything is handmade," Donna said, standing her ground and walking with her head held high, Mike and Jana right behind her carrying the unwieldy boxes.

Katie and Lisa caught up with them, Lisa announcing her horse's name was "Sandia."

"Where did you get that?" Donna asked as they shoved the boxes into the back of the station wagon. She looked surprised.

"That's the mountains isn't it?" Jana asked.

"Yes," Katie said, waiting for Lisa to tell her story.

"There was an Indian guy over there," Lisa said pointing to a covered porch (a portal) where jewelers were selling their wares, a place Jana and Katie hadn't ventured to. "He said I should name it after the mountains."

"Sandia means watermelon for the color of the mountains in the evening," Mike said, closing up the back of the station wagon. But he shrugged his shoulders and added, "Hey, why not. You'll always remember this trip, too."

He gave Lisa a pat on the back and everyone looked up as thunder cracked overhead. They hadn't noticed the storm coming in from the west.

It was pouring rain when they reached the university campus and had turned to hail by the time he pulled into the Twilight Sands parking lot. Jana watched the hail bounce off the water in the pool, making it look like a fountain as it sent the water shooting up with each piece.

"Let's wait here for a minute," Donna said.

"It'll cool things off," Mike said, watching the storm hit the windshield. "I doubt it will last long, though. Storms never do here."

"I'm hungry," Katie said.

"How about a Mexican buffet for dinner?" Mike suggested. "I saw an ad for a place called Pancho's Mexican buffet. Then everyone can taste a little of everything."

"Can we go now?" Katie asked. "I haven't had enough to eat today."

"I gave you a granola bar earlier," Donna reminded her.

"I know," Katie said. "I forgot to eat it. And if I eat it now, you'll say I won't be hungry for dinner…"

The rain had started to slow and Mike said, "Five minutes. Be back here in five minutes. And bring a sweatshirt tonight."

"Will it be cold at the buffet?" Lisa asked, looking her usual confused.

"You should always have a sweater," Donna reminded Lisa, who begrudgingly got out of the car to grab an outer layer from the motel room.

Everyone ate well at the buffet, filling up on not just chips but enchiladas smothered in red sauce– although Lisa was content with filling taco shells.

"You should try this," Katie kept urging Lisa with every new thing she put on her plate, Katie being the only one in the family who could convince Lisa that brussel sprouts tasted good. Not that Katie liked them herself but after Mike had explained the influence Katie had on Lisa, Katie used that to her advantage to build points with their parents for the days when she got in trouble and could remind them them they "needed" her help with Lisa. "It's really good."

Lisa looked over at Katie's plate, thought for a moment, and then shook her head, returning to putting together her taco. She had come back to the table with everything in separate piles on her plate.

"You know you could have put that together at the buffet," Mike said, looking like he was unsure what to make of what his youngest daughter had created.

Jana watched the scene, entertained by her family, enjoying her own plate of enchiladas, especially the combination of corn tortillas soaked in red chile with cheese and onion wrapped inside.

When everyone was full from a good dinner, instead of turning the car back to the Twilight Sands, Mike drove onto the interstate and headed toward the mountains.

"Uh, where are we going?" Katie asked. "I wanted to watch 'Knots Landing' tonight."

"Remember how I suggested you bring a sweatshirt?" Mike asked her looking through the rear view mirror and ignoring her television comment.

"Yeah, you just beat Mom to it because she's always afraid we'll be cold in a restaurant."

"Not this time," he said. "We're heading to the top of the mountain."

"That mountain?" Lisa asked, pointing where Mike had just pointed.

"Yep, to the tram it is."

The five of them boarded the Sandia Peak Tramway with as many windows as the lobby of the Twilight Sands, watched as the city disappeared below them, and they followed the line all the way to the top of the Sandia Mountains, moving away from houses into the national forest.

"Somewhere around here a TWA plane crashed in the fifties," Mike told Jana, pointing out the window in front of them.

"It did?"

"Not a big one but big enough," he told her, gesturing to the airplane pieces that were never removed from the mountainside.

When they reached the top, everyone pulled on their extra layers because of the ten-degree temperature drop and walked to the edge of the outlook. They could see the big yellow-orange sun starting its descent behind the solid-line horizon, the kind of horizon Jana remembered drawing in elementary school to show the difference between the sky and the earth. But here it stretched for miles, as if someone had an endless piece of paper. It was unlike any horizon she had seen at home. Only in Florida where the ocean separated the sky from the water did that look familiar.

"Don't get too close to the edge," Donna warned.

"I'm sure that's why they put these bars here!" Katie called back to her, rolling her eyes at Jana, who was standing on the other side of Lisa, who was sandwiched between them. "Geez, it's cold up here though."

Jana watched the twinkling lights of Albuquerque start to light up as the day grew to night. She loved the feeling of being so far above everything, of the inspiration she drew from these very lights. It made her happy. It made her want to write. What she didn't know though. But the urge was there.

"I have an idea," Katie said looking slightly sneaky, checking on their parents, who were behind them.

"What? What?" Lisa asked, shaking from the cold, jumping up and down to keep warm.

"Let's make a wish."

"But we can't just make a wish. We have to do something," Lisa reminded her.

"I know, silly little sister," Katie said. "Let's make a wish and as we do it, let's spit off the mountainside."

"What?" Jana asked, shaking her head, as if she weren't sure she her heard sister right.

"Yes!" Katie said, looking proud of herself, her thickly jelled hair barely moving in the windy high altitude air.

"Like this?" Lisa asked, spitting into the shrubs below.

"Yes, but did you make a wish?"

"No," Lisa admitted.

"Then you need to do it again," Katie told her.

"Do I have to say my wish out loud?" Lisa asked, looking serious.

"No! Don't say it out loud! Only do you say it out loud when it comes true!"

Lisa then spit again and looked at Katie for confirmation. "Did you wish this time?" Katie asked.

"Yes, stupid," Lisa said doing her best Katie eye roll.

"That's my good sister!" Katie laughed. "My turn."

She closed her eyes, took a deep breath, and spit further into the shrubs below.

"Did you make a wish?" Lisa asked, acting like a mini Katie.

"You better believe I did."

"Jana, your turn," Lisa said, both girls staring at Jana.

Jana felt a little stupid about it. Was this really going to work? She wondered. But she shrugged her shoulders and knew it was worth a try.

Bring me the most amazing story that I'm supposed to tell, she thought to herself and then she, too, spit off the side of the lookout.

"Let's go, girls!" Mike called. "We need to catch this tram back down to the base."

The three of them laughed, knowing the secret they shared, that their parents hadn't seen, and as they started to walk back to the tram, Katie said, "And may all our wishes come true."

*I*t happened again the next morning.

Jana had fallen asleep easily the night before, barely getting her journal written before she couldn't keep her eyes open. She didn't even open her magazine. Katie had been watching tv– Lisa long asleep with Chuck curled under her arm as usual and Sandia the horse propped up nearby on her pillow.

But then Jana found herself wide awake at 6:30 am. She could see it was light outside through the sliver between the curtains at the window and sighed.

Ugh, she thought, throwing back the blanket and sheet that covered her and sitting up. Her sisters didn't stir. Jana looked for something to wear in the dark and grabbed her notebook and pen and walked outside to the pool.

As usual, no one was there. Jana thought the air felt nice and cool, unlike Midwestern mornings where nothing would have cooled down during the night. These Albuquerque mornings were pleasant. One didn't feel exhausted from the heat. Instead, she felt rejuvenated by the cool air.

The chainlink fence gate by the pool squeaked as she let herself inside the pool area and she thought about how nice it was to sit by the pool by herself. That never happened at their neighborhood pool at home. Even if it was a crummy day, there was still a lifeguard watching. But here Jana felt like they had their own backyard pool because she had yet to see anyone but she or her sisters swim in it.

Jana sat there a moment and then looked toward the street and realized every day her only walk seemed to be from the room to the pool, the lobby, or the car. She stood up and walked outside the pool area and then to the sidewalk where she stood and watched a few cars drive by and the day begin as the sun continued to rise over the mountains and the city. To her right she knew was downtown and the university. However, she couldn't really see any of that although the Twilight Sands had been built on a part of Route 66 that had a higher incline than rest of it as it worked its way toward the Sandia Mountains on the east end.

What she could see were a variety of businesses, some old neon signs, some new– all turned off for the brightness of the day– like the 7-11 convenience store next to the Twilight Sands. It looked out of place next to the retro motel. Or the motel looked out of place next to the 7-11. Jana wasn't sure which one it was.

To her left she saw a large office building at a distance if she looked past the small block of buildings where the Laundry Basket was located. Nick had said the Western Skies was that way. Jana tried to imagine what it looked like, why it might be on the verge of closing.

But then she knew the Twilight Sands might be closing, too, and yet Nick had said he was looking for a buyer who would keep it up. But why would the Western Skies be closing unless the owner didn't care who bought it and what they did with it.

She watched a few more cars, wishing she had her bicycle so she could take a ride that way and see it all for herself.

Jana couldn't explain why she found it interesting but it was no different than curling up with those old *Life* and *Look* magazines at the college library. She wished she could enter a time machine just for one day to take her back so she could not just see what everything looked like then, but to actually be part of it.

She sighed and started to turn back to the pool when she saw her dad walking toward her.

"Good morning," he said, a slight look of concern on his face. "Are you running away?"

Jana laughed. "No." But she didn't know how to say it. Or what to say. While it all sounded good in her head, she thought to others it might sound stupid. "I just, well," she looked around, as if the words were somewhere and she just needed to see them so she could speak them.

Mike looked at her and Jana saw something she didn't remember from him before: a kind look of patience.

It wasn't that he wasn't patient or kind, maybe it was just that at home he wasn't there often enough that life was as relaxed as this. And on the Florida trips he always seemed to be on the golf course while Donna spent her days with the girls.

"Nick," she said, pointing toward the lobby, "yesterday he was telling me about the Western Skies and how it's closing. And I was standing here wondering why it was closing and hoping I could see it from here but I guess it's too far away."

Whew, she thought, her shoulders slumping.

"I'll take you there," he said suddenly with no hesitation.

Mike didn't wait for Jana, he started to walk back toward the rooms where the station wagon was.

"I need to get my stuff from the pool," Jana called, running after him to catch up.

"Then let's go," he teased, urging her on with a smile.

"Hmmm," he said, making a left out of the parking lot toward the mountains. "If I had known you were this interested…I wish we would have made this trip a long time ago."

"But maybe I didn't know I was then," Jana said. "Maybe it's all new. Maybe it's all because of this trip." Then she added, "And he said it has a new name, Mountain View Inn, I think."

"Maybe it's all about helping you figure out how you're going to get where you want to go."

They grinned at each other as he came to a stoplight.

"They had a nice lounge at the Western Skies," Mike said, tapping his fingers on the steering wheel.

"You were there?" Jana felt her eyes fly open. "You never told us that."

"I didn't know anyone cared. I had to bribe the four of you to watch my slides, remember?"

Jana giggled. "I'm sorry, Dad. This is different."

Mike reached out and tapped her shoulder softly. "I think this time is different. I could never have brought you here at Lisa's age. Maybe we're here for you."

That would be a first, Jana thought, feeling as if so much was always about Katie– because she was the oldest– and Lisa– because she was the youngest. Jana was smack in between, the place where she knew her parents hoped she would be the one to sit still while they chased her sisters, Katie running away, Lisa an endless ball of energy running in circles.

Slowly, the Sandia Mountains grew larger as they also drove a slight incline, one that would be hard to see until they turned around and started the trip back to the Twilight Sands. Suddenly they would see the downhill that they could barely feel or see now.

"There it is," Mike said, pointing to a big building on the right– with a big Mountain View Inn sign to match– surrounded on all sides with what looked like miniature hills. "There's still not much around here but back then there was even less."

He pulled into the parking lot– more full than the Twilight Sands but not by much– and parked the car.

"Are we going in?" Jana asked, instantly afraid.

"Why not?" He asked, giving her a puzzled look. "We didn't come here just to drive by."

"But we're not staying here, how can we go in?"

Mike laughed. "You definitely aren't Katie. If she cared, she would already have scoped it out. Let's go."

He walked quickly and Jana scurried to keep up with him, the smell of cigarettes long ago smoked greeting them as they entered the glass doors with worn red carpet covering the floors. "Wow," Mike said quietly. "This place hasn't aged well."

As Jana looked around, she felt like she had entered her time warp sans the clothes that everyone wore and the television playing "Good Morning America" in the lobby. The Twilight Sands had been kept up better.

No, she thought, there's no comparison. Despite the places where the paint was chipping– she had no idea that the desert sun did a number on paint with the hot, dry air– the Twilight Sands looked brand new compared to this place.

"It's a good thing I didn't book us here," Mike said quietly, leading Jana down a corridor. "I'm not sure your mom would have made it past the front doors."

73

It was quiet, eerily quiet, like the place was haunted because it had been worn down. They stopped by the darkened lounge, not looking like it was being used anymore, the chairs set on top of the tables, not unlike the Twilight Sands lounge.

"How sad," Mike said, shaking his head as they looked inside. "What a fun place this was. Danny and I came here with Gloria one night. She knew someone in the band who played here. We had a good time."

That was the first time he had mentioned Gloria in his memories, Jana thought watching him, wondering if he was thinking it wistfully or just as a matter of sharing a piece of his memories.

"Was that her name?" Jana asked, knowing full well it probably was.

"Yes," Mike said, quietly, as if transfixed in his memory.

"This place scares me a little," Jana said with a whisper as he led her further into the hotel.

Mike put his arm on her back. "It's not the same. Let's go look at the pool and then we'll go."

The pool was empty of water. Jana and Mike looked at each other and Mike shook his head. "I'm sorry this is what you saw. This isn't how I remember it."

"Is the Twilight Sands as you remember it?" She asked, thinking how it looked like it sparkled next to this place, but remembering that he said it wasn't. And yet now seeing the Western Skies, maybe he saw the Twilight Sands differently.

Mike shrugged his shoulders, leading Jana back down the dark corridor to the hotel lobby where the person behind the desk was yawning as he looked over a stack of papers. "I think coming back has made me realize that maybe my memories aren't the same as what really happened."

They climbed into the car and Jana looked back at the aging hotel, feeling sad for it, that no one had cared enough to preserve the history it held. She looked forward and could see– something she didn't remember from the day they had arrived or on their drive to the Western Skies– the incline of the road as it neared the mountains.

"Maybe we remember things only as we want to," he said, Jana not sure he was really speaking to her. It felt as if he might be thinking out loud, trying to organize his thoughts. Or maybe to understand them. "I've learned that we only hold onto what we want to, especially as the years pass." He paused and at the stoplight he turned to Jana and said. "I don't know. I'm sorry I don't have more. Maybe when you look back on this trip you'll have a better memory of it, especially if you're writing about it."

"But it's still just my memories, Dad. My version."

"And it should be," Mike reminded her. "You should only tell the stories you want to tell. Events as you saw them."

Those words resonated with her the rest of the day, one that saw Mike and Donna driving just a few blocks away to the Safeway grocery store to buy more food, especially snacks for the trip to Los Angeles.

"Don't forget the Cheezits!" Katie called from her lounge chair in the sun. "We only have a quarter of a box left."

"That's because you ate them all," Lisa reminded Katie, calling out her sister.

"You helped," Katie teased Lisa who gave her a dirty look that made Katie laugh.

"You better work on that," Katie said. "That's just going to make people laugh. Maybe I need to give you lessons."

Chapter 7

While they didn't get the early start the next morning that they had planned, Mike and Donna still wanted to take the girls on a trip out of town and Mike chose the drive to Jemez after conferring with Nick the hotel owner.

"Ugh," Katie complained as she showered and dressed after an hour at the pool. "I wish we could lay around more often."

Jana watched her sister from the bed where she sat catching up on her journal. Katie had a scoop of mousse in her hand and was about to run it through her wet curly blonde hair. It would dry crunchy, the way Katie liked it.

Jana always felt like Katie got the best of everything genetically. Her hair wasn't nearly as blonde as Katie's although when they were younger it had been much blonder and often they were confused for twins– more to the annoyance of Katie who liked to rub in the fact that she was the older sister by years, not minutes.

Jana's hair had been permed before but when just a few weeks later it went limp again, Donna stood in front of her daughter with her hands on her hips and sighed. "I'm sorry, it's just not worth the money. You'll have to keep the straight look."

One time, Donna had Jana's hair cut into layers so she could have the Farrah Faucet flip look but that, too, didn't last long enough. Especially because Jana couldn't get the hang of curling the layers just right.

"They don't make hair products strong enough to hold your hair," Katie often teased her, French braiding Jana's hair, the only way anyone could get it to have any sort of curl. And even then she had to mousse it up when it was wet so it would hold the waves when the braids were released.

Jana reached back and touched her hair, Katie having done just that after Jana had showered. She could feel the bumps and ripples of the French braiding. She didn't really like what she thought of as a severe pull back of her hair, leaving her face without anything to frame it but come the next morning, Katie would undo the braids and pull it up in a ponytail heavy with bounce and curl. That, at least, would last for the day.

"It's better than looking like Marsha or Jan Brady," Katie usually said, the ode to the long, straight hair that the girls wore on "The Brady Bunch" television show from the late 1960s.

Jana didn't really want to go anywhere either. It was getting hot outside and they already knew they'd be spending the following day in the car. But they all piled in right in time for Katie to miss "Days of our Lives" and remind Mike and Donna– who acted like they didn't hear her– that she was missing her favorite soap opera.

As Mike drove the car north on the interstate, Jana watched the mountains change with the population density. When they reached the far northern edge of the city, there was nothing in the way of seeing the base of the Sandias, no housing, no buildings, just the earth making a gradual incline of sand and sage, then rock jutting up over 10,000 feet at its highest point.

He would turn the car away from the mountains though, going northwest to the Indian pueblo that Nick had recommended, Mike telling everyone, because it was accessible and they had good fry bread.

"What's fry bread?" Lisa asked. "Do they take slices of bread and fry them?"

Jana didn't doubt that one day Lisa would give their parents a run for their money, more than Katie ever did. Especially with Katie as her mentor. Lisa had brought both Chuck and Sandia on the trip and was playing with them on her lap.

Mike chuckled from the front seat. "Not exactly," he said, "but good try. Soon enough you'll find out."

The scenery began to change again when they passed a small town called Bernalillo. Ahead, the mesas– the flat topped mountains– looked red.

Red earth, Jana thought, where have I heard that before?

"They've had some rain out here," Mike said to no one in particular. "Everything looks pretty green."

"Not as green as home," Katie said. "I would say everything is speckled with green."

And it was, not the heavy canopies of green where one couldn't see the ground but here plants were here and there, as if they had been planted spaced apart but never grew enough to take over and become the dense coverings they were used to in the Midwest.

As they entered the town and the "Welcome to Jemez Pueblo!" sign with its worn paint– Jana wondering why they didn't paint it more often if the sun faded it that much– the speed limit dropped and Mike slowed the car down.

There wasn't much to see on Jana's side of the car, the side where the road bumped up next to hills. Instead, she craned her neck to look out Katie's window at the houses made of adobe– matching the red earth– some with wood additions, a few trailers, and then something she didn't know about.

"What are those round things?" Katie asked, beating Jana to the question– not that Jana minded. Katie pointed out the window.

"Those are hornos," Mike said. "Spelled with an h but you don't say it. They're brick ovens. We'll get a loaf of bread here. Nick said to get the bread."

There weren't many people out and the pueblo looked sort of sad to Jana. She could see beyond the houses and dirt roads that a river ran along the edge of it. Mike drove past all the houses– the main area of the pueblo– and stopped the car at one of the areas that led to the river.

"Great fishing spot, it looks like," he said, letting everyone out of the car to stretch their legs. A few other cars had parked there and some men fished the river, standing in the middle of it on rocks and trolling their lines.

"A pueblo is like a little town?" Jana asked her dad as they stood and watched the small river flow lazily past them.

"Yes, a place where a tribe of Native Americans settled. I believe there are nineteen of them here in New Mexico."

Jana didn't say anything but she confessed to herself that she had no idea that one Native American was different from another. She felt kind of embarrassed that she didn't know this. And yet, she also questioned, how would she?

Back in the car, Mike drove about two miles back into town and made a left into a clearing where what looked like several wooden shacks with openings at the front had been built. They clearly had been there a while, some of them looking like they might fall down at any time.

"What's here?" Lisa asked, leaving Chuck and Sandia in the car and jumping out with the others.

"Fry bread," Mike told her. "Finally you can find out what it is."

A hand-written menu board advertised fry bread, tamales, Navajo tacos, loaves of bread, and sodas.

Mike and Donna conferred what to order, the girls watching. "Don't we get to pick what we want?" Katie asked, watching them.

Donna looked at her. "And you know what everything is?" She asked with a slight smile on her face.

"No," Katie said.

"We'll take care of it," Mike told her, waving her off.

A Native American woman with leathery skin stood behind the counter of the shack that Mike walked up to, choosing that one because it had the most items on its menu. A tray of dough balls rested in front of her and she smiled when he approached her. Her long black and silver hair was pulled up in a bun nearly on top of her head.

As Mike ordered, a young man appeared from behind the shack and started to get to work. Jana thought he might be the same age as she or Katie. He didn't really look up, keeping busy with their several orders of everything on the menu.

"It's like having Chinese food for dinner," Katie joked as the food was placed on the counter for them to pick up and Mike walked it over to the picnic table– the only one with a little bit of shade from a tree– while the family sat with sodas.

Jana had stayed behind a few minutes to watch how he made the fry bread, taking those rolls of dough and flattening them before tossing them into a well-used, cast-iron frying pan filled with oil and set on a camp stove. When he finished each piece, he placed it on a paper plate and the woman sprinkled powdered sugar on it.

For the Navajo taco, the woman added everything Lisa had put in her regular corn shell taco on a previous evening: ground beef, cheese, tomato, and lettuce, sending that out to the family where Mike placed it in the center of the table so everyone could have a taste of it.

The tamales, essentially corn (masa) wrapped around shredded pork and then a husk to keep it together– somehow had been kept warm. And, finally, a loaf of bread that had been dropped into a plastic bag and closed with a blue twist tie. That Donna set aside next to her purse to take with them.

"We can enjoy this on the road tomorrow," she said to Mike.

Jana couldn't stop looking around, though. A few other people had stopped– families looking much like hers– some license plates from Texas and Arizona, as well as a few from New Mexico. Now that their order was finished, the boy who had made their food walked out of the shack and over to the next one where he talked to a girl who also looked about their age.

"He's cute," Katie whispered. "Look at that dark skin and that jet black hair. Mmmm."

Jana laughed. "Only you," she said, shaking her head and taking another bite of the fry bread she had torn off, powdered sugar now all over not just her hands but her clothes, too.

She turned around and looked at the houses behind them, the little town right there. It looked sad and she wondered where the boy and the girl lived.

"I would hate to live here," Katie whispered as she finished her soda. "It's so poor."

We're really lucky, Jana thought, not saying it out loud but knowing it was true and that it was the very thing their parents reminded them of often.

They piled back into the car– the sun feeling hot and no one wanting to do anything but be inside the cool car– and Jana had the pueblo view on her side of the car for the drive back to Albuquerque. She saw laundry hanging on clotheslines, tires on roofs– to keep the shingles from flying off when the wind came her father would tell her. But the boy and the girl, they were beautiful people, Jana thought. While not a prayerful person, she sent them a prayer that their lives would be good to them.

That evening after dinner, Jana sat by the pool, dipping her lower legs into the water, letting her mind wander. Everyone else was watching television. And yet Jana didn't want to. She knew they would leave tomorrow and that made her sad in a way. There was something she liked about Albuquerque. Maybe it was just that it meant something to her dad and he had shared that with her. Or maybe it was all the history she didn't get to absorb.

As she stared at the glassy surface of the pool, she saw the Twilight Sands sign pop on, the lights standing out suddenly in the water. Jana jumped slightly when it happened, surprised. But then she smiled. Sort of a goodbye, she thought, not having seen the sign actually turn on since they were there.

The large cursive words also had a large plant in the middle– a yucca her dad had said– and then small stars all around it. She wondered how many people chose to stay at the motel because of the sign as they drove down Route 66, the night getting darker, and not wanting to go further into the darkness of the empty desert.

What would Los Angeles hold? She wondered. The trip had been interesting although she was looking forward to the ocean, especially because they went to Florida every year.

"Finally, we're taking you to the other ocean," Mike had teased the girls.

She started to feel sleepy and looked at her watch. It was already 9:30. Her dad had told them they needed to leave early in the morning so she said good bye to the pool and returned to the room where the repeating scene of Lisa sleeping and Katie watching television played out.

"Want to watch a little MTV?" Katie asked, sitting up with her legs crossed and a pillow in her lap.

"Sure," Jana said, feeling a little tired from thinking. Hearing some music and seeing Madonna would be a good way to end the night. And their time in Albuquerque.

Chapter 8

The next morning, they were scheduled to continue to their quest toward Los Angeles, but first breakfast. Jana knew they were going to eat at the motel restaurant and once again, because she was up early, she stopped in the lobby on her way to do a little final writing in her journal before they left.

The lobby was empty and Jana walked over to the desk– no Nick in sight– and picked up one of the newspapers there. While she had seen the Grand Canyon plane crash news the day before, she didn't pay much attention. Until now.

The headline read that they were recovering the bodies from the helicopter and plane that had collided, twenty-five people had died. Jana gulped. They were all sightseers, she was sure, because they were sightseeing tours.

And then she began to wonder, what if they had decided to do the Grand Canyon on this trip? What if that had been them? What if they all hadn't gone on the trip? Her mind started to spin and she stopped reading the story. She didn't want to think more about losing her family. Especially now. Everything was starting to feel different.

"Good morning!" Nick said, walking in with a stack of white folded towels. "How are you?"

"Hi," Jana said, smiling at him, instantly feeling comfortable. He was an older man, probably between the age of her dad and her grandfathers. But he had a calmness about him, as if he knew that despite anything bad in the world, all was still well.

That was a gift, Jana would learn about people as she traveled through life. And not everyone was blessed with it, but Nick would be the first person to expose her to it. At least that she was aware of.

"I guess no towels for you today," he joked, placing them on the counter next to the newspapers. "I hear you're off to Los Angeles."

"We are," Jana said, folding the newspaper up and placing it back where she found it.

She looked around for a moment and she thought that she was a little sad to leave the Twilight Sands. It's as if– even though she had been there several days laying by the pool and swimming in it– it hadn't been enough. But maybe her feelings were different with all that her dad had shared with her.

"Take the newspaper," Nick said, his hand flying through the air.

"No," Jana told him. "Not today. I think I've seen enough news."

She pointed at the headline about the Grand Canyon crash and he nodded. She suddenly felt the urge to be with her family and walked back across the parking lot to their room where Katie was finishing her hair.

"I guess no swimming for us today," she said sadly, although Jana knew she really meant the word should have been "tanning."

"Eat well, girls," Mike joked with his family as they all walked across the parking lot for bacon and eggs– and a tall stack of pancakes for Lisa that she barely finished. "We've got some travel to do today." Everyone groaned at his excitement of being in the car until their stop in Barstow, California, that night.

"We should be going to the Grand Canyon," Donna reminded him.

"They did on 'The Brady Bunch,'" Katie added.

"Everyone goes to the Grand Canyon," Mike said, waving them off with his arm. "Route 66 is much more interesting. The canyon will always be here, but I'm not sure all these motels will be." And he waved his arms at the Twilight Sands property all around them.

"Um, no, I don't think the Grand Canyon is a good idea," Jana said, recounting what she saw in the newspaper that morning. As the group went silent she felt a little sad that she had said it, seeing that it made their conversation stop.

To change the conversation, she thought back quickly to something else she had seen in the newspaper. "But 'The Cosby Show' is still ahead of 'Family Ties' in ratings,'" she said brightly, knowing this would spark a debate about favorite television shows.

As she watched them debate over breakfast– and listened– Jana sat back and smiled.

This is my family, she thought. Good or bad. I don't care. I'm glad to have them.

After breakfast, Donna, Katie, and Lisa all disappeared into their respective rooms to finish packing. Jana walked over to the pool, having packed the night before, and watched the Twilight Sands sign reflecting in the still pool in the sunshine. She thought about taking a photo of it because she didn't want to forget it. In fact, she worried she would forget what it looked like although she wasn't sure why

Her father joined her and together they stood, their hands on the top of the low chain link fence.

"Are you sorry to leave?" she asked him. "Do you want to stay here longer?" When he didn't answer, Jana kept asking questions. "Is there anything you wanted to see that you didn't get to?"

She stopped, thinking maybe she should give him a chance to answer. "Want to take a ride?" he asked suddenly.

Jana looked at him, noticing for the first time several silver hairs shimmering in the New Mexico sun on his head. His dark brown hair wasn't always going to be as she would remember it during her childhood. "Where?" she stammered, surprised. "Do we have time?"

"Of course we have time," he said, running back to the rooms. "Come on. Get in the car while I tell your mom. She needs at least an hour to pack anyway."

Jana climbed into the passenger seat and together they set off, Mike taking a left out of the Twilight Sands parking lot. She watched the businesses– mostly the motels– they drove by more intently because each time they felt like new scenery to her.

Mike drove left onto Wyoming and headed north, then over Interstate 40, and Jana could see that behind the businesses on Wyoming there was a residential area.

"Do you know where you're going?" she asked her dad, watching him maneuver through traffic.

"I hope so," he said. "I think so."

He took a right on Candelaria and then another right and another right. That put them in the midst of a housing area. The houses were built in the 1950s, resembling something more like the home Mike had been raised in than the fifteen-year-old two-story house where he was raising his family. These houses were all ranch style–one floor– but they had flat roofs, something Jana didn't know much about.

"It doesn't rain that much," he reminded her. "It's the desert. There's not as much need for a slanted roof."

Mike slowed the car down and Jana watched out the window on her right while her dad scratched behind his ear, the motion she sometimes saw him do when he was nervously trying to figure something out.

He parked in front of a brown house that looked like all the rest. The trees had long matured and towered over the houses, giving them lots of shade, especially on this warm Southwestern morning.

"Is this her house?" Jana asked.

Mike nodded, staring at it intently.

"How do you know this is it?" Jana asked, raising her eyebrows and looking around. "They all look the same."

"The bird feeder," her dad said, pointing.

Jana looked just off the front porch and there hanging was a light blue wooden bird feeder. "How do you know it's the same one?"

Mike laughed. "I know it well because I walked into it."

Jana started to laugh and couldn't stop. "How did you manage that?"

Her dad chuckled and looked away, his eyes turned to the residential street in front of them. He shook his head. "I went to pick her up to take her out one night. I don't think her dad had stopped laughing when I left."

"You must have been so embarrassed," Jana said, still laughing herself. But also feeling embarrassed for her dad.

"Gloria said she'd never seen her dad laugh that hard." Mike shook his head.

Gloria, Jana thought. She didn't know anyone named Gloria. There was Gloria Estefan of the Miami Sound Machine but she couldn't think of anyone else named Gloria.

A mail truck pulled up behind them, Mike started the car, and they began the drive back to the motel. Jana wanted to ask him why he didn't stop, why he didn't ring the doorbell but something stopped her, told her to be content with what he had just shared.

As Mike drove the station wagon out of Albuquerque– leaving the Twilight Sands and memories of Gloria behind– the conversation turned to the long day still ahead of them, "We get an hour back as we move into Pacific Time!" her father happily reminded everyone. Yet Jana couldn't stop thinking about her dad. And Gloria. She wondered if there was a sadness inside him, something he always wondered about had he made a different choice.

Mike kept the car on Central and they passed through downtown with a few tall buildings and not much else, looking somewhat like a ghost town.

"That's nothing compared to downtown Chicago," Katie joked, craning her head out the window to look up and see which building was the tallest.

That led to Old Town– the place they had visited several days before– and then a variety of businesses, small motels, and finally, empty mesa.

"I guess we'll need to get back on the interstate here," Mike said to no one in particular from the front seat.

The view from I-40 wasn't much different from the one they'd just left, mostly empty land. Jana pulled out her Walkman and headphones from her bag and slipped them on, still choosing the newest Heart tape to listen to, settling into staring out the window at the mesa which seemed to stretch forever, no trees to hide the distant land.

She continued to think about her dad, feeling like something had changed in their relationship because he had chosen to share with her. It was something she knew that Lisa didn't know about and she was almost positive that he never told Katie– mostly because she would have rolled her eyes and covered her ears, saying, "I don't want to know!"

Jana wasn't sure if her relationship with her dad had been different than the one he had with her sisters. She peeked over at Lisa who was asleep with Chuck under her arm, leaning on Katie who was probably sleeping, her sunglasses covering her face, and her Walkman playing Madonna's "Like a Virgin" tape, using Jana's copy because she had worn out her own.

Mike still played with Lisa, as he had with her and Katie, but he was older and often joked that he wasn't sure how much his back could take after carrying her across the house not long ago. "I might need to retire from that," he had said, rubbing his lower back after setting her– and Chuck– on the ground.

What Jana did believe was that her parents tried to treat each of them equally and fairly, something she knew was especially important to them because her mother's family had revolved around her older sister– Aunt Emily– who was supposed to be a genius and they expected her to go to Harvard.

That was until she ran off with her high school boyfriend the summer after her high school graduation and ended up pregnant. While she came in and out of the family's life after that– by her own choosing– each time she appeared at home, she was welcomed with open arms as if nothing had happened.

Donna worked hard at school and then college to become a nurse, meeting Mike at the hospital when he was starting his career in pharmaceutical sales. He asked her out, following her around an entire floor until she said yes. It was the story they always told, looking at each other and giggling, as if it had just happened the day before. Jana liked hearing it because a look appeared in their eyes, one of absolute love, as if remembering that day was what kept their marriage together. If that was true and they needed at times to remember it frequently, then that was okay in her book. However, lately that hadn't been the case with more frequent arguments and clear hurt feelings between them.

Even though all hadn't been as well recently, she was grateful to have two parents who appeared to not just like each other but love each other. Now that she knew what happened in Albuquerque, Jana wondered if he always felt he had left a piece of his heart there in 1964. Maybe this trip was the only way he could get that piece back. Maybe something would be different for him because of it. Or was it already different? Or maybe he just needed to see if the piece were still there.

Then she wondered– the same scenery repeating as if she were watching a Flintstones cartoon on television– if you left a piece of your heart somewhere, eventually did it heal up and you didn't realize it was missing anymore?

Jana looked at the back of her dad's head, everyone quiet in the car, the radio playing softly, the Albuquerque news station 770 KOB AM now starting to filter in and out with the usual static that came as one drove away from the location of the station.

Jana peeked ahead between the back of her mother's seat and the side of the car and she could see red mesas just ahead. The road started to curve after going straight for some time. And then they began a slow climb into not a mountainous area but definitely one of higher altitude.

After passing several semi trucks, Mike pulled the car off the road into a scenic overlook.

"We're there already?" Katie asked sarcastically from the back seat. "That was quick."

"No," Mike said. "Just a little break I thought everyone would enjoy."

He pointed to the north side of the overlook where sitting on a big hill off in the distance was the Laguna Pueblo. The white washed buildings covered the side of the hill with a church– obvious from its cross– set to the left.

Jana looked for a moment when she opened the car door and climbed out but then saw some little buildings nearby. She began to walk toward them when she realized that they were Native Americans selling their jewelry– plus bread in one, pottery in another. She began to wander through, mesmerized by the silver and turquoise she'd just seen for the first time a few days ago in Old Town.

She spotted a silver bracelet with four triangular pieces of turquoise in it and started to touch it but then remembering her mother would tell her not to and started to pull her hand back.

"It's okay, you can pick it up," the Native American girl behind the counter of the little wood building said. Jana looked up and saw a girl– probably her own age– smiling at her. She had long, black hair twisted into a braid down the back of her head. When Jana didn't instantly reach for the bracelet, the girl did and handed it to her. "Really, it's okay."

"Did you make it?" Jana asked, not thinking twice, just a question falling from her brain and forming in her mouth.

"I wish," she said, rolling her eyes slightly– although not as dramatically as Katie, no one could beat the dramatics of Katie's eye roll. "My dad did. I'm still learning. He said maybe by the time I get as old as him I'll be even better than him." She laughed and Jana smiled, slipping the bracelet onto her wrist and liking both the way it felt and the way it looked.

"I'm saving my dollars for Los Angeles malls," Katie said quietly, walking by, Lisa skipping along behind her.

Jana ignored her sister and the girl kept talking. "I hope to go to college. I don't really like standing out here all summer in the heat selling jewelry."

"Oh," Jana said, her fingers resting on the bracelet on her wrist, but her mind listening to the girl. This was a world she knew nothing about, it wasn't even close to the reel-to-reel movies they watched in elementary school about Native Americans– or the film strips with photos set to a tape recording that their teacher had to advance the frame every time they beeped. The films showed Native Americans living very rural lives in very traditional clothing. Jana looked at this girl with her shorts and t-shirt, not unlike what Jana was wearing.

They stared at each other for the moment and Jana realized how lucky she was. It wasn't *if* you going to college in her family, it was *where*. After all, she had learned early on, there were to be no more Aunt Emilys. That meant no one was treated like a queen either, but everyone was treated fairly and equally.

Jana really wanted the bracelet. While she wasn't totally clear about her reasons in that moment, she knew she didn't want to forget this moment. Or this girl. She wished she could stay there and talk to her, to learn more.

And just before she could say she was going to the car to get her money, she heard a voice from behind her. "How much is it?"

Jana looked behind her and saw her dad standing there, pulling out his wallet from his back pocket.

"It's forty dollars," the girl said, her dad walking in just then from an open door where Jana could see clearly led to nowhere– after all, there was nothing behind these buildings– except the pueblo they could see off in the distance.

"Hello, sir," the man said, slightly tipping his head at Mike and then at Jana. "What brings you to New Mexico?"

There wasn't room or time for Jana to protest. The girl held out her hand for the bracelet and Jana handed it to her, the girl taking a cloth and shining it up brighter than it was before.

"Family vacation," Mike said, reaching to shake the man's hand. "I came this way in '64 and wanted to bring my family, too."

"Ah, the Route 66 trip?" the native man smiled. His hair also was long but pulled into a ponytail, streaks of silver running through it. His dark brown eyes looked kind, like he was a good man and good to his daughter.

Jana kept watching the girl polish the bracelet, then saying to Jana, "I'll include a polishing cloth so when it tarnishes, you can make it shine again."

"Yes. All the way from Chicago." Jana looked up to see her dad smiling as he recounted a few of his adventures.

"I haven't done that. I've been too busy trying to make a living off all of you driving through," the man laughed. "But I hope she can do all the things I didn't get to do," he said, pointing at the girl who was placing the bracelet in a black cloth pouch and pulling the drawstring closed before handing it to Jana.

"Thank you," Jana said. "It was nice talking to you." She wanted to add, "I wish I could stay and talk more," but she felt a little shy saying that around her dad.

The men talked a moment more and then Jana felt her father's hand on her back. "We better go. We're heading to Barstow today."

"Do you have air conditioning?" the native man asked, looking at the several cars, and a semi, parked along the dirt road and wondering which one was theirs.

"Yes," Mike said. "Last time I did this I didn't. I wouldn't do that again."

They shared a good laugh and Mike and Jana started walking back to the car where Donna and Jana's two sisters were waiting to get back on the road. Lisa was using the tip of her left foot– mostly her big toe– to draw "Lisa was here" in the light brown dirt.

"Lisa," Jana heard her mother say sternly. "Cover that up. We're on these people's land. That's disrespectful."

"Thank you, Dad," Jana said, looking up at her dad who smiled at her and gave her a squeeze from the side. "I had enough baby sitting money for it though."

"You're welcome. I don't want you to ever forget this trip."

"I won't," Jana said, quietly taking the bracelet out of the pouch and slipping it onto her wrist, knowing that at this moment her reasons for remembering the trip might be different from what her father was thinking.

The sun had continued its steady rise into the upper sky and Jana noticed, as they continued the drive west, that the shadows she saw on the mesa when they had come into Laguna were now gone and the sun was fully drenching them with its light and rays. They passed through Gallup on the western edge of the state, Mike pulling off the interstate and taking Route 66 all the way through town.

It started on the eastern edge with a series of small motels and ended on the other side with the same, none looking as big as the Twilight Sands, except the El Rancho in the middle of town where Mike stopped the car, letting them walk around the rustic lobby with its rustic cabin décor and 8x10 autographed black and white photographs of movie stars displayed on the walls.

"They filmed a lot of westerns here," Mike explained to the girls as they recognized names like Clark Gable and movie swimming star Esther Williams.

Then on the western edge of town came more motels, everything looking a little more rundown than the area where they had stayed in Albuquerque. While Jana noticed Holiday Inns and Days Inn had sprouted up at the interstate entrances and exits, she wondered how many stories all these old motels could tell. If these stars had come through town, they had stories but so did everyone else who might be taking a trip across Route 66. Just like her dad.

"I think I'll get gas here," Mike said, turning to Donna, who nodded. "That way we're good to go across Arizona."

He pulled into a chain gas station and Jana opened her door to get out and stretch one last time before they started what Mike had warned them would be a long drive across Arizona. A state Jana only thought of in the spring when the Chicago Cubs went to spring training there, many people from Chicago packing up and following them for the sunshine they'd been missing during the Midwestern winters.

"Dad," she asked, looking to her left and seeing a new Red Roof Inn motel and then looking to her right and seeing another little motel, half the letters missing on the sign, something about wishing everyone happy holidays but instead saying H p y Holi a s, Jana thinking Vana White from "Wheel of Fortune" must have stolen the letters for the game show. "Can I walk over there?"

"Sure," Mike said, shrugging his shoulders as he pumped the gas into the car. "Just stay where I can see you." He paused. "For your mother's sake," he added.

Jana nodded and walked across the hot pavement to the motel, passing the motel office and the property opening up to her when she passed it.

The two-story motel itself was set to the back, everything paved around it. And right in the middle of it Jana could see there was a playground with what looked like a swimming pool to the back of it. She walked over, just a few cars in the parking lot and Mike still able to see where she was, and stood there at the chain link fence looking into...an empty pool.

Wow, she thought, the scene of an empty pool. Desolate was the first word that came to her, trying to give the benefit of the doubt that maybe they hadn't filled it yet.

Still she continued to stand there and look, her mind formulating what it might have looked like filled. And with families swimming in the pool, ready for a day of rest after traveling across the hot and dry desert, much like Jana's family.

"No water," she heard her father say, coming up next to her.

"Sad," Jana said.

Mike waved his hand in front of him. "Not unexpected though. These places are dying, like I said the other day."

"But they all have stories, don't they?" She asked, wondering how many people remembered jumping into a motel swimming pool after a day in the car.

"And think how refreshing it was after not having air conditioning in the car all day," Mike laughed, as if his and Jana's thoughts crossed and he had started to speak but couldn't stop to answer her because his thought was already on its way out. "The convertible didn't have air conditioning," he reminded her.

"That must have been awful, "Jana said, making a choking noise. "And hot with the top down and the sun hitting you."

Mike shrugged his shoulders. "You don't miss what you don't know that you don't have."

He pulled the car back onto the interstate and everyone craned their necks out the windows to get a good view of the red rock mesas on either side of them, as if the mesas had split just for the interstate to travel through the middle of it.

Jana thought about her dad's words, that you don't miss what you didn't know existed. It made her think about how much she took for granted. She knew her mom wasn't happy about all these motels but one day long ago they all had been sparkling and new, a time when Donna would have been happy to stay at them.

She'd never thought about her dad as such a nostalgic person except that she knew she should have simply because of how much he liked to show the slide show as if sharing it with his family each year kept it alive in his mind.

Maybe he didn't want to forget, Jana thought. Maybe he didn't want to forget what had happened in Albuquerque.

She looked at Katie, who was staring out the window of the other side of the car. Did Katie think of her boyfriends like that? What really went through Katie's mind when she said she wanted to forget them? Did she really do what she said she was going to do?

Jana didn't have any experience like that. There was one boy, John Monroe, whom she had liked in seventh grade. He moved that summer, not coming back to school in the fall, and

Jana found out from someone else that his father had been transferred to Dallas, Texas. Jana didn't think about him. She felt as if she had moved on and looked forward, not at what she couldn't have in the past. She'd never see John Monroe again.

She looked up at the back of her father's head– getting to know it well on this trip– and thought that something must be different if her father didn't forget Gloria. Why would you keep the memories of someone you weren't going to be with in the back of your mind? she wondered. Wasn't that painful?

Katie reached into the very back of the car to the box Donna had filled with snacks and pulled out the familiar red box of Cheezits. Jana happened to look up– her headphones glued back onto her ears– and Katie motioned her finger toward the box.

"Want some?" she asked.

Jana shook her head and motioned instead for the Twizzlers, their other travel snack, and Katie pulled out the large bag, the second of three that Donna had bought for the trip.

"We can always buy more," Katie joked, knowing full well that wouldn't be enough for them. In Florida– because they flew– Donna always took a trip in the rental car to the local grocery store and stocked up on their favorite snacks to keep the girls away from the expensive vending machines at the hotels (much to their dismay).

They'd crossed into Arizona and Jana munched on the Twizzlers– Lisa having fallen asleep again, this time her head laying on top of Chuck– while Katie ate the Cheez-its.

Signs for the Grand Canyon started to appear and Jana happened to be between songs– that empty space when one ended and before another one began– and she heard her father say, "That's for another trip."

Jana realized the end of that side of the tape had run out and heard the conversation continue as she forwarded it to the end– each side never even because the lengths of the songs were never the same.

"We can be like the Bradys," Katie laughed, bringing them up again. "But I don't want to go to Hawaii if we're going to get some weird wood dude who has bad voodoo."

Jana shook her head, not sure if their parents knew she was still referring to the Bradys. Or because they were so used to her comments that they simply ignored her.

That's when they passed the first big green sign indicating Los Angeles was ahead: 454 miles.

The second side of the tape began and Jana felt herself slipping off into sleep again although the road began to wind more as they traveled through a mountainous region of Arizona. And Mike insisted on pulling off the interstate and traveling the Route 66 roads through towns like Williams.

There wasn't much to see and Jana could hear the sighs her mother let out, each time he did it, not sure if– like when Katie made her comments– that her father was ignoring her mother or simply didn't hear her.

I'm sure there never was a lot to see, Jana thought, making a slight laugh to herself. Although, she wondered, maybe it didn't look so rundown because there were more people traveling through it so there was more of an expectation to make it look nicer. Just like Gallup, each time they pulled off the interstate or back onto it, there would be a small group of motels and restaurants, mostly fast food, along with modern gas stations and convenience stores.

Jana was beginning to realize that most people would never see what they saw on this trip, despite the inconvenience of taking the road less traveled.

*J*ust before they crossed the state line into California, they stopped at a rest area in the desert.

"There are signs everywhere about snakes," Katie noted out loud. "Yuck."

And then to tease Lisa, she quietly said, "There's a scorpion over there." And knowing full well that Lisa had to use the bathroom, Katie added, "I bet they're all over the bathroom."

Lisa screamed and went running back toward the car.

Donna sighed– looking hot in the sun that made them all appear to melt into the concrete– and glared at her oldest daughter.

In the dense desert heat under the clear blue sky– even with the sun starting to shift across the sky into the later afternoon, the temperature hovered well over 100 degrees– the five of them walked around, everyone mesmerized by the unique landscape. The heat, the sun, and the desolation all came together to form an unfamiliar landscape. There were no lush lawns with dads pushing the mowers every Saturday morning.

"It reminds me of the old 'Star Treks,'" Mike said to Donna, who nodded in agreement.

"That weird show you always watch on weekends?" Katie asked.

Mike ignored her and started to walk across the light brown sandy dirt, following Lisa, who had been convinced by Mike that there were no snakes or scorpions in the bathroom and that she should follow Jana who she could trust to save her. This time Lisa ran to the bathroom believing if she made the trip quicker, her chances of being bitten by something would be much much less.

"Don't let her run so much! I don't want to her to suffer heatstroke!" Donna called from shade under the rest area building eaves where she was reading up on information about the area.

Jana watched her family: each of them a unique personality. Each of them allowed to be themselves, even when it came at the expense of irritation of the others.

"Two more hours," Mike told Jana, squeezing her shoulder as he walked by her on the way back to the car. "Then we'll spend the night in Barstow."

"Do you know where we're going to stay?" Jana asked, feeling slightly shy that she was asking questions she knew her dad would quickly realize she hadn't cared about before.

"Not sure yet," he admitted. "I couldn't remember the place where Danny and I stayed." He shrugged his shoulders, squinting his eyes in the sunlight because he'd left his sunglasses in the car. "We'll find somewhere. It's like Albuquerque in that way– Route 66 has plenty of options. But first we have another stop."

She nodded and everyone climbed back into the car. Jana pulled out her Walkman and slipped the headphones on her ears, the metal piece that slipped over the top of her head tangling her hair. She picked out a mix tape filled with songs she'd recorded off the radio a few months ago, mostly because she didn't have the albums themselves, and looked out the window, not hearing her dad whoop it up when they crossed in California.

Outside the sun was still bright in the sky although it was heading toward late afternoon and a few boats lingered in the river below them as they crossed the bridge that divides the states, using the Colorado River as a marker.

There isn't much between the state line and Barstow, Jana thought, unable to believe how much land was uninhabited. And amazed at the heat. When they passed Needles, she thought of the Peanuts character Snoopy whose brother Spike "lived" in Needles and occasionally made an appearance in the daily newspaper cartoon.

Spike's life with cactus didn't seem far off from what Jana saw. Needles disappeared into the rearview mirror and all Jana saw was a bluish-purple light that made up the shadows of the mountains. She could see for miles even though it looked like she could reach out and touch the mountains with her hands.

She pulled her headphones off and bunched her pillow up between her head and the car window.

But it wasn't long after that Mike once again pulled the car off the interstate, a sign pointing to the left that said, "Amboy."

"Really, Mike?" Donna asked, clearly hot– although the car was cool enough to be comfortable with the air conditioning running full blast– and ready to be finished for the day. "Do we have to?"

"We do," Mike said, ignoring her comments and turning the car south on a true two-lane road. The difference was this one looked more desolate than anything they had been on yet.

Jana sat up and watched the road unfold like a ribbon in front of them, rolling slightly along the terrain of the earth which made her realize that everything was only truly flat when humans made it that way. There were cacti and scrub everywhere but it was different than New Mexico because off in the distance here the mountains almost gave off that bluish purple hue, one she didn't remember seeing in New Mexico.

The road also hadn't been paved in some time, making it bumpy in places, a few pot holes scattered haphazardly through the drive. Everything looked the same, maybe how the United States as a whole looked before any civilization, Jana thought, or just like a science fiction movie. A cross between westerns and science fiction.

Maybe where they meet, she thought, the car quiet, knowing her dad had turned off the radio some time ago because there was nothing but static. She let the nothingness of where they were permeate all her senses.

"Mike, this makes me nervous," Donna said, looking at Mike who Jana could tell was incredibly happy to be taking this drive. "What if the car breaks down? What will we do? Did you bring a jug of water?"

Mike shook his head and let out a slight laugh. "Donna, remember I did this before." He gave her a quick look and then back at the road, mostly to stay on it because there surely wasn't anyone coming or going for miles in either direction. "And obviously Danny and I made it just fine in a convertible with no air conditioning."

Donna shook her head. "But you didn't have a wife and three kids in the car. This seems dangerous."

"People travel this all the time," he reminded her.

Jana looked down and touched the turquoise and silver bracelet on her right hand. Each time she heard her dad say something that surprised her, she felt herself wanting to touch the bracelet, as if it would help her remember it and savor the memory for the future. Maybe that was better than a camera, she thought.

Up ahead, Jana could see a few buildings even in the slight descent the sun was starting to make. A sign for "Amboy." And, finally, several white buildings that made up the town. And a big sign that towered over everything: Roy's Café and Motel.

"We aren't staying here are we? Is this Barstow?" Katie asked, taking her headphones off and clearly not having been paying attention.

Mike laughed as he pulled the car to the side of the café, not to the gas pumps where gas was two dollars more a gallon than they'd paid previously because of the cost to get it to the small town– and yet being a savior for those who hadn't planned accordingly. "No. I won't make you stay this far into the middle of nowhere. But go walk around. If anyone wants a milkshake, meet me in the café."

The wind blew because there was nothing around it to stop it. Jana stood by the car door for a moment, taking it all in.

Who had stopped here before? she wondered, looking at the little cabins that were the motel rooms, each separated rather than built into one long line like a strip mall, as they used to.

The lobby sported a sixties look to it with tall glass windows on one entire side and an angled roof. Jana walked all the way to the end of the cabins, passing the big sign that she knew must have been a beacon in the darkness for the people crazy enough to travel the road at night.

No swimming pool, she thought, glad they weren't staying there and hoping wherever they stayed that night did have a pool.

Lisa came running over– this time not fearing any snakes. "Dad wants to know if you want a shake," she said.

Jana nodded, told her strawberry, and then walked back to the café with her sister where the bar inside the diner took up most of the length of the building.

"Feel free to go sit outside with those shakes," said the older man working– the owner's son– Jana would learn, waving them outside. "But drink them fast before they melt!" He teased.

Jana walked over to the stretch of concrete that fronted the glass side of the motel office and sat down where she could dangle her legs slightly with space between her and the ground. Everyone joined her, only Donna not having her own milkshake and drinking some of Lisa's chocolate one.

"Did you stay here?" Jana asked her father, still not having seen a car go by since they arrived.

"No," Mike said with a slight laugh. "We had to get to Los Angeles so we had to make it to Barstow that night. But I remember going through here."

What Jana really wanted to ask was if he felt sad that day, leaving Albuquerque which also meant leaving Gloria even though they would stop there for one night on their way home.

They all piled back into the car for the final stretch to Barstow and Jana found herself looking back at what was left of Amboy as they pulled away and Mike continued the car east.

Stories, I bet that town has a lot of stories, she thought, once again drifting off to sleep.

"Next stop, Barstow," Mike called from the front seat.

When Jana woke up, Mike was pulling the car onto Route 66, the main drag in Barstow.

"Does anything look familiar?" Donna asked, her usual worried self. "I don't want to wake up in the wrong part of town and our car is gone." The sun was quickly going down although it wasn't cooling anything off.

"It'll be fine," Mike reassured her, as they passed through what was a nearly empty downtown. "This was a railroad town. And a Route 66 town. All of that going away changed it." He sighed.

Jana watched the little motels with their unique signs– although not as unique or as fun as the ones in Albuquerque– and played a game with herself, trying to pick the one that her dad would pull into.

She didn't get it though, mostly because he chose one on the left which was his side of the car, not hers– the Desert Inn– its vacancy sign still lit up and the light on in the office window.

"Are we there yet?" a sleepy Lisa asked from the front seat.

"Yes," Donna called back. "We're there. We're just waiting for Daddy to bring us the keys to our rooms."

"We got lucky with first floor rooms," Mike said loudly, oblivious to the fact that his family was nearly asleep. He backed up and pulled in front of the rooms, handed Katie one key, and told everyone they needed to be ready to leave at eight.

"Can't we go swimming?" Lisa asked.

"You can swim in Los Angeles at our motel tomorrow afternoon," Mike said, turning her toward the room when she began to drift across the parking lot to the swimming pool. Katie grabbed her from there and the three girls never brushed their teeth that night, choosing sleep before anything. And no one complaining about the musty smell or the dated furniture.

At least it's cool in here, Jana thought as she quickly drifted off to sleep.

Chapter 10

"There's a place across the street that I thought we'd try," Mike said, pointing, the next morning as everyone gathered back at the car with their belongings. "Guillermina's Steaks and Mariscos."

"What's a mariscos?" Lisa asked, looking perplexed.

"It's shell fish in Spanish," Katie explained, tapping her sister lightly on the head.

As their dad packed up the car again, Jana walked Lisa over to the pool. "Let's go look at least," Jana suggested. Lisa skipped happily next to her, Katie following them. She, too, was disappointed they didn't get to swim but they'd been too tired to care the night before.

"This place is a dump but at least it's California and not Oklahoma," Katie said, peeking through the fence with slats of white offering privacy from the outside world. "At least if you live here you're just a few hours to fame and fortune in LA."

LA.

Jana thought about what LA meant to her, what she thought they would see when they arrived there later that day. Everything always looked perfect in LA. It meant Hollywood, the beach, tanned skin, blonde hair, perfect bodies, cool clothes. And she thought it was a place where anyone could be famous. And rich.

"Chorizo…red chile…," Mike said, repeating various items off the menu at Jenny's– clearly an old Denny's, but now a local restaurant that offered chips and salsa. For breakfast.

"It might be hot," Donna warned about the sauces, having been too surprised in Albuquerque by a salsa that made her eyes water.

Mike laughed at his wife as he took a chip and dipped it in the green sauce. "You worry about everything."

"Someone has to," she reminded him.

The restaurant slowly filled with locals: railroad workers, immigrant families, all cultures, all walks of life. Donna looked uncomfortable in such a multi-cultural setting; Jana wanted to know what everyone speaking Spanish was saying.

"Erik Estrada must be here somewhere," Katie whispered to Jana, setting her off laughing. Jana looked out the window at the faded town around them.

"We'll be in LA in about two hours," Mike said as they waited for their dishes to arrive.

Eggs, chile, meat. Jana took a bite of her chorizo and eggs– no one flinching as she ordered–wanting to do something completely different than Lisa, who stuck to cereal, and Katie, who had an omelet. With just cheese.

The taste melted in her mouth. It was like the food in Albuquerque in some ways. But lighter, as if it needed to be because it was even hotter here.

"Good, isn't it?" her dad asked.

Jana nodded.

He drove Route 66 as far as he could through town, catching the end of I-40 and the start of I-15, and once again they found themselves back in the desert. For a while. As they neared Los Angeles, much like Chicago, the area began to spring up around them. Slowly at first, then getting denser as they got closer.

*****

"And here it ends," Mike said, the finish of Route 66 as anticlimactic as where they had started back in Chicago, the blending of streets with no fanfare except to those who were traveling it. Jana had a silly thought that maybe it would be like the end of big race where there was a ribbon to break.

Santa Monica.

"The home of 'Three's Company,'" Katie giggled as everyone looked around at the new surroundings. "Come and knock on my door…," she sang.

"Maybe we'll see Mrs. Roper," Jana joked with her sister about the television show.

"We wouldn't miss her with those giant tents that she wore."

Donna helped Mike find their motel, The Sea View Motor Hotel, which of course didn't have a sea view because of all the apartment and new condominium buildings that now lined the ocean. He pulled into the parking lot and came back with one key from the office.

"That's disappointing," Katie said, looking bummed.

"It's a suite," he told them, shaking his head. "Two bedrooms with a living space and kitchen. It was too expensive any other way. This is Los Angeles, remember?"

It was also dark and somewhat damp. Jana looked around, feeling as disappointed as her sister looked.

"It's expensive here," her mother said, pinching Jana's upper arm slightly. "But there's a pool and the beach is two blocks away. We won't be in here much."

"Let's go swimming!" Lisa begged, both Jana and Katie quickly joining in the idea.

"You can go to the ocean, too," Donna told her daughters.

"I want to go to the pool," Lisa said.

"We'll have dinner nearby and go for a walk along the ocean later," Mike said, flopping down on the couch and looking relieved that they had finally arrived at their destination.

Jana thought he also looked proud of himself. After all, they had just traveled the entire length of Route 66. He'd accomplished his goal of taking his family on a Route 66 trip. The rest of the trip would be icing on a cake.

*****

As they sat in an Italian restaurant a block off the ocean, Mike and Donna talking about everything that they had planned for the next few days, Katie showing Lisa the best way to eat a meatball without making a mess– getting a glare from Donna across the table– Jana looking around the aging restaurant.

They had been placed in a black vinyl booth, the fabric cracked in places, the table covered with a red and white checked tablecloth. Jana ran her fingers across it, reminding her of the oil cloths they had used in elementary school to keep from making a mess when they painted. Hers was white with turquoise and blue flowers, Donna having picked it out one day from the fabric store for her.

The restaurant was busy, more of a locals' haunt, and Jana jokingly wondered if Jack, Janet, or Chrissy from "Three's Company" might wander in for dinner.

She looked over at her parents and watched them. Her dad hadn't said much about Los Angeles and his trip. He hadn't said much about anything relating to the past since they'd left Albuquerque. He looked happy with Donna, but Jana thought that maybe, just maybe, he didn't want to think about what had transpired since leaving Albuquerque.

Maybe he didn't suggest they eat at any of the same places because he didn't remember where they ate. Or maybe he didn't want to remember Los Angeles. And it wasn't until he reached Albuquerque just a few days ago that he realized this wasn't going to be as fun as he thought it would be. But now they had left Albuquerque and he could leave the memories behind, too. Out of sight, out of mind, Jana thought.

After dinner– everyone full from their heavy pasta dinners– they walked across Pacific Coast Highway to the beach.

"There's the famous pier," Mike told the girls, Jana wondering if his excitement and his smile were true or he was hiding the sadness he had felt from his prior trip.

The family walked across the beach– Lisa leading and eventually taking off running– as the big round yellow sun had started its descent, like it was going to disappear behind the ocean for the night, resting like everyone else, before reappearing in the east in the morning, ready for a new day.

There weren't that many people out, most of them on the pier or staying near the sidewalk. Donna and Katie stood together, near where Lisa frolicked in the waves, not a care in the world. Jana walked a distance, then stopped and stood, away from the others.

This is Los Angeles, she thought, trying to recall everything she knew or had thought about the city. They had yet to see Hollywood: the sign, the studios, Beverly Hills. So far, just the end of Route 66 and "Three's Company."

"Beautiful isn't it?" A voice said behind Jana and she realized it was her dad. She looked up at him as he walked up next to her, wrapping his arm around hers that she had folded across her chest from the cool ocean breeze. He pulled his side close to her and she felt his strong arm not just keep her warm but give her strength, as if to give her strength for everything life might hand her.

"It is," she said quietly. They stood together in the silence of the beach, only the sound of the water lapping onto the shore, bringing with it the cool breeze.

Jana turned her head, pushing her hair out of her face as the breeze blew it toward her skin, to see how far her mother and Katie stood away from them. Not in earshot, she confirmed. Then she looked back at the ocean and took a deep breath– hoping her dad wouldn't notice– before speaking.

"Does it make you sad to be here?" she asked him, nervously glancing at him before she said it, then quickly looking back at the sun setting before her words had a chance to sink in.

She knew he looked at her, opened his mouth, then closed it. "Your mother says you're an old soul," he finally said. "I never understood what she meant. Now I do."

"What do you mean?" Jana asked, having no idea what he was referring to. And why was he turning the conversation back on her?

Mike laughed and squeezed her tighter. "You're a lot more aware of not just the world around you, but the feelings and emotions of others. That's a huge maturity that most people never understand. And that's why your mom says you're an old soul."

Jana nodded, kind of knowing what he meant and yet still wanting to know if her dad felt sadness about what he had left behind.

She felt his chest move, as he took a deep breath, then he pulled slightly away so he could look at her. "Yes," he said, finally, turning back to face the sun and the ocean. "I do feel sad. I didn't think that I would. But I do. And yet I'm still happy to be here in Los Angeles, that we made it all the way across Route 66."

They stood there silent together for a moment, Jana stepping closer to him and leaning on him, wanting him to know she was sorry, and knowing it was something that needed to remain unspoken. She couldn't talk to the rest of the family about any of it. This was something her dad had shared with her that wasn't meant to be open in the family.

"I have a great life," he said. "I love your mom, I love the three of you. I have everything I could have imagined and more. We live in a great place. I make enough money and more so we have a nice house. But yet something deep in my soul is missing. I now know– after being in Albuquerque– what it is."

He then again pulled slightly away from Jana and looked at her. "I want for you– and for your sisters– but for you something slightly different. I know that you aren't like everyone else. That pink notebook your mom got you says it right there." He took both of his hands and placed them on each of her shoulders as they faced each other. "You have something to share with the world, you understand something that others don't. What I want for you more than anything is for you to be that person you're supposed to be. And don't ever let anything– or anyone– hold you back."

He took a deep breath. "I know that I would have completely altered my life had I made a different choice. I felt like I couldn't leave Chicago. Life will put lots of doors in front of you and you'll have to choose which ones to open, knowing you're leaving others closed. That will be the hardest part. But open as many as you can while also making decisions that don't leave regret behind."

Jana tried to swallow everything he said to her, but it was slightly overwhelming. She wasn't even sure she could remember all his words as the evening went by– Lisa interrupting their conversation when she came running up with a rock in her hand.

It's the best rock I've ever found," she announced. "I'm taking it home."

"I think it is," Mike told her, Jana knowing his face looked slightly pained in the now near-darkness on the beach, only the lights from the buildings and Pacific Coast Highway, the PCH, lighting up the beach. The darkness in front of them as the lights ended where the ocean started. She knew he hoped that Lisa hadn't heard anything– she had figured out there was no Santa Claus at five years old when she snuck downstairs late on Christmas Eve and found her parents placing the gifts under the tree. Her inquisitive nature had been hard for them to contain at times, especially with Katie to egg her on.

As Jana listened to her sister talk about the rock, she knew Lisa hadn't heard anything. After all, she was more concerned with how excited she was about the rock.

The three of them walked back to Donna and Katie and together they returned to their motel and the stuffy rooms, grateful for the open windows that let a breeze flow through the suite.

Still, Jana couldn't sleep. As her sisters lay contentedly in the next bed– Lisa still insisting on sleeping with Katie which Katie acted like she minded but didn't really– Jana lay awake thinking about what her dad had said to her.

"Was he lecturing you?" Katie had teased her after they had gotten back to the motel.

Jana shook her head, knowing she wouldn't reveal what he had said, but also knowing that her father often had to remind Katie about everything he wouldn't tolerate, especially each time she brought a new boy home.

As Jana lay there, she thought about how she and her sisters were so different. But she didn't realize how different she was from the other two until her father told her all that he did this evening. She drifted off to sleep wondering what her life would be like as she got older. And thinking about what she wanted it to be.

And– still– what was that story she was supposed to write?

She only had the notes, but no clear path of a story yet.

The seagulls talking in the air woke Jana up the next morning. Lisa was practically hanging off the next bed, Katie almost laying across it as if to make part of a diagonal. Jana curled up in a ball on hers. She heard her parents talking in hushed voices in the common area of their motel suite.

She stretched and pulled herself out of the bed, grabbing her toiletries to take a shower before her sisters. She walked out into the common area where a carton of orange juice and a box of Dunkin' Donuts sat in the middle of the table.

"Breakfast," Donna said, holding out her hand as if she were Vannah White on "Wheel of Fortune."

After Jana showered, her sisters were still sleeping. "You get the pick of donuts," Mike said. "After us, that is." He held the *Los Angeles Times* back up and continued reading the newspaper while Jana selected a jelly donut.

"These aren't as good as the ones by Grandma's house," Jana told her mom, who looked up from her word search.

"Nothing is as good as those," Donna said with a smile.

This is life, Jana thought as she looked for something interesting to read in the newspaper, not realizing how slow it could be, how the pace as an adult wouldn't always be as exciting as she thought it would. Often it would be routine and her parents seemed content with that.

Maybe it's easier that way, she thought, feeling a breeze come through the window by the table where she sat. She smelled the salt water of the Pacific Ocean. Maybe most people don't want more, she wondered. But she knew she did.

Later that day as they began to tour Hollywood and Beverly Hills, she would begin to see that wasn't true for everyone– that there were others like her who did want something more from life than the routine. They had sent Lisa across the street with $5 to buy the movie star home map, Donna holding her breath until Lisa came back through the throngs of tourists and homeless people wandering Hollywood Boulevard.

Mike held onto the map while they turned into Mann's Chinese Theater.

"Oooh, I've wanted to see this," Katie said, whipping her camera out of her bag. "This is as close as I'll get to a dead movie star." She quickly began looking at the hand and feet imprints, many of them made back in the 1940s and 50s.

Jana looked at almost every one, recognizing some but not others. When she came to Marilyn Monroe's she stopped and spent extra time examining it, as if her handwriting, her hand prints– where Jana placed her own hands, finding out how much smaller hers were– and the imprint of Marilyn's heels– could tell her something. Jane Russell was to her left, Sophia Loren above her, but none of them gave Jana the sense of anything except Marilyn herself.

For a moment she was transported back to Mrs. Gallagher and the college library and the paper that she had written just months before, that now seeming like years ago since the events of the past week and their trip.

"Ah," she heard her father behind her. "Gentlemen prefer blondes."

"Is that true?" Jana asked, still staring at the concrete that had been there since 1953, an anniversary almost to the day, June 26. "Do men prefer blondes?"

He chuckled. "I'm afraid I'm not one to answer that." Jana turned to see him shaking his head. "It's all about what's inside the person that makes you love them."

She nodded her head and took a quick look at Donna, who was out of earshot but Jana imagined she was explaining to Lisa who someone had been. Every photo Jana had ever seen of her mother– even the black and white ones– Donna's hair had been consistently brown.

"How I got blonde daughters, I have no idea," he laughed.

Even though they kept walking, looking at the other movie stars whose hands and shoes had been immortalized in the cement, Jana continued to feel her eyes drawn back to Marilyn.

This was as close to Marilyn Jana had gotten, only reading about her in old *Life* and *Look* magazines in the little college library back home. The black and white photos from the 1960s plus the articles told Jana stories she wouldn't have heard elsewhere. Jana looked at her dad, talking with her mom as they stood over Clark Gable and thought about how many stories he had to tell.

Her brain began to feel a little overwhelmed and she took a deep breath, trying to listen to Katie, who was talking endlessly about James Dean and watching him late one night on television when their parents had been at a wedding.

"When we get home, I'm going to rent the rest of his movies," she was saying, adding, "not that there are many because he died so young."

People sometimes do want more, Jana thought, as they walked back to the car. But sometimes what they get isn't necessarily what they want. Marilyn was the case of that. How do you make sure you get what you want and not something you don't?

All around them at the parking lot, other families and couples were getting in and out of cars, doing much the same thing as the Danielson family. Jana could see that they were like any other family taking a trip that summer.

But I believe I'm different, she thought, looking around at all the station wagons like theirs.

"Thank God we're not in a minivan," Katie said again, also scanning the cars. "Thank you parental units for not buying a minivan," she called out to Mike and Donna in the front seat.

"Parental units?" Donna asked, swinging her head around, her sunglasses on so Katie couldn't see the look stemming from her eyes. "We're not aliens. Or robots."

Lisa found this hysterically funny and leaned on Katie as she laughed so hard she doubled over and said her stomach hurt.

I'm still different, Jana thought. I believe I'm supposed to do something greater than all of this.

She didn't think she could be content to live a life like her parents. She believed there was something greater for her to do.

"Where should we start?" Mike asked, Donna unfolding the map, the three girls clamoring behind her to see what was on it. He clutched the wheel, watching his family, pointing out the Capitol Records Building with its familiar round structure and long antenna stretching off the top of it, and then the Hollywood sign.

All these places, Jana thought, she'd heard of but never thought she'd get to see. And now that she saw them, she wanted something more from them. What though? Were there story ideas that might stem from them?

Jana saw Joan Crawford listed in the names on the map, but not Marilyn Monroe– not realizing at the time that her house hadn't been in Beverly Hills but was in Brentwood instead. Jimmy Stewart, Lucille Ball, all stars the entire family was familiar with.

"Roxbury Drive," Mike said, as he made a left onto the street and Donna pointed out Lucille Ball's house. "Home of many stars."

Manicured lawns, mansions built fifty or more years ago with extensive driveways and gates to keep people from wandering up to their front doors. Donna continued to list the names and Mike kept driving. Some houses looked older, Spanish style with tile roofs and brown stucco walls, Jana remembering a few they saw in Albuquerque like that.

I want it, all of that, she thought, wanting to be part of what she saw from the outside, knowing nothing about what it was like on the inside. Just believing there was something there for her, as if she could just open one door and inside she'd find exactly what she was feeling but couldn't yet describe.

That evening, after a dinner of burgers and fries from down the street, all eaten at a table by the swimming pool, Lisa begged Katie to take her back to the beach. After Katie relented and they took off, Donna collected the trash and walked back to the room, Jana knowing they'd find her reading her book on the couch when they all returned to the suite for the night.

Jana pulled out her pink notebook from her yellow canvas tote bag and opened it, taking the cap off her pen, but then set it down on the lounge chair where she lay and glanced over at her dad who looked as if he were in a far-off place, watching the water.

Everyone thinks swimming pools are television sets, Jana thought, knowing she did it, too. What was it about the water that was mesmerizing? she wondered.

She looked at her dad and he didn't take any notice of her at all.

"Dad," she said, quietly.

Mike turned his head slowly and looked at Jana, a smile coming across his face. "Yes?"

Jana took a deep breath. "How did you meet Gloria?"

She fully expected him to shut her down, to shrug it off. But when he registered what she had asked, his face turned, not to something upsetting, but to a relaxed place. To a memory that appeared to make him happy.

"It was at the club at the Twilight Sands," he said. "Didn't I tell you this?"

"You did," Jana admitted, gulping. "But...well, I don't know. I'm sure there was more than that. You obviously saw her again since you went to her house."

Mike shook his head. "She had jet black hair– her mother was Hispanic and could cook like you wouldn't believe. The food we ate in Albuquerque last week was mediocre compared to what we ate at their house." He laughed, mostly to himself. "I learned how to make eggs from her. My mother's eggs were never very good but Gloria's mother– Maria– taught me how to tilt the frying pan just right to cook them perfectly."

Jana laughed, thinking about how many times she had seen him do that, never knowing what he was doing.

"Gloria had a laugh, the kind where she threw her head back and it went all the way to her belly, her body shaking. I felt appreciated by Gloria and I think that's what it was about. She let me into her life fully." He stopped and Jana tried to picture everything he said in her mind. "I just wish we had thought about what we were getting into before we started to spend those few days together." He shook his head. "I was so caught up in her energy. And I think she was caught up in mine."

"Why didn't you just stay and not come to LA?"

"I couldn't do that to Danny," he said, shrugging his shoulders. "We planned this trip together. I couldn't just let him have to drive home all by himself."

Jana nodded, knowing her dad always tried to explain the importance of being a good friend to her and her sisters.

He nodded as he continued to look at the pool.

"Did you love Gloria?" Jana asked shyly.

Mike didn't answer right away. Jana watched his mouth open, then close, as if he were going to speak but then decided differently.

"I think that my idea of love has changed since then," Mike admitted. "But, yes, I loved her. And I think that today I still love her. But I also know that I'm probably in love with what

I remember, not with what I would see today. Just like the Twilight Sands isn't as nice as I remember. I'm in love with the memory of what it was. And that memory of what it was involves Gloria so it's all jumbled together."

He was quiet again, the pauses long as he formed the exact words he wanted to say. "What I see in your writing is that it will morph and change as you experience love and relationships and everything else in your life."

Jana tried to absorb all that he was telling her. She wished she could take notes or record it in some way so she didn't forget it. But she also had more questions.

"Dad, what happened to Danny?"

Mike looked a little stunned that she had asked. Jana once again regretted that she'd said anything. Maybe that was a sore subject, she realized, swallowing her regret. But why didn't Mike talk about Danny who was in all the slides with his short blonde hair? He was a stocky guy, the kind who was a little shorter but had shoulders that looked as if they could lift a couch.

Mike let out a soft laugh and shook his head. He looked at Jana. "You know, I don't know. And it's been a long time since I've thought about him."

"But he took a job here– in LA, right?"

Mike looked out at the pool. "He did. When your mother and I married he and his wife– her name was Betsy– they flew in for it." He smiled at the memory. "Betsy always told me how grateful she was that Danny and I took that trip because she loved living here. She loved being near the ocean. And she didn't miss the Chicago winters."

"Did you keep in touch?"

Mike shook his head. "I guess it's no different than with anyone else in my life. You get married, you have kids, and you're busy. Your immediate concerns are making sure the bills are paid and everyone has what they need. You start to socialize with the people around you, like the people you work with or your neighbors, probably because it's easier because you're busy."

Jana thought about all he said, especially about socializing. They'd moved into their house when she and Katie were young, before Katie started school. Jana didn't remember their old house although Katie sometimes mentioned it because they had to share a room.

She pretended she hated sharing a room with Jana but Jana knew that was a lie. Katie was always inviting her into her bed to tell her stories. But she played around with Katie's fake drama, holding out for the day when she'd remind her none of it was true.

There were neighborhood barbecues although not so much now that the kids were getting older. The neighborhood had been new when they moved there and as most of the kids aged, Lisa was now one of the younger ones on their block.

"As far as I know, they still live here," he said.

"Do you remember where they last lived?" Jana found she couldn't stop asking questions. It was like she had to find the end to this puzzle.

"They had an actual Los Angeles address but that's all I remember."

"Let's look them up in the phone book," she suggested.

Mike laughed and reached out to touch her arm. "You're relentless."

Jana shrugged her shoulders. "We're only here a short time. Do you want to go home regretting that you didn't try to find your friend?"

She thought– no, acknowledged– that it was different with Gloria. That was a love. And for as much as Jana wanted him to find Gloria, she had some understanding of why he didn't. But why not look for Danny?

"Come on," he said, standing up and waving his hand. "I have an idea."

Jana grabbed her things and followed his long purposeful steps in his worn loafers that he wore with no socks– like everyone else– to the lobby.

"Can you believe this guy's name is Harry?" Mike whispered as they came into sight of the bald man behind the desk.

Jana started to laugh out loud.

"I hope that at one time he did have a head full of hair or his parents played a cruel joke on him with that name," Mike added, opening the door to the lobby and Jana biting her lip to keep from laughing each time she looked at Harry.

Harry stood up from writing something down behind the desk and Jana watched and listened to their conversation.

"I need a Los Angeles phone book," he said, Jana looking outside and seeing a public phone booth, wondering if a phone book were inside it.

"Are you sure you're looking for someone in Los Angeles" Harry asked, tapping his fingers on the formica countertop and looking skeptical.

"We're from Chicago," Mike laughed. "We know how this works. How many books are there?"

Harry gave a weak smile. "We only have two of the three. Someone took off with the third and we haven't gotten a replacement yet."

"What about the phone booth?" Jana asked, pointing outside.

"Someone stole those."

"Hmmm," Mike said, thinking. "Let me see the ones you have. Is there a library nearby?"

Good one, Dad, Jana thought giving her dad silent kudos.

While Harry pulled out the phone books and dumped the heavy paper volumes onto the countertop, he gave directions to the nearest library, just a few blocks away.

Mike thanked him and took the books across the lobby to the little waiting area with the 1960s-era furniture, Scandinavian chairs with burnt orange cushions that hadn't been recovered since their original fabrication in the early 1960s.

"Dad, did you stay here?" Jana asked, realizing that he didn't talk about where they had stayed in LA.

As Mike opened the book and started looking for Danny's name, he said, "No. The place where we stayed is now a Travelodge or something. They tore it down to build something bigger."

Jana nodded and grabbed the other phone book, feeling a sense of urgency and wanting to help. "What was Danny's last name?"

"Bolton."

After a few minutes, Mike sighed and closed the book. "No luck here."

"Or here," Jana said. Lots of Boltons but no Daniel or Dan or Danny.

"Let's go quickly so we'll be back quickly or I'll need to go tell your mother where we're going," he suggested, once again walking briskly down the couple blocks to a little building that looked like it had more than served its purpose as a library with books crammed everywhere. It wasn't spacious like the new one at home although Jana reminded herself that this one probably looked new once, too.

"There are four volumes now," said the librarian with her glasses on a chain roped around her neck. "We don't stop growing." She snickered slightly.

Again, they each took a volume and looked. With no luck. Jana watched her dad stand there, his hands holding the volume in his hand as if it might fall off the solid counter where it rested.

"I'm sorry, Dad," Jana said, as they retreated back to their motel, passing by a few houses and small apartment buildings on the way.

Mike slowed his walk down, Jana feeling as if the purposefulness of it had been sucked away by not finding Danny.

"I thought for sure you'd find him."

Mike smiled and patted Jana's shoulder. "It's okay. It's been twenty years since I've talked to him. They could be living in another city in the LA area. And that could take all day with all the phone books they had there."

Jana nodded, thinking of the three shelves of phone books that the librarian pointed out held all the names, addresses, and phone numbers for the entire Los Angeles area.

He shrugged his shoulders and they walked by Harry– still behind the lobby desk– and back to the pool, not stopping there, and continuing onto their suite. "Or he might have gotten a job and moved across the country. More than anything, I just hope he's well and happy."

Jana nodded as he used the room key to open the door to their suite where Katie greeted with him with, "Good grief. Where did you go? We're starving for dessert."

"We want to go to the mall," Katie announced the next morning as they ate pancakes at a diner several blocks away from the motel.

"The mall?" Mike asked, raising his eyebrows. "We come all the way to Los Angeles and you want to go to the mall."

Lisa giggled. Jana tried to stay out of the conversation. She secretly wanted to go but a part of her didn't want to disappoint their parents. Not that this was new, at least to their mother.

"You can go to the mall at home," he reminded them.

"Dad," Katie said, raising her eyebrows. "This isn't just any mall. This is a mall in Los Angeles."

Mike looked at Donna, who shrugged. "We aren't teens, remember? They've been good about doing all your Route 66 touristy things. Let them have the mall today."

"And when do I get to golf?" he asked, looking slightly annoyed.

"You golf, we go to the mall," Katie said, her face brightening up like a lightbulb.

Donna nodded approvingly. Mike thought for a minute and said, "Okay. You have a deal."

"See," Katie said, looking proud of herself. "Everyone is happy."

Mike talked to the hippie guy at the front desk– it must have been Harry's day off– calling him "Rainbow Eddie" because of the tie dye he wore each day they saw him and found the Santa Monica Mall and a golf course in a span of twenty minutes.

"The good news is that you can always take the bus back," Mike said as he dropped his family off in front of the Sears entrance of the 1960s-looking indoor shopping center.

Donna glared at him and Jana gulped, hoping an argument wouldn't break out because of the comment.

"You'd think they would have updated it, being LA and all," Katie said, quietly, as they waited for Donna and Mike to finish discussing the details.

"It looks like a time warp," Jana said, shrugging her shoulders.

But inside something looked brighter than home. Was it the light? Everything looked white, as the sun swooped through the large skylights on the ceiling. The mall didn't have the dark brown of their own mall at home. This was California, of course it was different.

Even though Katie and Jana made a beeline for The Limited, not realizing the items were the same as the ones at The Limited in their mall at home, it would be different to buy it in California.

"We don't have Broadway," Katie reminded her sister, leading her across the mall and past a slew of stores, to a department store they had never heard of. "Let's go check it out."

Donna and Lisa were nowhere to be found, Donna making sure the girls knew they had two hours and were to meet her back where they started.

"Yeah yeah yeah," Katie had said, antsy to get started, as if the clothes might disappear on them. "We'll be back." She pointed at the plastic Swatch on her left hand that she had converted to Pacific Time. "Right here."

They walked into Broadway and stood for a moment in admiration and awe: a section of swimsuits stood in front of them. Bigger than they'd ever seen before.

"Oh God," Katie said, her eyes bouncing around. Jana immediately felt overwhelmed with colors and patterns.

"Where do we start?" she asked her sister, hoping she could lead the way.

"I'm not sure," Katie said. "But I think we both know what we're going to buy with our money. I believe we have reached the pot o' gold at the end of the rainbow."

In that moment, Jana knew that all those Saturday nights babysitting the Lancaster kids had been worth it. The boys weren't hard to handle, that wasn't it at all. Jana didn't mind the Disney movies that Mrs. Lancaster always rented to keep everyone happy– or the pizza– until bedtime. In fact, usually the hardest part was coaxing them to bed after they fell asleep watching the movie– and eating too much pizza. No different than Lisa at home who was just a few years older than them. And that was just so Jana could have the couch to herself and finish watching classics such as the Herbie the Love Bug movies about the beloved VW beetle car and its adventures. The same movies they showed the day before vacation breaks in elementary school.

She had saved the money for this trip and while she'd bought a paisley pencil skirt at The Limited before they left, something had told her to save the rest of it. Now she knew why.

Ocean Pacific. Jana saw the label in an entire section. Everything sang "California" with the sun-drenched oranges, yellows, and blues. And florals, too. This was what she wanted to take home. This was the life she wanted to live.

Katie and Jana shared an extra-large fitting room, going through a pile of swimsuits, Katie having convinced Jana to try on a bikini.

"Come on," she told her sister, pointing at the OP rack. "I see you ogling those. We won't be able to wear bikinis forever. Look at Mom after three kids. She's afraid to show anything. Let's do it while we can. And, remember, it's California."

When Jana pulled on the first one, turquoise with orange piping, and had adjusted it for her body, she looked at Katie first.

"See, I told you. Look in the mirror," Katie said with a big smile across her face.

Jana turned– seeing her sister looking behind her– and realized she didn't look bad.

"You can get some color on that white stomach," Katie teased, pulling on yet another suit. Her pile was up to ten, of which she knew she could only afford three, max.

Jana nodded and was happy to hand over the cash to the unhappy sales clerk, who looked miserable in her job.

You live in California, Jana thought. Sunshine. No winter. Why aren't you happier?

As she and Katie– who had taken twenty minutes to pick out her three suits– walked back to where they were supposed to meet their mother and Lisa, Jana thought about how if she lived in California she always would be happy.

No winter, she thought again. The sun shines most days. That was the life.

She wore the suit the next day to the beach with her sisters and her mom nodding approvingly. "I like it," Donna said. "The colors are perfect for you." Donna then adjusted the white shorts she had pulled over her own navy blue one piece.

As Jana watched her mom, she realized she was glad that her sister had convinced her to go with the two-piece swimsuit. What if I can't wear one the rest of my life? Jana thought, thinking there was some sort of unwritten rule somewhere that said once you had children– or were of a certain age– you didn't wear two-piece suits.

It was a day that Jana didn't look forward to and hoped she didn't have to follow those rules.

Chapter 14

"Tomorrow is a day off," Mike announced at dinner that night at a place called Norm's.

"It's like an oversized Denny's," Katie remarked, looking through what seemed like an endless menu.

"A chain local to Los Angeles," Mike said.

"What does that mean?" Lisa asked, looking confused.

"Like Portillo's to Chicago," Mike told her, his eyes peeking out from the top of the menu.

"A hot dog," Katie said. "A hot dog sounds good." She sighed, still looking through the menu. "But I guess I'll settle for a burger."

"What do avocados taste like?" Jana asked, feeling a little tired of eating in restaurants, wishing they were home at the dinner table eating her mom's baked chicken and potatoes.

"I've never had one," Donna admitted, looking at Mike.

"Order it on the side," Mike told Jana. "Then you can try it."

She'd always heard about guacamole but she knew this might be her one chance to try it, choosing the guacamole burger with the guacamole on the side.

"You can dip your fries in it if you like it," Mike told her as they waited for their order. "If not, I'll eat it."

But when everyone tried it– each one dipping a fry into the thick, chunky dip in the brown bowl– Jana realized there wouldn't be much left for her.

"We should order another side of it," Donna suggested, Jana knowing she sensed her disappointment.

Jana felt relieved to get back to the motel that night although she really wished she could have some time alone. She missed her room, her bed, and the way the sun streamed through her windows in the morning. Much to her mother's annoyance, she never closed her curtains.

"Someone could see you!" Donna would complain, her hands on her hips, as she stood in the doorway.

"It's the second floor," Jana would say, shrugging her shoulders.

She didn't care about that. What she loved was the sun coming up in the morning and reminding her it was a new day and that there was always more to look forward to. Katie, however, loved the darkness and always shut her curtains. And the ones in the motel as Jana been enduring for the past week.

"Who can sleep with so much light?" Katie asked as she shut them.

As Jana lay there in the darkness that she hated so much, she tried to distract herself with the story she wanted to write. The trip was half over and she still hadn't done more than write in her journal and make a bunch of messy notes and ideas. She had written descriptions about people, about places, about whatever she had found inspiring. She didn't know what to do with it now, though. Jana felt herself drifting off, thinking about her dad and Gloria and the life they almost had. But what if they did have it? she wondered. What would it have been like?

The next morning– her sisters still sleeping, as well as her parents when she walked into the open area of the suite– she quietly snuck outside to the pool where she sat down at the table and began to write.

The first few lines she wrote were a struggle, like stop, start, stop, start. She had to think up names and details, turning back to the pages and using what she'd been writing the past few days. She crossed out several lines, finally starting again on the next page, reminding herself that she would throw that page out. She then tore a page out to write details on it so she wouldn't forget the names and other information she needed to remember about each of her characters.

She knew the story was inside her and she stared at the quiet pool, the mirror image of the palm trees and everything in the courtyard reflecting back at her in the water. She heard traffic on the other side of the building, a few doors opening and closing. And a maid with a cart getting restocked with clean towels to start the day.

I'm not here, Jana thought, letting her imagination take her back in time.

Finally, she began to write, filling up several pages easily, and feeling as if she were finally overflowing with a story to tell.

"Jana," a voice called, she realized, jolting her out of the another time and place. Jana looked up to see her mother waving at her from the door of their second floor room. "Are you hungry?"

Jana shook her head, waved her mother off and kept writing. "I'll be up shortly," she said, wanting to finish the scene.

This must be how it feels, she thought, putting a period on the last sentence where she thought she could stop. This must be how it feels to have a book to write.

She ran her fingers over the imprints that the ink creating words had left on the pages, shut the pink notebook, and then returned to the room where everyone was awake.

"It's a beach day," Katie said, already wearing her new pink and yellow bikini, the tags still on it, her hands on her hips. "Get ready and we can go now."

"First, the grocery store," Donna said, holding a piece of paper and pen in her hand.

"Ugh," Katie said, rolling her eyes and flopping onto the couch.

"Jana why don't you come with me?" Donna asked, Jana knowing she couldn't say no. "Katie and Lisa you can go to the pool until Jana gets back and then you can go to the beach."

"Why can't Dad go with you?" Katie gave Jana a sad look. "We won't go to the beach without you, don't worry."

Jana followed Donna to the car and they drove just a mile or so to the Safeway, Mike having gotten directions for Donna. Jana really wanted to ask her mother why she couldn't do this alone but she didn't want to make her mad.

Remember all that she does for you, Jana told herself, trying to act like it was okay that they were delayed going to the beach.

"I want to make sure I get the right snacks for you girls," Donna said as she pulled into the supermarket parking lot.

"But you always do that without us going with you?" Jana felt slightly confused as she followed Donna– who was walking quickly– and pointed to Jana to grab a cart from the line of them.

Donna stopped for a moment and looked at Jana. She wore a nice dress, as if Los Angeles were a reason to wear more than the shorts she might be sporting at home or if they were in Florida. When Jana looked around at everyone else though, it seemed as if her mother knew instinctively how to fit in. Her dress sported stripes that traveled in several different directions in browns and oranges, not as bright as the clothes that Jana and Katie wore, but stylish enough especially for an adult.

"This trip has made me realize you girls are growing up fast." She sort of laughed. "Faster than I thought. I'm trying to let go. I can't do it all the time but I'm working on it."

Jana instantly felt bad for anything she and Katie might have said, especially recently. She pushed the cart behind Donna, who continued her fast clip through the store, dumping items into the cart, asking Jana questions, and making sure they could still have plenty of beach time.

I wonder why I know so little about my mom, Jana thought, as her mother grabbed several boxes of Cheez-its, smiling at Jana as she did, knowing how much the girls liked them. But she also knew that her father opening up to her as he did made her question why her mother hadn't as well.

They're different people, she reminded herself, helping to unload the items onto the checkout stand. Just because they're married and they're my parents doesn't mean they're the same and that they share the same things. Nor does it mean it all resonates with me.

Chapter 15

Their parents heading off to explore Los Angeles, the three girls made their way to the beach, on the north side of the Santa Monica pier, where it was early enough that they had their pick of spots in the sand.

They each carried a tote bag and towel plus Katie held the cash their father gave them to get something to eat for lunch.

"Be back at 5:00," he had said while Katie stood there with her hand out, "otherwise we're coming to find the three of you."

As they had walked out the door of their room, Katie had whispered, "Yeah, I bet he wants us out of the room." She jabbed Jana in the side, who barely reacted, now realizing she knew something about their parents' relationship that Katie didn't. And yet, she had no plans to share with Katie what that was.

They set up their towels on the beach, someone not far away with a boom box playing the Top 40 pop music they liked. "We'd have to move if it was country," Katie had joked, Jana agreeing with her.

Jana peeled of her white California t-shirt and denim shorts to reveal her new Ocean Pacific bikini, turquoise with orange trim. It didn't show as much as Katie's string bikini but Jana still felt self conscious in it.

"Be confident, Sister," Katie said, her hands on her hips, in her trademark pose. "Flaunt it while you can before we get married and have kids and hate the way we look."

"What do you mean?" Lisa asked, sitting in the sand in her purple suit as she let the dry sand filter through her fingers and drop all over her legs. Donna had pulled Lisa's long hair into a ponytail.

"You'll thank me later," Donna had insisted. "And make sure you wear lots of suntan lotion. All three of you. No one comes back with a burn. This California sun is a lot stronger than our Midwestern sun up north."

Jana slathered on the SPF 8, not really wanting to be a lobster, Katie only doing so after watching Jana. "Why do you always listen to her?" she sighed.

"Because sometimes she's right," Jana said, with a laugh. "Sometimes."

"Can I go in the water?" Lisa asked, looking like she was getting hot.

After she said that, and before Jana or Katie could answer, a girl ran by holding onto her bikini top.

"Hmmm," Katie said, watching the girl run and a guy chasing after her. "Watch out for your ties." She looked at Jana who looked down and realized her bikini was a lot more secure than Katie's.

"Yes, you can go," Katie said, ushering Lisa to the water where just a few kids frolicked in the waves. The beach was starting to get crowded and Katie looked to their right and saw the lifeguard in his red shorts and white tank top setting up for the day in the grayish blue lifeguard stand, one of many that dotted the Los Angeles County beaches. "There's a beefy dude," she laughed.

Jana shook her head and made herself comfortable on her towel. She yawned and laid on her back, using her right forearm to shield her eyes from the sun after she determined her sunglasses weren't up to the job, making her wonder if sunglasses sold in the Midwest were different than those sold in the West.

She was almost asleep when she heard Katie talking. "You know you need to do a sport."

After a moment, Jana sat up, took her arm away, and squinted at her sister. "Are you talking to me?"

"Duh," Katie said. "Who else would I be talking to?"

Jana said, "What are you talking about?" She replaced her arm with her sunglasses, Katie playing with her own hair, making it poof out further than it already did.

"You have to do a sport at school," Katie said. "Or be a cheerleader. Or something."

"But why do I need to do a sport?" Jana asked, knowing full well being a cheerleader would never be her thing. Nor would she believe her sister would want to share that with her.

Katie sighed and shook her head. "Look, you don't want to be uncool and all the cool kids are involved somehow."

"But you know I'm not very good at lot of things. I want to write books."

"I know. I know. You're the bookworm writer girl. But that's even more reason for you to do something. You'll meet more people, get more ideas about what to write about. I don't want you to run out of ideas because I fully intend that one day I'm going to sponge off your wealth."

"So what do you suggest?"

Around them more people arrived, mostly teens, and Katie was scoping out all the guys as she talked to Jana.

"Well, there's volleyball but I know you suck at that." She rolled her eyes, both of them remembering a backyard game when Jana broke her arm, tripping over a tree root, as she dove for the ball. "There's cross country. Those are the skinny people who run all the time." She paused, watching a guy wearing blue and yellow board shorts and no shirt talking to his friends. "Tennis!" She turned to Jana. "You could play tennis."

Jana fell backward and laughed. "Seriously? Didn't we take lessons once and I hit some girl in the stomach?"

Katie waved her off. "That happens. Maybe it was her fault. Think about it. I think it's a great idea."

"Because it's yours."

"Yeah, but you were better than you remember," Katie said, looking hopeful. "You won that little tournament we had to play at the end of our lessons, remember?"

Jana laughed. "I had no idea what I was doing."

"You got that little trophy," Katie said, holding out her hands as if to remember the size of it. "Do you still have that?"

Jana shrugged her shoulders. "It's probably in a box in my closet. I have no idea."

"You still have time to practice this summer," Katie reminded her. "You don't have to get a job like I do. Babysitting doesn't take up all your time."

Jana quickly dismissed the idea and looked at her pink notebook. She laid back down again, shutting her eyes, focusing on where she left off with the manuscript, as if she were saying a prayer about where to go next with it. She drifted off. The sounds of the surf, of people around her having a good time, of the music playing from the boom box were drown out finally by the thoughts in her head.

It was getting hot with the sun now fully above them. While she wished they had an umbrella, she also knew this was her chance to get a good start on her tan and that would be beneficial as summer went on. She lay there, uncomfortable in the heat, trying to distract herself with thoughts of her writing.

I'm too hot, she thought, sitting up again and looking around. There were a few trees planted along the low concrete wall that bordered the beach. She was reminded of the opening theme of "Three's Company" that took place nearby.

Some people biked, some roller skated, and others walked along– what was it called? She tried to remember from vocabulary in school- a promenade?

She spotted an empty area under a tree where someone had been sitting and had gotten up to leave. Jana turned to see Lisa playing in the water with two other girls looking like they were near her age. Katie worked on her tan, periodically flipping herself over to make sure she baked evenly on all sides.

"Nothing like an unevenly baked cake," she always joked when they laid out in the grass on their beach towels in the backyard.

Jana took her notebook and pen, walking quickly over to the spot before someone nabbed it. Straddling the low wall, her notebook resting on the concrete for a flat surface, she began to write again, oblivious to the world around her. She filled several pages before she looked up, grateful for the shade.

The sun inspires me but this might be too much, she thought, looking out at what appeared like sparkles bouncing off the ocean from the sun hitting the waves.

"Are you writing the great American novel?" a voice asked her.

Jana looked up to see a guy with curly black hair watching her. His surfboard rested on the wall underneath his legs and feet. She hadn't noticed him. Was he there before she had sat down?

She smiled and then laughed. "I am," she said.

"I guess that's what everyone wants to do, right?" He finished a drink in a red and white Coke cup, slurping down the rest of the liquid from the ice like they all did.

"I don't know about everyone else but it's what I want to do," she said, slipping her sunglasses off her face and onto the top of her head so she could see him better. He wore yellow board shorts with different colored circles on them and an Ocean Pacific t-shirt. He lives here, she thought.

"It's a beautiful, sunny day," he said, waving his hand at the scenery, the ocean, the people enjoying the beach and the surrounding area.

"I'm enjoying it," she said, tapping her pen on the notebook. "I tried to write in the sand but it didn't work so well."

"Have you been in the water?" He asked, raising his black eyebrows that matched his black hair.

Jana thought for a moment and he laughed. "If you have to think about it, then the answer is no."

He stood up. "I need to get in the water. Good luck with your writing."

Jana laughed and waved as he picked up his board and walked away. She noticed his board shorts and the white t-shirt didn't exactly match but it wasn't as if anyone cared. That was the look. He caught up with a group of guys, disappeared into the crowd, and that's where Jana lost him.

She tried to keep writing but now she found herself watching the water, looking for him. Him. He didn't have a name. Of course, nor did she.

Jana realized she should head back to what Katie called "Ground Zero"– where they had plopped down all their stuff– because she might be looking for her. And when she sat down– Katie laying on her back, sunglasses on, looking like she'd browned several shades darker in that short time Jana had been away– Jana looked up and saw him and his friends in the water.

She watched them for a while, paddling out past where the waves broke and then straddling their boards as they waited for the perfect wave.

Whatever that is, Jana thought, getting a little bored watching and returning to her writing.

Until Lisa came running up from the water.

"I'm hungry," she announced.

"That's nice," Katie said, not moving an inch.

"I am, too," Jana admitted, nudging Katie for the money, Katie pointing to her tote bag.

"Get me a Coke, please," Katie said.

By the time Jana and Lisa returned to their Ground Zero spot, the surfers had shifted north in the water and Jana couldn't see much other than bobbing figures. She stopped watching and pulled out the magazine she had bought when they were at the mall.

She first held the paper to her nose, sniffing the perfume ads, reminding herself of the department store, especially the other day.

"I'm going to buy you some Obsession for your birthday," Katie teased her, sipping her Coke and taking the crust of Lisa's pizza slice that she didn't want to eat.

"And then I'm going to buy you some Ralph Lauren," Jana teased back.

They looked at each other and laughed.

It was 4:00 pm when the beach started to empty out, the sun moving across the sky but still a few hours from hiding behind the horizon line for the night.

"I'm ready to go," Katie said, yawning. Lisa looked like she'd gotten too much sun and Jana leafed through the notebook, happy she had made some progress on her writing. "And if we're back before 5:00, there's no chance Dad will come looking for us."

The girls weren't excited when Mike and Donna announced they wanted to drive down the coast and check out some of the missions the next day. "It'll be a good cultural event," Mike said, taking a fry off Lisa's plate at dinner.

"Dad!" She said. "Eat your own fries."

"I have salad, see?" He pointed at his plate. "That's what happens when you get old– you have to eat salad."

Lisa made a face and pulled her plate closer to her.

"Something to look forward to," Katie said, before taking another bite of her cheeseburger. "Iceberg and carrots. And maybe a celery stick."

"You got too much sun today," Donna frowned at Lisa. "Did you make her put on suntan lotion?" She asked, looking at Katie and Jana.

"Twice," Katie said. "I guess she didn't get any brown pigment in her skin," she teased.

Lisa glared at her sister.

"Can't we go back to the beach?" Katie asked, Jana also wanting to ask but letting her sister be the one to ask first.

"You had a day on the beach," Mike said, ignoring them and frowning as he took a bite of his salad and then looking for more Thousand Island salad dressing.

"Maybe we should let them have another day," Donna suggested. Jana thought it was a rare time their mother suggested they do something without the girls around. "They did just fine today."

Jana watched her father's reaction and waited, still not sure if she should chime in on this one.

She didn't have to.

"Okay," he said. "One more day but after that we're going up to Malibu as a family," he said.

"Are we going to see where Malibu Barbie lives?" Lisa asked, innocently.

"Really?" Katie asked, looking amused and nudging Lisa with her elbow. "She's not real, you know."

"Yes, she is," Lisa announced. "She's at home at our house. Maybe I should have brought her so she could show us where she lives."

"Add that to your list," Katie told their parents. "You should ask around and find out what house Malibu Barbie lives in and we can drive by like we drove by the stars' homes."

The following morning Mike and Donna left early, wanting to get a start before rush hour traffic. Mike gave the girls extra money to pick up something for breakfast although Donna insisted they eat the leftover donuts and orange juice.

"I'm too lazy to go find food," Katie admitted pulling herself out of the bed. "We might as well eat what's here."

"I want a hot dog for lunch," Lisa announced, her face still looking red from their time in the sun the previous day.

"I think we might need to find you a hat today," Katie said, looking at Lisa, who was still in the bed. "Or Mom will lecture us again."

In the darkened motel suite, they dressed and found the donuts and juice before leaving for the beach.

"We're even earlier than yesterday," Jana noted quietly, seeing there were fewer people on the beach. But more surfers in the water.

"We can watch the surfers!" Katie exclaimed, peeling off her shorts and t-shirt to show off another bikini– this one the one she'd brought from home. "Way cool!"

Jana didn't look at her plastic Swatch; she kept her eyes peeled on the scene around her, thinking about how she wished some form of this could be her everyday life.

You'll have to work, she thought to herself. It's not like you can hang out on the beach all day.

But why not? she seemed to be responding to herself. Maybe there is a way to make it all come together.

When Lisa announced she needed to go to the bathroom later that morning, Katie offered to take her. "I need a walk anyway," she said, letting out a deep sigh. "The boys aren't really biting. I must have boring Midwestern girl written all over me."

Jana returned to her deep thoughts that she was writing in her notebook when a dark shadow loomed over her, at first feeling as if someone had placed a beach umbrella right behind them. Then she felt drops of water and looked up to see him. He was standing over her, board in one hand, dripping wet, and raining water all over her.

"Did you get in the water yet? I was wondering if you might melt if you got water on you," he teased.

"I did get in the water yesterday," Jana insisted– she had played ocean beach ball with Lisa for a while.

"What about today?"

Jana smiled and then laughed. "It's still early."

He looked at her, looked at the water, then looked back at her. "You don't come from where there's an ocean," he said, rubbing his chin. "How about a surfing lesson?"

Jana looked at him and her face lit up. But then she backed off, her face turning dark. "I don't think I can do that," she admitted, waving at him.

"Why not?" he asked. "Because you don't know my name? It's Scott." He stuck out his hand. "I don't know your name and I'm willing to teach you surfing," he said.

"Jana," she said, standing up and wiping the sand off her legs, the inevitable sand that gets everywhere at the beach. "I'm Jana. But girls don't surf."

"So? Do you care?" He shrugged his shoulders. "Are you scared? I'll be with you."

"What if I get hit in the head with the board?" She asked, cringing at the thought and of her experiences with sports before. She always seemed to be the one who caused some sort of accident. Jana knew her mother would never let her surf if she were there now. Donna felt much better that Jana wanted to write, not bounce around doing cartwheels like Katie.

He laughed and shrugged his shoulders, his skin quickly drying in the warm sun. "It could happen but how will you know if you don't try? You'd rather stay on the beach?"

Go go go, Jana told herself, looking around and realizing that Katie and Lisa still weren't back. They'll see I'm in the water, she told herself, shrugged her shoulders, and dropped her sunglasses into her tote bag.

"Good thing you wore a one-piece suit today," Scott said looking at her white and fuchsia striped swimsuit, grabbing his board, and leading her to the shore.

"Why?" Jana asked, not knowing a thing about what was about to happen.

"Less rash on your skin from the board," he said, rubbing his hand across his hairless chest. "When you pop up."

Jana looked at the board. It appeared he had waxed it that morning but she could see sand stuck under the wax and wondered how that might feel when she rubbed against it. Maybe this wasn't a good idea. It sounded painful.

They walked along the shore until they arrived a bit north where it wasn't so crowded in the water.

"The surf isn't so good now– it's really died down– so there won't be many surfers– but it's a good time to learn," he said, plopping his white board with a red stripe down the middle onto the sand.

Jana found herself lost in what Scott was saying and showing her, giving her all the lessons of what he had learned about surfing.

"It's you and the ocean," he said, waving at two guys who came out of the water– with boards– who waved at him.

"I guess you started young," she said shyly, wanting to ask a billion questions but remembering how impolite she'd been told that was.

"My dad brought me out when I was like six," Scott said, looking out at the water, as if he could see the memory there. It reminded Jana of her father doing that very thing when he talked about Gloria when they were in Albuquerque. She wondered if everyone found their memories that way.

A part of Jana found it hard to concentrate at the same time though. She heard the words but she wasn't always sure what they meant because she kept thinking about how scared she was.

"Let's practice the pop up," Scott said.

He got down on all fours and showed her on the beach how to jump up on the board and balance herself. Jana watched, hoping she could remember everything that Scott said. He made it look easy but she knew that wouldn't be the case with the ocean underneath her, rolling at its own rhythm. Part of her just wanted to watch him because she could. He was cute with that curly black hair. But the other part of her wanted to impress him. She didn't want him to think she was an idiot.

"Don't worry," he said, as if he could read her mind.

I'm too tentative, she thought, that's why he's saying that.

Jana tried to look confident and when she did, she instantly forgot about anyone on the beach who might be watching.

Before she knew it, Scott had slipped the surfboard leash onto her right ankle and he picked up the board, walking next to her, making sure that the two of them didn't get tangled up.

"How do you know it goes on that ankle?" she asked looking slightly confused.

He looked up from where he was attaching the Velcro strap and said, "Because when you fell forward on the pop up, your right foot went first. And you write with your right hand."

"Very astute," she teased. Confident, she thought, this is what it feels like to be confident.

"Using SAT words are you?" he teased, standing up and wiping the sand off his hands.

Jana laughed. And when she did, something changed inside her. But what she didn't realize at first was that really it had changed how she presented herself to the world. For one, she was no longer on the outside watching, here she was in the thick of the part of something. She was the action, not watching the action as she usually did with Katie and her family.

In doing that– the part she wasn't aware of– she was showing herself off as someone different to the world. And that meant Scott, too.

He gave her a few more tips, she did what he told her to do, and suddenly she found herself in the water, Scott helping her onto the board, the waves mellow. "Like Hawaii," he said, "it's a great ride in Hawaii." Once they were past the breaks, Scott swimming alongside side her and holding onto the board, he said, "I'll call out exactly what you need to do."

Jana nodded her head, the butterflies starting. Was she really doing this? she asked herself, barely any time to process what *this* meant, how everyone would react when they found out.

But she hadn't surfed yet. In fact, she hadn't done anything yet.

Scott's eyes focused mostly on the horizon, watching the incoming waves. "I don't know how you see anything," Jana admitted, unsure how he could judge something that was forming so far away.

"You never totally understand the ocean," Scott laughed. "My dad said that's the ultimate nirvana and if we got there, there'd be no reason for living anymore. We spend our entire lives chasing it though."

At first Jana thought about her dad and how he often remarked that about golf, but then she said, "Maybe like chasing writing the perfect book."

Scott turned his head to look at her and smiled. "Exactly." He paused and then quickly said, "Okay, here comes a good one. Paddle paddle paddle!"

Jana cut her hands through the cool ocean water, not thinking, just listening to what Scott said to do and doing it. She had no idea where the wave was but then he called out, "Nope. Not good."

This went on for a while, the sun hot, the water cool, Jana forgetting about anything else in life, any anxiety that left her wondering what life was all about, nor did she see the people all around them, not thinking how some of them were watching the pair.

It was there on the water that she learned the most about Scott, about his life in Los Angeles, about how he was going into his junior year in high school– like Katie– how he worked at a pizza place in the evenings, how his parents had gotten together young and bought a little house right near the beach before he was born and how they still lived there. And that his dream wasn't all about being one with the ocean, but about traveling the world and seeing what it had to offer. "Like those guys in 'Endless Summer,'" he said, again watching for a wave.

"What was that?" Jana asked, thinking it was a Beach Boys movie.

"The ultimate surfing movie," Scott laughed. "I should have known you wouldn't know."

Jana made a note to remind herself to ask her dad about it. He seemed to know more about California culture than she'd ever been aware of.

"Here we go!" Scott called. "This is it finally!" He gave the board a shove and let go.

Jana turned her head back toward the shore and Scott called, "Paddle paddle paddle!"

Don't think, just do, she told herself. She felt a rush of energy behind her, not knowing it was the wave rolling underneath her.

"Be one with the water," she remembered Scott saying. Surfing was all about catching that energy, that rush, and going with it.

"Pop up!" He called, Jana somehow pushed her body off the board while at the same time balanced it on the balsa wood that floated on the surface. She looked straight ahead like he said to do, not down. And while she saw people on the beach, they were just figures. She focused on the buildings beyond the beach, keeping her eyes level with her body as she balanced herself.

"Yesssss!" She heard him call from behind her as she surfed the wave. Surfed, a word she never thought would ever describe her own life. The water under her, Jana stayed steady with her arms stretched out as she and the board headed for shore and finally landed in the sand where the wave ran out and retreated back to the ocean.

When she looked up in front of her, she instantly saw Lisa and Katie cheering. And their father. Jana laughed and smiled and Scott came swimming from behind. "You did it!" He exclaimed, giving her an awkward hug as she stood next to the board, the waves still crashing to the shore, and their bodies getting tangled in it all to celebrate. "You did it! I knew you could do it!"

Jana couldn't stop smiling and started to laugh. "Can we do it again?" She asked, then realizing that her dad was calling her name and motioning her to him. "Oh, that's my dad," she said, a little disappointed. She didn't think it was that late in the day yet.

"You're not in trouble, are you?" Scott asked. "Do I need to leave quickly?"

Jana laughed but shook her head. "I hope not!" She ran her hand through her wet hair and Scott detached the Velcro on the leash and carried the board toward her family, minus Donna, who Jana believed must have been back at the hotel.

"Look at you!" Mike exclaimed, but Katie and Lisa hugged her first. When she got to her dad, looking halfway cool in his sunglasses but also looking like he had just stepped off the golf course in his khaki shorts and dark green polo shirt. "I didn't know leaving you at the beach meant you were going to learn to surf. Maybe we finally found a sport for you."

"I couldn't find you," Katie said, looking a bit exasperated. And then, "I wish we had a surfing team at school. That I know you could do!"

"I saw you," Lisa reassured Jana. "I knew where you were. Katie needs glasses."

Jana forgot about Scott until her dad said, "And who taught you how to surf?"

"Oh," Jana said, now embarrassed.

But Scott beat her to it. "I'm Scott Morgan, sir," he said, stretching his arm and hand to Mike. Jana watched them shake warmly.

"I hate to be the bearer of bad news but your mom is waiting for us to go to dinner," Mike said, "so I think your surfing adventure is over." Then he turned to Scott. "Maybe you'd like to join us."

Jana was so excited about surfing she didn't think much about Scott and was surprised about her father's offer. She felt Katie's finger in her back.

"Thank you," Scott said, "but I have to work tonight."

"Well, maybe again before we leave," Mike said.

Jana suddenly felt tongue tied and later she was grateful for Katie who at that point stepped in. "We're going to Malibu tomorrow but we'll be back early enough to go to the movies," she said.

Jana had no idea what her sister was talking about but Katie's finger in her back indicated to be quiet.

"We want to see that Ferris Bueller movie everyone is raving about," Katie said, sounding knowledgeable. "After all, we are from Chicago."

What Jana also didn't see was that Katie had sent Lisa to Ground Zero and she came running back with Jana's pink notebook and pharmaceutical pen, shoving them at Scott.

"Jana will call you," Katie said.

"I get to write in the coveted notebook," Scott asked, writing his number on the back. With his name and "Surf Teacher Extraordinaire" underneath it.

"We need to go," Mike said, ushering the girls toward the promenade. "Thank you again," he said to Scott.

"I'll walk with you to the sidewalk," he said, Jana lingering behind, Katie pushing everyone to move ahead so the duo could have a few moments alone.

"I didn't know my family was going to show up or do that," Jana whispered, a little embarrassed.

Scott waved it off. "It's cool. When they reached the sidewalk, he pointed to the right. "My house is that way. I guess I'll talk to you tomorrow?"

Jana nodded, feeling awkward, having no idea what to do, finally looked up and said, "Thank you. That was great."

"*You* were great," Scott said, giving her a quick hug and running off with his surfboard under his arm as she turned to go the other way and catch up with her family.

When she reached the trio, Mike put his arm around her and squeezed her. "You really surprised me," he said with a chuckle and a smile. "Katie I'd never have thought twice about getting on a surfboard but I never thought that's something you'd do."

Jana shrugged her shoulders. "It wasn't my idea," she admitted. "I was pretty scared."

"But I bet you'd do it again?"

She laughed and nodded, feeling exhilaration she wasn't sure she had had ever felt before.

When they reached the motel, Lisa threw the door of their suite open and exclaimed, "Jana surfed a wave!"

Donna closed the paperback book she was reading and looked up, confused.

"She did!" Katie said, proceeding to tell their mother all about it.

Jana lingered in the kitchen area, looking for a donut. All the time on the water had made her hungry. And now she was feeling a bit tired, too. The excitement had taken its toll.

"Don't snack," Donna warned Jana. "We're going to dinner soon."

"She was on the water for God knows how long," Mike said, holding up his hands to show he had nothing to do with it. "She really surfed."

"Jana?" Donna asked, forgetting about the snacking comment as Jana ate a powdered donut.

"Our Jana," Katie laughed. "I'll even let you have the shower first," she told Jana, gesturing toward the bathroom.

"Just this once," Jana said. "I'm sure it'll never happen again."

"Never."

As Jana shut the door of the white-tiled bathroom and turned the shower on, looking for the hottest water possible, she sat on the side of the tub and sighed, looking in the mirror across the room above the sink, seeing her dark blonde hair streaky light blonde from the sun of the last two days, her cheeks also a bit red– she didn't know that being in the water brought on a greater reflection of sun and thus it was stronger ("I should sunbathe on a surfboard," Katie said when she found that out).

She almost didn't recognize herself. But she knew it wasn't because she looked tanned and her hair blonder, it was because she had just done something that she didn't know she could. And that would reverse the course of her life.

Still there was another factor she hadn't been able to soak in yet. Scott.

What did Scott mean in all of this? *Who* was Scott in all of this? She thought about the way about him, easy was the word that came to her. Very California. Very laissez faire, a word she remembered from history about businesses not getting involved in politics but it was the idea of letting go that made Jana think of it relating to Scott. He didn't frazzle easily. But yet he didn't seem like what she had always thought was the typical surfer, the lazy California guy. Scott was motivated.

She stepped into the shower and let the hot water warm her skin and remove the salt and sand that had stuck to her.

"You were due for such a great day," Katie would say later, on the trip home. "I'm happy for you."

For all her eye rolling, Jana thought, her sister really did care under that exterior.

"You're more authentic than me," Katie had said during that same conversation as they passed through the mountains of Western Arizona heading back toward New Mexico. "Somehow you're more comfortable in your skin than I am." She had then turned to the window to look out at the scenery.

Jana watched her sister for a moment, wanting to tell her that wasn't true, that she felt like she couldn't be herself, that she wanted to be as confident as Katie was to call out cheers and do cartwheels in front of large audiences of people. But the words wouldn't come out. Something told her it wasn't the time to say that. And she, too, turned to look at the scenery, but from her side of the car, Lisa asleep between them.

The next morning– after Jana lay awake until after midnight staring at the popcorn ceiling of the motel room unable to completely process the day enough so she could sleep– she heard a soft knock at the door of the room where she and her sisters were sleeping, then the faint light coming through as someone opened the door.

"Jana," said a voice, her father's voice quietly. "Jana."

"Dad?" She asked sleepily, sitting up in bad, neither of her sisters stirring.

"Get your swimsuit on," he said in an encouraging way. "I want to take you to the beach."

"But it's only…" she looked at the clock next to the bed and saw it wasn't even 6:00 am. Surely the sun was still coming up. She'd been getting up early but not that early. "It's too early. No one will be on the beach."

"Yes, they will," Mike said. "Come on. Don't think, just do."

That phrase, "Don't think, just do" was something he always told the girls when he wanted them to trust him. And yet the girls knew they didn't trust him when he used the word "trust" thus one day he changed the way he phrased it and never told them to trust him again, just to not think, just do.

She heard him yell, "Ow!" from the living room area of the suite and she cringed, guessing that he had just stubbed his toe on the couch or another piece of furniture. The coffee table, too, was made of a heavy wood and Lisa had run right into it and jammed her knee, leaving her in tears, while Katie reminded her that she was supposed to walk around furniture, not into it.

Mike then swore and Jana bit her tongue from laughing, wishing Katie were up to hear it because it always made them laugh together.

"I know we shouldn't laugh," Katie would say, holding her hand over her mouth. "But it cracks me up. It's the only time we ever hear him swear."

Good grief, Jana then sighed in her mind, forgetting Mike swearing, climbing out of bed, and looking for her swimsuit. Because it was still dark in the room, she grabbed what she could find, the one piece she'd brought from home and slipped it on, throwing a large summer Limited t-shirt over it and then carrying her flip flops out to the living area where Mike was sitting on the arm of the couch waiting for her.

"Dad," she said, still sleepy– and yet happy about the events of the day before– "What is this about?"

She watched him take a look at her and then grab her beach towel from the back of the counter bar stool where she had left it the evening before to dry.

"Come on," he said, urging her out the door into the morning air.

The walk was quiet, the shadows long, the air feeling cool and different as Jana looked between the buildings and saw the light making the ocean visible again.

"This better be good," she said, wishing she were still sleeping.

"It will be," he said, Jana not realizing he was smiling as he looked away from her and at the ocean.

"Are you thinking I should join the swim team and you want me to go for an ocean swim?" she asked, completely confused about what was going on.

Mike just laughed and they turned the corner to the beach. Jana looked at the ocean– as if to drink it in would fill her energy depleted by her sleepiness– and saw figures in the water.

Surfers.

"Dad?" Jana asked.

"Don't think, just do," he repeated. "Isn't that what you did yesterday?"

She felt Mike's reassuring hand on her back, pushing her slightly forward. "I'll leave now if you want. Or stay."

"You can stay," she said, feeling slightly terrified suddenly.

All the surfers looked the same out there, just outlined shadows straddling their boards with the sun hitting the water just right that it sparkled, as if someone had dropped a jar of glitter on the ocean. Jana stopped walking and she felt Mike's solid hand push her slightly forward again. "Go right to the water line," he whispered, walking slightly behind her.

She realized she couldn't see where he was looking with his sunglasses hiding his eyes, but she could see the rest of his face looked determined. Part of her wished that Katie were with her instead of Mike. The boys would flock to Katie but here she was showing up with her dad of all people. She felt slightly embarrassed. When Katie had an idea– even when Jana didn't completely agree with it usually because it made Jana step out of her comfort zone– it at least seemed cool.

In that moment, the cold sand under Jana's feet, her hands shaking as she carried her flip flops, she didn't feel cool at all. But yet she didn't want her dad to leave her. They stood at the water line, Jana letting the water rush over her feet, but standing far enough away that she didn't think any of the surfers would come her way.

And then she heard her name.

"Jana!"

Scott.

Jana looked to her right and saw Scott surf a small wave to the shore, grab his board, and run over to her and her dad. "What happened to Malibu?" he asked, smiling, looking at both Jana and Mike.

Just then Jana wondered, what did happen to Malibu, and couldn't speak. She opened her mouth to ask but found all she could do was stare at her dad. Mike smiled, patted Jana on the shoulder and said, "We'll go tomorrow. Jana, go surf some more. I believe you have a great teacher here."

"Thanks," Scott said with a big smile and still looking at Mike.

Jana finally spoke. "But how did you know?"

"I know a little more about things that you think I do," Mike told her. "I'm going to send your sisters down to the beach when they're up." He handed Scott some bills. "Get her some breakfast, okay? She hasn't had much of a chance to think since I woke her up."

"I will, sir," Scott said, taking the bills and shoving them into the snapped pocket on his red and blue board shorts. "Come on," he said to Jana. "The waves are perfect for you right now." He used his hand to indicate the smoothness. "Rolling nice and long for a good ride. Let's see how many we can get in before the wind picks up later today and they get choppy."

When Jana looked back, she saw her dad had already turned to leave and was walking toward the street. I didn't get to say thank you, she thought, knowing she had to remember to do that later.

Everything suddenly felt like a blur and later when she would try to remember that day, it felt as if it had holes in it because there were only portions that would remain in her mind.

It felt natural when Scott took her hand and part of Jana– probably the writer– felt like she had just entered a scene of one of those 1960s beach movies that her father watched on television. Frankie Avalon would grab Annette Funicello's hand– the other arm carrying his surfboard– and they would run toward the water.

Scott's hand felt strong, pulling her forward but not too hard, just enough, as if he knew how much pushing Jana needed.

"Your dad is a cool guy," Scott said, when they reached a pile of the backpacks and clothes strewn across a small area of the beach, the beach spot for Scott and his friends.

"I know," Jana said quietly, still feeling dazed and not wanting to tell Scott that she, too, was surprised.

The air continued to warm up as the sun rose and Scott said, "Leave your stuff here. Let's get in the water."

As Jana waded into the coolish water, Scott walked next to her, maneuvering the board to his side. "I was afraid I wouldn't get to see you again," he said, not looking at her, instead looking straight out at the incoming waves.

"Why? I was going to call you later." She didn't tell him she was terrified to call him later, that she, too, was afraid she wouldn't see him again.

Scott then looked at her, Jana now noticing his wet curls flying all over his head, the water sending them in different directions. He shrugged his shoulders. "Sometimes you don't know. My dad says that the beauty of life is that you don't know. You just throw it out there and let it happen. And I guess that's what happened today. Thanks to your dad."

He smiled at Jana and she smiled back.

"And knowing that you're leaving, let's see how many rides you can get in before you go back to Chicago. Deal?"

"Deal," she laughed and he pushed the board toward her in the waist-deep water to jump on it.

"I'll teach you more about choosing waves today, too."

When Jana looked back at the building waves behind them– at the endless horizon of water– she had the sense that the ocean was calmer on this morning than the day before. There were a number of surfers in the water (although she didn't see any other girls) but no one appeared to be taking the few waves coming along. They sat there in the water for some time, having a conversation.

"It was really good when I got here," Scott said. "The sun was just coming up, too. Talk about amazing. I never get tired of it." He paused, both of them watching the horizon and then suddenly he said, "Ah! Here's one! Paddle paddle paddle!"

Jana hoped she would remember what to do from the previous day, feeling Scott pushing her board from the back, but she didn't dare look back. Why look back? She thought, just go forward.

Forward forward forward. She tried to paddle hard enough that she and the water moved at the same pace, that they became one. Suddenly, she felt movement under her. The wave.

"Pop up!" She heard Scott call. "Pop up!"

Stay in the center, keep the board balanced, she told herself. Jana looked forward, balancing her arms as if she were Ralph Macchio in "The Karate Kid" standing on a stump.

And there it was. Again. She'd managed to hit the wave just right, to get on top of it, to meet it in just the right place. She was gliding across the water until she ran out of surf and the ocean retreated, the fin of the board stuck in the sand.

"You did it!" Scott called, running through the water toward her. She stepped off the board and waited for him to get to her.

Without thinking, they embraced and laughed.

"That was awesome," he said.

By then, most of the surfers had started to leave the water. Jana saw her own fingers had turned wrinkled as if she had been in the water too long, knowing they had been in longer than she. And she not realizing how long she and Scott had been out there together.

"Are you hungry?" Scott asked, carrying his board back to the spot where they had left her things.

"Yes," Jana laughed, her stomach growling. She had no idea what time it was– not that it mattered– but she was past ready to have breakfast.

Several of Scott's friends had already gathered there, resting from their morning jaunt in the ocean. They all looked about the same age, Jana feeling as if she were infringing on guy time and wasn't surprised when Scott started to introduce her and the first comment was "We don't want any scared girls here," a tall blonde guy named Jeff said.

"I'm not scared," Jana snapped back, surprised by her own confidence. Usually it didn't happen that quickly but on this morning she began to acknowledge that she had changed. At least a little.

Suddenly he backed off, pushing his hands as if showing he was backing off– a half-peeled banana in one hand. "You're right. You did have that wave behind you this morning and you didn't back down from it."

"Yeah, dude," another guy said, glaring at him. "That was one of the biggest waves this morning."

Scott just laughed. "Come on, how about a bagel or a donut?"

As they walked away, Jana heard the conversation continue, the guy sitting down continued to defend her. "I bet those gymnast girls would be great on boards with all the flying through air they do on balance beams."

Jana and Scott sat together near the same place where they had met, each one with a bagel and an orange juice. At first they were quiet, just watching the beach fill up with people, Scott sometimes pointing out something about the now lagging surf that he noticed.

Jana didn't see her sisters, wondering if they were still sleeping because surely Katie would have wanted to be on the beach as soon as she heard what Mike had done that morning. And Jana also wondering if her dad had stayed around, watching her with Scott.

"You're really lucky to have a dad like that," Scott said. "Is your mom like that, too? You must have really cool parents."

Jana laughed. "Hmm." She didn't know how to put it in words and she looked out at the ocean as if the answers were there. She just needed to see them and grab them. And in that same moment, she realized she *was* lucky. She was here with Scott because of her dad. He knew something she didn't; he made sure she didn't miss an opportunity. And it felt like the first time in Jana's life that everything the family did on that day was altered because of her.

"We didn't get to go see Malibu Barbie's house today!" Lisa called, running up to Jana, Katie running behind her, waving her arm, trying to get Lisa to stop.

"Um, I'm sorry," Jana said, still processing all that had happened, too caught up in being with Scott that she had blocked it out of her mind for, at least, the time being.

"We're going to tomorrow," Katie said, grabbing Lisa's shoulder and pulling her back to the beach. And then turning back to Jana, "We're by the guard stand. Dad said we needed to be back at 4:00."

Jana nodded and watched her sisters head back to the beach, Katie clearly giving Lisa an earful.

After they had disappeared into the sea of people who had gathered on the beach that late morning, Jana started to talk. "I never thought of my dad as cool," she laughed, Scott reached for her crumbled bagel wrapper to place in the white paper bag they had been given at the bagel shop. "He's fine but who thinks their dad is cool?"

Scott laughed and said, "I get it." He stood up and took a few steps to throw away the bag in a large trash can and came back.

Suddenly, Jana– and she didn't know where it came from– started to talk about her dad, about the trip, about Gloria, about how differently she saw him now.

"Wow," Scott said. "That's a lot to absorb."

"I know!" Jana laughed.

"Is that what you've been writing?"

She laughed again and shrugged her shoulders. "I think I have a story. We'll see."

Because Katie had made it clear what time they were due back at the motel, Jana and Scott walked back to the spot where his friends were, a few of them having left, and happened to glance at her right forearm which was now turning red. Along with the rest of her. "Oh no," she said softly.

"Yikes," Scott said, looking around to see if anyone had anything. "We aren't so good about that around here."

Jana walked over to Katie– Lisa was back in the water– and sat down with her for a moment. "I need some suntan lotion," she said, holding out her arms.

"Oh no," Katie said, quickly digging into her bag. "Dad gets you up this morning and he obviously didn't think about that."

"That's why he has Mom," Jana laughed. "They each have a different perspective of the picture in front of them."

When Jana got up to leave to go back to be with Scott, Katie said, "Hey. We're still going to see that Ferris Bueller movie tomorrow night."

Jana nodded.

When Katie asked her what they had talked about all afternoon, Jana didn't know what to tell her sister. It seemed like so much yet it didn't. She had fallen asleep at some point on the beach, too, although she didn't know how long. If it weren't for the sun moving in the sky or the people changing around them, it was as if time stood still that afternoon.

"You know," Scott said, looking at his watch, "It's almost 4:00. You better go. Your dad's been good to me. I don't want to piss him off."

Jana suddenly felt a little sad that all was coming to an end and started to pull on her t-shirt coverup.

"I'll walk with you to the motel," he said.

"Like yesterday?" Jana asked, trying to be hopeful.

"Like yesterday."

"I still don't like you," Lisa said to Scott when they arrived at ground zero, Katie shaking out the beach towels.

"Get over it," Katie told her. "You'll see it tomorrow. It's less than twenty-four hours away." Then she turned to Scott. "And we're going to see 'Ferris Bueller' tomorrow night," she said again, clearly hinting for him not to forget.

"Promise?" Scott asked, looking at Jana.

"Promise," Katie answered, Jana grinning at Scott.

"Good thing I'm off again," he said as the four of them started their walk toward the motel.

"I hate goodbyes," Katie mumbled when they reached the motel and grabbed Lisa's hand to pull her away. She nudged Jana and then Katie and Lisa quickly disappeared around the corner behind a tall hedge that led to the pool area and the rooms.

"Call me tomorrow," Scott said, tapping her arm lightly and smiling. His hair had dried but it was still all over the place, Jana wondering how badly she looked, especially now that she was slightly red. And then there was the lecture she'd get from her mom. "I better go," he said. "I left early this morning. My mom knows where I'm at but I generally don't stay at the beach that long and I'm sure she's home from work by now."

This time Scott– and his surfboard– disappeared leaving Jana standing in the parking lot by herself. She happened to look into the little motel office and saw Harry the bald owner buried in a magazine, only the top of his shiny head visible to her as she continued to disappear around the same hedge her sisters had a few minutes ago.

Donna didn't ask Jana anything, barely looking up from her book when Jana walked into the room. Katie and Lisa laid on the couch– feet to feet– watching MTV. No one said a word– although Katie looked up and smiled at Jana– and Jana went into their room and then showered. She felt a little strange and she didn't know why.

"Where's Dad?" she asked when she came out, dressed for dinner, hoping she didn't look as red as she thought she did.

"He'll be back," Donna said, finally looking up. "Oh dear. You got a little red. Your father forgot to have you put suntan lotion on when he woke you up this morning."

Jana shrugged her shoulders, and brushed her wet hair into a ponytail– catching a view of herself in the mirror by the kitchenette and seeing her now sun-kissed hair from several full days outside by the ocean. She thought it looked as if she had squeezed lemons on it like she had heard that models did.

"I'm going to the pool," she said to no one in particular– because no one seemed to notice– taking her notebook and pen to the empty pool area and settling in to catch up in her journal.

Jana didn't know how long she sat there, watching the still water as she always did, collecting her thoughts and weeding her way through everything that had happened over the past two days. When she couldn't decide where to start, she thought, duh, start at the beginning.

And she did, trying to put down as many details as she could remember, no, as many details as felt important to her about meeting Scott. And surfing. And her dad. And where did it stop?

"You're writing like mad," she heard her dad say, appearing out of nowhere in his navy polo shirt and khaki shorts. He slipped into the white plastic chair across from her.

Jana looked up, stopping mid-sentence, having just gotten into what it felt like to surf the wave that morning– what turned out to be the only one she surfed that day because the ocean was changing and she'd been lucky to get one at all.

"Did you get a wave this morning?" Mike asked.

Jana forgot that her father was sitting across from her. He looks happy, she thought, his fingers wrapped together, dropped into his lap. His face looked tanned; he looks good tanned, Jana thought.

"I did," she said with a smile. But she didn't want to talk about the wave. She knew she wanted to ask him some questions. "How did you know?"

Mike laughed and looked away and then back at her. "I've been here before, remember."

Jana shrugged her shoulders. "That was a long time ago. You knew something. And you don't surf."

Her dad smiled at her and sat up to lean forward toward Jana. "You know what? No matter what happens in your future, I want you to have as many experiences as you can." He pointed at the notebook she was writing in. "I know that the more you experience, the more you have to write about. And if I had let you sleep in this morning, you'd be short more to write about."

"I don't understand," Jana said, feeling confused, but knowing she was so overwhelmed with thoughts and experiences in that moment that it wasn't hard to be confused.

"Your life is always going to be a balance of writing and experiencing life." He held out his hands as if they were balanced scales. "I realized on this trip that as your dad it's my job to help you have as many experiences as I can to give you more to write about."

"Did you just decide this?"

He smiled again. "After seeing you out there with Scott– that's his name, right?– yesterday, that's when it hit me on the head. And I wanted you to have another crack at that today."

"So you uprooted the whole family day for me?"

"We never do that for you, Jana, you know that. Your mom says you're the old soul in the family, you sort of sit back and watch most of the time, as if you're taking it all in so you can write about it later. This time I wanted you to know what it felt like to have it be all about you, to have an experience no one else in the family will have."

She was starting to feel tired, as if someone had taxed her brain from all this information or she had been studying too hard for a test and felt as if things were starting to fall out of her brain because there wasn't room for anything else. Her brain was like a plate of spaghetti and meatballs piled so high that the meatballs were sliding off.

They sat there for a few moments, Jana still thinking, watching the empty pool, her father doing the same.

"You know," he said, still watching the water as he spoke, his fingers still intertwined. "I realized after we left Albuquerque– after all we did have quite a few miles to think as we drove here– that life is about embracing everything you can. You can't always have what you want, you won't always get what you think is supposed to be yours or supposed to work out. And yet how lucky are you that you've had that experience at all."

Jana listened, hoping she wouldn't forget his words, not all of them resonating with her in that moment although she wished she could record them so she could write them down as quotes. And keep them close at hand forever.

"No matter what happens, Jana, I want you to have the experience of a lifetime. And then build on that experience, that the next time you have the chance you surf twelve waves or whatever it is. I want you to look back on this trip and see how these experiences are helping you form who you're supposed to be. And what you're supposed to contribute to the world."

"You mean as a writer?" She asked, quietly, running her pen along the distorted wire edge of her notebook.

"That and whatever else life holds for you."

Jana nodded her head. And for a reason she didn't understand, she thought she was going to start to cry. She was happy, absolutely was she happy to have met Scott, but what she hadn't told anyone was how scared she was because they were going to leave in two days. Part of her wondered why she was getting herself into something that was going to end in less than 48 hours.

And she thought of Katie who always dove right into situations and never looked back. She might be dramatic about it but she didn't let anything stop her from going full-speed ahead.

Jana had never been like that. Her dad was right, she was usually the one watching from the sidelines.

"And you know what else?" Mike asked, leaning forward again.

Jana sniffled and looked at him.

Mike smiled. "Seeing you up on that surfboard was the highlight of this trip for me." Jana smiled and thought his eyes looked watery as he got up, ruffled the hair on the top of her head, and walked back up to their room. "My hope is that it's just the first of many great adventures in your life."

Jana wiped her own tears, finished the sentence in her notebook, and followed him back to their room.

$\mathcal{U}$nder more ordinary circumstances– as in, had Jana not surfed the day before– she knew that going to Malibu would have been a more exciting activity for the following day. Only Lisa seemed genuinely thrilled about it, still talking about driving by Malibu Barbie's house– until Katie informed her it was in a gated community and they wouldn't get to see it.

"Think about it," Katie explained as they traveled north on the Pacific Coast Highway, passing by first the boats of Marina Del Rey and then the LAX airport, "if you were Malibu Barbie, would you want everyone driving by your house and gawking at it?"

Lisa didn't flinch. "Yes," she said.

"That didn't work," Katie mumbled, then to her parents, "I guess we have to go past Malibu Barbie's house. Wink wink."

"We got it," their father called from the front seat, turning his head partway back at them as he maneuvered through Los Angeles traffic.

Jana bit her lip to keep from laughing thinking it was like Lisa to believe that Santa Claus still existed– although she didn't– and they were taking a drive by his house in the North Pole. She didn't want to ruin anything for Lisa so she turned her head to look out the window even though it was Katie's side that was getting the ocean view.

When she had awakened that morning, she had to pinch herself to realize that the past few days hadn't been a dream. It was one of those days in one's life that are so few and far between that only seemingly happen just a handful of times in one's lifetime.

As she watched the cliffs they passed on the right side now that they reached Malibu itself, she thought about how she wanted to create more events like that. Jana let her mind wander as her father drove, the car quiet, everyone focused on the scenery and probably the sleep they wished they were still getting that morning.

I created that one, didn't I? she asked herself. I did it by doing something I didn't think I could do.

She glanced down at her tote bag and saw the pink notebook peeking out of the top.

That's how I create more, isn't it? Reaching outside what's comfortable for me, what I know I can do, to do what's unfamiliar.

She felt as if someone else were talking in her mind, someone who felt familiar but whom she didn't know. Then her mind drifted into how she could incorporate the surfing adventure into what she was writing. Maybe what she wrote wasn't what she thought it was going to be.

But Jana stopped thinking about everything as Mike turned the station wagon into a large parking lot that butted up against the beach.

"Here we are," he said. "Surfrider Beach. A very famous surfing beach, I might add." He turned the ignition car's off and gave his usual blurb about where they had arrived as if he were their tour guide with a microphone at the front of the bus. "There are several famous beaches in Malibu and some movies you probably haven't ever seen were filmed here. I can name a few."

"'Beach Blanket Bingo,'" said Donna with a smile on her face.

"Those silly sixties movies," Katie said. "Phhfffttt."

"We'll stay about two hours so go get your sun," he told them.

"Maybe you can get me a surfing lesson with a hot guy today," Katie said to Jana as they walked across the parking lot.

Jana smiled at her sister and didn't say a word. She didn't want to say that she had beaten Katie to something but that was the reality of it. Katie was the girl who always met a slew of boys no matter where she went. She was cute but she was also funny, making people feel at ease, even with her eye rolling. Jana was the one who stayed in the background, who observed, who made mental notes. Katie lived life where Jana knew she was observing it.

The previous day though, Jana knew she had made a step towards living life and not just observing it. While she could have easily said no and stayed on the beach, it was like an invisible hand– belonging to that familiar but unknown voice– had pushed her forward to go learn to surf.

And there was Scott, of course.

He didn't think twice about helping Jana learn something new, about being part of that experience with her. She liked him for that, that he wanted to share it with her. What she didn't know was if she could put any of this into words. At that point it was how she felt, no more.

And she didn't know if she would see him again.

"Look at all the surfers," Katie said as they made a spot with their parents on the beach. Donna and Mike sat behind the girls, both opening books to read, while Lisa ran down to the water, hoping to find a "Malibu rock."

Jana watched the water on that clear California day– the fog having burned off on the ride up from Santa Monica– and the greenish blue hue it radiated from the sun's reflection. It was water as she had never seen it before– it never had this greenish hue in Florida– and it made her happy, to feel good. Then she looked up behind them at houses up in the hills, some of which they would explore later when they went to find Malibu Barbie's house (a modern house Mike would point out, saying it was Malibu Barbie's house and no one in the car daring to challenge him). Lisa was happy and quiet the rest of a day, a smile stuck to her face because she had gotten exactly what she had wanted.

It would be nice to live here, Jana thought.

The sun motivated her. She laid back for a few minutes, listening to the lazy waves crash and the people talking around them, but she sat up a few minutes later and opened her notebook.

First, her journal, then her novel, she told herself.

But her mind kept drifting back to Scott and after writing in her journal, not really able to describe much about how she felt, she slipped it back in her tote bag and sat up to watch the surfers down the beach.

"Let's go watch," Katie suggested, lightly throwing a little sand at Jana to get her attention.

They wandered toward the south end of the beach and sat in the sand without their towels, Jana admiring how easy the surfers made it look. She wasn't sure it was that easy, Scott had made it easy for her, but she realized that it would be different if she were out there by herself. She didn't see any girls in the lineup past the breaks, all guys, most of them wearing brightly patterned board shorts, and a few sporting t-shirts as well.

"Listen," Katie said, interrupting Jana's surfing thoughts.

Jana looked at Katie but Katie kept her eyes on the water. "We need to get you back to Santa Monica," she said.

"What?" Jana asked, feeling confused.

Katie finally looked at her. "We're leaving soon. We need to make sure you see Scott again."

"Why do you care?" Jana asked, surprised by her sister's sudden interest in her life.

Katie laughed. "My dear sister. You have a surfer dude who really likes you. A genuine California boy. You are going to have the time of your life telling everyone this story when we get home."

"You aren't going to steal it for your own story?" Jana teased her sister, knowing that while Katie rolled her eyes often, she wouldn't do that. Ever.

"You're having the better vacation than me," Katie laughed. "The least I can do is help it along." She paused, turning her entire body toward Jana, both of them forgetting there was anyone else on the beach. "You have to call him when we get back to the motel."

Jana shook her head. "I can't do that," she said, looking out at the water again but not really seeing anything. The idea of having to call Scott sounded too difficult. Scary.

"Why not?" Katie asked, letting out a low snort. "He doesn't have your number, remember? You have his? I goofed yesterday. I should have made sure we did that the other way around. But I didn't so you're going to have to be the one to make an effort here."

Jana sighed but agreed, her stomach flip flopping the entire afternoon, especially as she waited for her parents to be done with the beach. Or Lisa to be done with the beach. When Lisa got tired, they knew they could leave. And red. As soon as Donna saw Lisa turn red, they'd need to leave.

"But I put suntan lotion on you three times," she would say to Lisa, who just shrugged, looking right back at her mother.

Jana watched Katie pay Lisa off as they stood at the water line. No exchange of funds took place on the beach but Jana knew it would later. Katie was the queen of that.

"Yeah, we should probably beat the traffic anyway," Mike said when Lisa feigned tired and wanting to leave.

"I can't call him from here," Jana whispered to her sister in their room after they'd gotten back as their parents sat in the common area both reading books again. "Mom and Dad are right there."

"I'm not going to torture you that way," Katie laughed. "There's a pay phone outside the motel office. We'll go call him there."

The two girls announced they would be right back, that they were going to check the pool before dinner, their father not looking up at all, their mother giving them a funny look but returning quickly to the romance novel she was almost finished reading.

Katie stood guard slightly in earshot while Jana nervously dialed the phone, a rotary that hadn't been updated to a push button. It felt like it took forever to dial his number. As it rang, she thought about throwing up. And all the possibilities. What if he does answer? What if he pretends he doesn't know me?

But a side of her looked at Katie, who was watching a buff shirtless guy walk by, and thought about what Katie had told her. "No guy would teach a girl to surf– or teach her to do anything– if he didn't like her. Trust me, he likes you."

"Hello?"

Scott.

"Hi Scott," she said, feeling as if she were jumbling all over her words, glad he couldn't see her running her fingers along the metal coil of the phone line. "It's Jana from the beach yesterday."

"Hey," he said. "I didn't see you today."

"I know," she said. "We had to go to Malibu." She stopped herself before she told him that they had to go see Malibu Barbie's house, biting her tongue as her transition to something else, something that wouldn't be so embarrassing.

"It wasn't the same without you," he said.

"Well, we're going to see that Ferris Bueller movie tonight," she said, looking up to see Katie smiling and nodding her head, her hands on her hips like a proud coach when a routine has been perfected. "I guess there's a movie theater not far away…"

"You name the time, I'll be there," Scott said without any hesitation.

Jana tried not to let out a big sigh but she was happily relieved and when she hung up the phone, Katie began to dance around the paved parking lot. "He likes you! He likes you! I told you!" They walked back to the suite and while Jana went to their room to change into another outfit, she heard Katie asking their parents if they could just get pizza by the beach and then go to a movie.

Jana peeked out and thought her parents looked relieved, as if having time alone, probably just to watch television, seemed like the greatest evening in the world.

"Why not?" Mike asked Donna, Mike shrugging his shoulders. "There are a lot of people around. They'll be fine."

"Okay," Donna said, a little more tentative but okay with it.

"Oh, and…," Katie added, as she started to walk away, then turning back to her parents, "Scott the surfer guy. He's going to join us."

Jana hoped she was out of range, that her parents couldn't see her. Her mother's face looked almost flat but her dad let out a smile. "Great," he said, nodding his head.

"But…," Donna started to protest, looking at Mike at which he patted her arm from where they sat together on the couch and said, "He's a good kid. It's good for Jana."

"Mom thinks you're going to run off with him or something," Katie teased when she had returned to their room.

Jana shook her head but knowing that had happened with Aunt Emily was one of Donna's biggest fears for her own daughters.

Yet they had a surprise waiting for them when they re-emerged from their bedroom at the motel. Donna was wearing a sundress, what looked like a new dress. Katie and Jana– Jana happy to have something to distract her from her emotions about Scott– looked at each other, believing they knew everything in the walk-in closet their mother shared with their father.

"Um, that looks like a new dress," Katie said, looking not just surprised but also admiring what she saw.

"She got it at the mall," Lisa said from the couch where she was looking through a magazine about Los Angeles, Chuck under one arm. "She said you can see her cleavage."

Jana tried not to laugh but Katie did, both girls realizing it did take a low turn between her breasts. "Go Mom," Katie said, letting out a whistle. "I don't think I've ever seen you bare so much of your chest."

The dress went low at her cleavage and showed much of her back, too, freckled from years of the sun she was trying to avoid for her girls. The stripes ran diagonal in opposite directions, brown on a white background with shade of beige between. A small fabric belt tied in a bow at the front waist pulled it together.

"It was on sale," Lisa added as if she were dictating the conversation. "Like on sale a lot."

Donna blushed. "Oh girls," she said.

"I'm taking your mother out tonight," Mike said, appearing from around the corner wearing khakis and a pink polo shirt.

"Our California cool parents," Katie laughed, nudging Jana who giggled.

"I'm keeping her mind off what you girls are up to tonight," he whispered after Donna had already walked outside the room and was waiting at the balcony.

Katie looked stunned at first but quickly regained her composure. "Wait!" She suddenly walked toward the kitchen bar where Donna had left the camera. Katie grabbed it and made Mike and Donna pose for a photo. And then she added Lisa and– begrudgingly– Jana.

"You'll be glad I included you," Katie said, urging Jana next to their father. "I think this might be an important day that we'll want to remember."

"We'll be back before you," Mike warned as they took off toward the steps and the car for dinner somewhere near the beach.

"I can't believe he actually got her out," Katie said, smiling. "I think you might have inspired it." She nudged Jana again. "I don't know what you did but you need to do more of it."

I was myself, Jana thought, believing she and Scott just happened to be in the right place at the right time.

"I hope they have fun," Katie said, putting the camera down and looking at her watch.

Taking Lisa with them, the three girls walked back to the main area of the beach and picked out a small pizza spot, Lisa happy she could have more pizza– and still on a cloud from seeing Malibu Barbie's house– where they took their slices and drinks to the low wall where Jana had originally met Scott.

As they ate, Jana watched the crowd, looking somewhat older than during the day. "All the 'Three's Company' people who live here home from work for the day," Katie joked as a blonde woman roller skated by.

Out of nowhere, Scott appeared.

"Hey," he said, looking just as cute as the day before, this time wearing a surfing t-shirt with different board shorts.

Nonetheless, Jana felt her heart do a little skip as he smiled when he saw her. She felt her own face light up.

"Hey," he said, sitting down next to Jana whom Katie had purposely put on the end.

"Who are you?" Lisa asked, handing her crust to Katie.

Jana saw Katie elbow Lisa out of the corner of her eye. "You know him," she seethed at Lisa.

"Scott," he said, not skipping a beat and then to Jana. "I'm glad you called. I was afraid I wouldn't see you again."

"Well, it wasn't as if I know the motel phone number," Jana said, then feeling Katie handing her something and looking down to see a postcard in Katie's red nail-colored hand.

"Now you do," Katie said, waiting for Jana to take it which she did. And hand it to Scott.

"Oh, the place down the street," he said, pointing behind them.

A few guys walked by and waved and said hi to Scott as the four of them sat on the low wall, the girls finishing their drinks.

"You look like Skipper's boyfriend," Lisa said suddenly. Then adding, "His name is Scott, too."

Katie and Jana looked at Lisa, then at each other, both of them realizing at the same time what she was referring to. Scott looked confused.

"She has a doll– Skipper is Barbie's sister," Jana explained. "And Scott is Skipper's boyfriend."

"Scott has a skateboard though," Lisa said. "But he has the same black curly hair as you."

Scott made a face at her. "Well, I could probably get a skateboard. Would that help?"

Lisa laughed. "Then that means Jana needs roller skates and a pink body suit with a long purple skirt."

"I think we need to get to the movie," Katie said, shaking her head. "Lisa has quite the imagination," she explained to Scott, pulling Lisa along so Jana and Scott could walk together.

"Is your whole family like that?" Scott asked as they walked along.

It was Jana's turn to shake her head but she did with a laugh. "Pretty much. Except my mom. I guess it's her job to keep us at least acting normal in the outside world. Obviously she hasn't succeeded with Lisa yet."

In the movie theater, Katie slightly shoved Jana to the other side, taking Lisa with her.

"Your sister seems cool," he said, as they settled into the seats.

"Yeah, I've learned a lot about her on this trip," she admitted and changing the topic. "So I hear this is about Chicago. That's where we live."

Scott nodded and the lights went down, he taking her hand and holding it during the movie.

When it was over and the four of them met up outside the theater, Katie said to Lisa, "We should get you back."

"But I'm not tired," Lisa told her, looking irritated.

"That's why we should get you back to the motel," Katie said again, taking a confused Lisa by the hand and leading her away.

"I shouldn't stay long," Jana said as they took their flip flops off and walked across the nearly empty darkened beach to the water's edge. "But Katie will let them know I'm with you." She was happy to be with Scott but she also felt awkward. This was all new territory she had ventured into and yet she would only be there a short time before they started the drive home the next morning.

"Your dad seemed cool," Scott admitted, both of them glancing at each other at the same time.

With the sun down, the sand felt cool, just like the dirt at home would feel in the darkness, earthy.

"Yeah," she laughed. "I had no idea how he would react but I guess you could say my sister paved the way for me. I think she's been boy crazy since the day she turned ten."

"Girls like your sister are a dime a dozen," Scott said, taking her hand again– this time somewhat shyly, Jana not used to the hand of anyone but Lisa's recently.

"They are?" Jana asked, surprised. "I thought all boys wanted girls like Katie. She's fun, she's confident, she looks good."

Scott laughed. "They peak early. They aren't always happy inside. Everything you see on the outside is because they're making up for what they don't believe they have inside. I've watched guys older than me get together with girls and sometimes marry them and a few years later you can see it's not working."

Jana listened quietly, absorbing what he said as she listened to the ocean and voices of the few other people on the beach with them. She hoped that wouldn't be true for Katie. She wanted Katie always to be happy.

"You're different, Jana," he said, the first time she'd heard him say her name. "You don't pretend to be something you're not. That's cool."

"It makes me dorky," she laughed, knowing her mother would tell her to accept the compliment but somehow being unable to. She bit her tongue at her own lack of confidence in the moment.

"Dorky pays off later," he said.

They stood in silence listening to the ocean wash the waves to the shore, seeing the white caps on top of the waves, somehow standing out in the darkness.

"I want something more from life," Jana said, not sure why she said it, just feeling as if maybe she could share that with Scott. But she hesitated to say more. How could she tell him that she wasn't sure she wanted a family or to live in the suburbs, the life she saw her parents had.

It's what I'm supposed to want, she thought, feeling if she said it, it might send Scott away.

"Life is what you make it."

He turned to her and she looked into his eyes; she could see– even in the darkness– the whites surrounding the brown of his pupil, almost like a fried egg. A brown fried egg. She tried to dismiss the thought quickly before it made her laugh.

And then he leaned forward and kissed her, catching Jana by surprise.

As he pulled back, smiling, she smiled back at him but inside she worried she had done that all wrong because she hadn't seen it coming.

And where were the stars, the bells? All that jazz everyone said happened when you were kissed? That felt like a sloppy mess, she thought, hoping her confusion didn't read across her face. At the same time, she felt closer to Scott, like he had shared something with her that he had chosen to, not because he had to, and that alone made her happy. Maybe the sloppy mess was all part of getting to know someone.

"I better get you back to the motel or your dad really will come looking for me," he laughed, taking her hand and leading her back to the sidewalk.

Be in the moment, Jana told herself, wanting to kick herself to remember they were leaving in the morning. She wouldn't see Scott after this evening.

They stood in front of the motel sign, a place where Jana knew her parents couldn't see them until they walked outside the room looking for them. She also knew that Katie would keep them in the room for that reason.

"I know what it's like to have them spying," she would say if Jana asked.

"Here," he said pulling something out of his pocket. "Here's my address. Maybe we can keep in touch," he said.

Jana smiled, wishing she had something to put her info on and remembering the postcard Katie had handed her and that they had pens in the little office. "Wait, let me get you mine," she said, holding up her hand for him to stay there while she walked into the office with the neon "open" sign and waved at Harry, who barely looked up from the newspaper he was reading.

She grabbed one of the pens on the counter, he shook his head, his reading glasses nearly falling off his head as he did, and she went quickly out the door, before he could ask, reminding herself that it had been her sister who had been taking everything before. Not her.

Scott laughed. "You should send me a postcard from Chicago."

"No, silly," Jana told him, sitting down on the curb by the flower bed, to write her info down. "A place to write my address down." After she did, she handed it to him.

He kissed her again, under the motel sign light, standing together as nearly one in the shadows.

What a scene, she would think later, adding it to her manuscript. Not for her though, but her main characters.

There still weren't any bells or whistles or anything but at least she didn't feel blindsided by it. She tried to let him lead, as she'd been taught about dancing. And yet she wasn't sure what she was supposed to do there either. What she liked most were his arms around her, his hands touching her back, his embrace holding her close.

"I better get home," he said, stepping back and looking up at the sky. "It must be close to ten now. Your dad definitely will be looking for you."

"Bye," Jana said, feeling conflicted about watching him leave.

"Start heading toward your room," Scott said, turning her lightly around. "It's as if I took you home from a date. I wouldn't drive away before you got into your house." And before they parted, he said one last thing. "Hey, always stay the way you are."

Jana smiled, not remembering that anyone had ever said that to her. She smiled and for a moment they looked at each other. It was then that she felt her stomach jump. A little.

Jana nodded at his thoughtfulness. "Thank you," she said and before she turned the corner by the swimming pool to take the outdoor stairs to the second floor where their suite was, she waved to Scott who was still standing in the shadows under the sign. She last saw his hair– the gelled curls making their own outline– as she turned the corner and disappeared.

But before she went to the room she stood outside it hearing the television inside; it sounded like "Miami Vice" was playing.

Jana watched the water in the pool, someone must have gotten out of it recently because the top didn't look glassy; it seemed to move, distorted by both the underwater pool light and also the lights above it.

She looked at Scott's information in her hand. Do I write? What do I do? She wondered, worried something was wrong with her because she hadn't felt anything from the kiss. Katie would tell her what to do. She hadn't been wrong so far.

The door opened behind her and she turned to see her father come out. He stood next to her, the light ocean breeze blowing their hair off both of their faces.

"Hi," he said. "I was getting a little concerned. I thought I would look outside the window and there you were."

"Yeah," Jana said. "I'm sorry. I should have come back earlier."

He didn't ask anything, Jana didn't say anything. She found she didn't know what to say. Her mind felt jumbled. Maybe she needed to write in her journal, to sort it out, and then maybe she'd be able to say something. But telling her dad about Scott? It all seemed a little weird and better left unsaid.

She wasn't sure how much time went by but he pulled her toward him for a side huge, squeezed her and gave her a kiss on the top of her head.

"I love you Jana," he said simply.

And with that he went back inside leaving her alone in the darkness watching the pool as it finally became a mirror against the dark sky and lights. She went in a few minutes later, ready to face Katie's questions and the blank pages of her journal.

Chapter 18

*D*onna gently shook the girls in the morning. "No sleeping in today," she said as they stirred groggily in their beds. "You can sleep in the car."

"Of course I want to know," Katie had said the night before, quiet enough to make sure their parents weren't listening. "But you can tell me later. You might not want to tell me while Mom and Dad are nearby. The walls in these places are paper thin. Mom probably has a glass on the wall to listen."

"Know what?" Lisa asked, looking up from the book she was flipping through, Chuck under her arm. Lisa rolled toward space between the two beds where Jana and Katie were facing each other, Jana with her legs crossed, Katie with them flat on the floor, as if to ground her as she questioned Jana.

"Nothing," Katie teased Lisa, playfully pushing her away. When Lisa started to laugh, Katie whispered, "Shhh. They'll definitely come in if they hear any giggling."

Jana wasn't sure where to start. She knew her dad would have been happy to listen and maybe she felt a sense of obligation to him because of all that he had shared with her. She had laid awake part of the night trying to untangle her thoughts and confusion, not feeling much better about it in the morning.

As they showered and dressed, having packed their suitcases the night before, Mike started to pack the car in the early morning silence. A few cars sped by on the street but few people were out.

"How about a last view of the ocean before we leave?" He asked, everyone standing at the back of the station wagon– everything packed into it– his hands on his hips.

Jana walked quietly, her parents having a conversation about the drive. Katie and Lisa bantered about a new song they heard on the radio, Lisa saying how much she liked Madonna, Katie telling her she knew very little about Madonna– which wasn't true because Katie loved Madonna– which made Lisa start spouting out details about the singer.

There were a few people out jogging, but mostly it was quiet as the sun came up over California and a new day. Jana couldn't help but keep looking in the direction where she saw Scott head after he left her the night before. That must have been where his house was, she figured. And part of her expected him to come out at any moment.

And yet he didn't.

There was no curly hair, no smile appearing from around the corner.

You didn't expect to see him today, she reminded herself, taking off her flip flops as she went from concrete to the beach. Donna stayed back at the little wall, urging the rest of the family to go on. "But don't get your clothes wet," she warned Lisa. "You're not going swimming this morning."

"Why can't we go swimming this morning?" Lisa kept asking.

Mike laughed at his daughter. "Because we have to get out of town before traffic hits. This makes Chicago traffic look tame."

Jana stood at the water line, letting the rolling waves of the tide that was going out cover her feet and then leave them filled with sand. She watched the motion of the water and the sand over and over, then looked up and out toward the horizon where daylight made the difference between the water and the sky visible.

There weren't any surfers out that morning, the water looking flat– like glass as the sun came up and turned the sky from darkness to orange and shades of pink then finally to clear that looked blue from any distance.

Must be because the water is flat, Jana thought, realizing there would be no waves to surf. She didn't understand the tides or waves, wishing she had asked more questions before she went home. No regrets, she told herself, shaking it off.

I'll be back, she thought. I'll be back one day. And I'll learn more.

What that had to do with Scott, she didn't know. She thought it would be cool though. Maybe it would happen. But she remembered boys she had met before in various places, through friends, and how they always vowed to keep in touch. And never did.

But they weren't Scott.

Then Jana asked herself, Do I want to hear from him? What do I want from him? There's a big world to explore and many guys to meet. Maybe one day Scott would be a blip on her radar, she would remember him for the boy who took her surfing, a story she would tell as part of dinner party conversation, but that would be all. Or the basis of a character.

"You're lost in thought this morning," Mike said to Jana, joining her at the waterline while Katie helped Lisa find a new rock to take home. A last time on the beach for a California rock.

"It has to be perfect," Lisa kept saying, rejecting each one that Katie picked up.

There weren't many other voices on the beach that morning, making Lisa and Katie's conversation obvious.

Jana shrugged her shoulders at her dad's comment. "I don't know."

"Don't know what?" He asked, smiling.

"I don't know. I guess I don't know about anything."

He raised his eyebrows and acted surprised, "The writer doesn't know what to say?"

A few minutes passed and they stood and watched the surf, a few surfers appearing out of nowhere. Jana looked but didn't see Scott. "I guess it's too flat to surf?" She asked her dad, thinking that maybe the surfers knew something Jana didn't, something more than what met the eye.

"It's very flat," he said, nodding his head, Jana seeing him only out of the corner of her eye. "You wouldn't get very far on the board. I imagine you could look down and you'd see the sand below you. And anything else that might be swimming by."

Jana cringed. Those were the things she hadn't thought about: creatures in the ocean swimming by.

"Are you sad?" Mike asked. "Are you sad we're leaving?"

Jana shrugged her shoulders and gave him a weak smile. "I don't know."

He looked to see where Katie was and then said, "I remember when your sister had her first break up. We thought the entire world was going to end."

Jana started to laugh, nodding her head. "I remember that. She cried for weeks it seemed."

"We thought she was easier to console as a baby," Mike said, shaking his head at the thought. "I'm still not sure how we survived that. The worst of it was that she felt rejected by him. What was his name? Brent?"

"Yes, then she called him 'Brent the Dent.'"

Mike laughed and they shared a moment of the memory together.

"I bring it up because it was one of the hardest moments to endure for a parent, to watch your child's pain, knowing there was nothing you could do. No reassurance that they would find that true love would come, that this was just a step in the road."

"I don't know that I'm sad, Dad," Jana finally said. "I'm sad about leaving LA but I'm not sure about him." She shrugged her shoulders. "Maybe I'll never hear from him again. I don't know. And it was fun but it kind of disrupted my writing," she admitted. "Yet he was different from any boy I've met before."

Mike looked at her and laughed, pulling his sunglasses out of his shirt pocket. "Do you know how many parents would be filled with joy to hear that their child felt a possible relationship disrupted whatever else they wanted to do? Still, I know for you that each experience you have gives you something else to add to your writing."

Jana shrugged her shoulders and they heard Donna calling from behind them, all four of them starting to make their way back to the concrete to find a nearby outdoor shower to wash the last of the sand off their feet.

That was part of the struggle, Jana thought, taking one last look at the ocean, but knowing it wasn't her last look at the Pacific. There would be many more to come. The struggle would be finding balance between living life and writing about life. She knew writing would bring her the life she wanted to live, the one that was becoming clearer each day on this trip, and yet she would need to live life to make sure she had life experiences to write about.

"I'm thinking of playing tennis this fall at school," she said to her dad as they walked back to the motel where the car was. "Because there's no surfing team, you know," she teased.

"Yes! I won that!" Katie called from behind her.

Jana didn't want to give her sister any satisfaction so she ignored her and kept talking. "Do you think you could help me when we get back? I know it's not golf…"

"Of course," Mike said, patting her shoulder and she looked past her father to see her mother look back, her face filled with relief that it wasn't volleyball.

They inched their way out of the Los Angeles area, everything turning sparse within an hour of leaving. Jana kept her eyes peeled out the window, knowing there would be no more ocean to see, but taking in every last bit of Los Angeles and its surrounding area that she could.

The freeway traffic slowly built up both ways and it reminded her of driving around the Chicago area, the closer they were to the city, the heavier the traffic, but as they motored their way toward Naperville and the outskirts, everything opened up. The only difference here was the scenery.

"We have a full day of driving ahead of us," Mike announced from the front seat, everyone looking dazed but not asleep yet after Donna passed out fruit and granola bars. "We'll stop in Holbrook for something to eat and then hopefully just for gas and the bathroom until we get to Albuquerque around 10:00 tonight."

It was a long trek to Holbrook but somewhere along the way after they had arrived into Los Angeles Jana heard her dad say to her mom how someone had suggested they stop in Holbrook on the way home.

"They have one of the old motels. Each room is a teepee."

"Not to be confused with toilet paper," Katie reminded everyone.

Jana bit her lip.

"How can each room be a roll of toilet paper?" Lisa asked.

"Fix it, Katie," Donna called from the front seat before Mike had a chance to actually say what a teepee was, Jana knowing her father was probably excited to do that.

"It's a Native American thing," Katie told Lisa using her hands to show what they looked like. "Kind of like igloos with a point at the top of the roof."

"We're going to stay there?" Lisa asked, getting excited. Jana was glad she couldn't see the deep breaths their parents were taking.

"Not this time," Mike told her. "Maybe on our next Route 66 trip."

"Can we do this again next year?" Lisa asked. "Maybe Malibu Barbie and Ken will be home. I don't understand why they had to go to Mexico."

Michelle L. Rusk

Jana took a peek at Katie, who was hiding her mouth behind her pillow, ready to burst out laughing.

"I'd be happy to do it again," Mike said hopefully.

"We'll talk about it" was all that came from Donna and the conversation ended, the car going quiet until Mike pushed his Beach Boys cassette into the car's tape player and everyone started to sing along to "Surfin' USA."

"A song for Jana!" Mike called.

"We should go back and help Jana surf on all those beaches," Katie said. "You should buy her a surfboard for Christmas," she suggested to Mike and Donna.

Jana put her head in her hands, overwhelmed from all the ideas. I surfed twice, she thought. Maybe it won't be the same the next time. If there is a next time. No, she thought, there will be a next time.

The land had turned to desert and Jana felt herself doze off until they reached the rest area just across the Arizona border, the one with the signs for the snakes.

"I'm too scared," Lisa said, not willing to get out of the car because Katie had scared her so much on their way out there at the same rest area. "I'm not leaving the car."

"You need to go," Donna said, coaxing her daughter from the front seat where she had turned her head to watch. "Katie, you need to fix this."

Donna looked irritated, probably from the heat that had overwhelmed them once they entered the desert, not a cloud in the sky.

Katie sighed and pulled Lisa's arm. "Come on, I'll save you from the snakes."

Lisa was satisfied by that and let her sister lead her to the bathroom.

"But not if they get you in the toilet stall!" Sending Lisa running back to the car, Katie following her, and Donna with her head in her hands.

Jana bit her lip to keep from laughing, not wanting to be in trouble, too.

*****

It was late enough when they reached Holbrook. The sun was starting a slight descent into the sky; it would be dark soon. Mike pulled into the McDonald's drive through, not looking pleased about it, but Jana knowing that everyone in the car was getting hungry.

"Let's just go in," Donna said, looking anxious to get out of the car.

He managed to maneuver the station wagon out of the drive through and into a parking spot. The girls grabbed a table outside and Lisa ran around, carrying Chuck with her.

"We better make sure she doesn't leave him," Katie said, looking tired herself.

But when they were back in the car and took a right turn down Main Street– and Route 66– of Holbrook, everyone's spirits picked up at the sight of the Wig Wam Motel. Still in service, the "no" had been lit up in the vacancy sign. In front of each of the teepees, all serving as rooms, there was some sort of classic car. Except for the minivan parked in front of one.

"Looks like a classic car trip across Route 66," Mike said to no one in particular as he parked the car so everyone could take a look.

"Do you remember this from your last trip?" Jana asked as they all walked around the parking lot, it getting too dark for photos.

"Hmmm," he said. And then turned to her and said, "No." They shared a laugh and the family packed back into the car for the final push to Albuquerque.

When they reached the New Mexico border Mike reminded them of what was still ahead.

"And tomorrow we'll drive to Joplin, Missouri, then onto home the next day."

"Home," Katie sighed, sounding like she missed it. "But I'm not the one with the story to tell this time." She turned to Jana and gave her a quick grin. Jana smiled back but she wasn't even sure what story she *would* tell.

Katie knew how to spin these things so they were believable, even if she embellished the details. But what would Jana say? "I met a guy, he taught me to surf, we went to the movies, and then I never saw him again." That seemed lame. It would have been more interesting if she could add, "And I'm going to visit him at Christmas."

But that would have been Katie, not Jana. Jana wondered what the future held for her boy-crazy sister. Sometimes when she watched her, she thought that either Katie would end up becoming the doctor who found a cure for cancer– she did do well in school because that was what Donna and Mike expected for all three girls– or she would finish college, marry her college sweetheart, buy a house, have a bunch of kids, and live happily ever after. As far as Jana could tell, Katie wanted a life just like their parents, just like everyone else. The life she made fun of but what else did you do when you got married? How did you keep life interesting when you settled into a routine?

Jana knew Mrs. Crenshaw was anxious for her to come back to start babysitting again so she could go back to work part-time at least for the summer.

"I've got to get out of the house," she would sometimes say as she practically ran out the door to her garage when Jana showed up to take care of five-year-old Carrie and her four-year-old brother Mason for a few hours.

Jana would look at the two kids, busy coloring and oblivious to their mother leaving and think, "Is this what it's going to be for me?"

She tried to accept it and thought that maybe by babysitting all summer she would have a better appreciation that that would be her life one day, too. A nice house, a nice husband, cute kids.

That's all?

What about a life in Los Angeles? What about a nice house near the beach? Books on the best seller list? Did it have to include kids?

They were getting close to Albuquerque, at least that's the what the big green signs indicated, as the number of miles continued to dwindle. Jana looked around and thought everyone was asleep. Her mom's head bounced against the window of the front passenger side of the car where she sat and Lisa had curled up against Katie, who was using her pillow so her head didn't bounce against the window like Donna's was.

"Dad," Jana said quietly, shifting her body forward to be closer to where he sat driving.

"Hmm," Mike said, not able to take his eyes off the road but acknowledging her presence.

"Are you sad to go home?"

She heard him chuckle and she knew she probably wouldn't get the answer she wanted with her mother right there. Mike looked to his right– as if to see if Donna were sleeping and how deeply– and then shook his head before speaking.

"I don't know that sad is the right word. Work is important to me, especially because I have to think about how I'm going to pay for college for all three of you." He was silent for a moment and Jana watched the same scenery that he saw as he kept his foot on the gas, motoring east on the interstate. "But this trip was very different than all our other trips. We've always taken you girls somewhere that we could rest, not where we would sightsee or obviously drive to."

They passed through Grants, only visible by the numerous lights that made up the town in the darkness.

"I enjoyed this trip more than any others we've taken." He nodded his head as if for confirmation. "That I know. And I also know that I'll always look back on this trip with happy memories, especially as I watch you girls continue to grow. I do believe we chose the right time– meaning the ages of you girls– to take this trip."

They were quiet for a moment, everything getting dark again as they approached a rural area, leaving the lights of Grants behind.

"And you?" He asked. "Are you sad to go home?"

"I don't know," Jana said honestly.

And then she didn't know what else to say because she really didn't know.

"When you were young," Mike said, short of chuckling. "You used to talk so much. Not as much as Katie but we always thought you were trying to keep up with Katie. But then one day you stopped talking as much. We could see that you had pulled back slightly, as if you realized that you weren't the same person as Katie and that if you stopped and looked around– and listened– you would experience more of the world than she did."

Jana listened, also wondering if Katie heard this, too. Jana looked back and before she could see anything, Mike said, "She has her headphones on. She's not hearing a thing. I'm sure she's listening to Madonna again."

He continued, "Your sister doesn't look before she leaps. You look first because you want to take it all in and I'm sure it's because you know there might be a story in it one day."

"Have I always been that way?"

"Since you were about four and handed me a pad of paper and a pen and told me to write down the story you wanted to tell."

Jana laughed. She had heard this story from her parents before although she didn't remember it. The story, something about two sister bears, hung on the bulletin board in the kitchen, by what they called "Mom's Desk" where Donna kept the family organized and took all her calls.

"When I feel sad or feel like I'm not sure what to do, sometimes I go look at that story," Jana admitted, feeling slightly stupid.

"You do?" Mike asked. "All these years it's hung there haven't been in vain?"

She giggled. "No. I guess it's my way of remembering how important writing is to me."

"When we get home we're going to get you a typewriter," he said. "But don't stop writing in those journals. It doesn't matter what you write, just keep writing," he said.

They were quiet again and suddenly they came up over a hill and saw the lights of Albuquerque appearing like a pool of glitter in front of them.

"Oh wow," she said, surprised.

"Amazing, isn't it?"

Out of nowhere it seemed, there lit up in the near darkness, was the city, the Sandia Mountains barely an outline in front of them. With thirty miles still to go, Jana started to feel slightly sleepy.

"Thanks, Dad," she said and then she curled up in her corner– her nook she began to think of it– in the car and dozed off for the rest of the drive.

*****

"Here we are, back in Albuquerque," Mike said, pulling the car into the Twilight Sands parking lot.

"Déjà vu," Katie said, sleepily.

Jana opened her eyes and immediately saw the lit-up sign reflected in the pool. She couldn't say it– especially with Katie there– but something about it *did* feel like home. Still no one had the energy to argue; they would sleep and be on the road at some point midday the following day.

"Sleep in, girls," Donna told them, standing in the open doorway of their room, the lit parking lot behind her, turning her body into a shadowy outline especially with her curly hair on top. "We're not in any hurry to leave tomorrow."

Jana curled up into a ball in the bed closest to the window where she could see the Twilight Sands sign lit up in the crack of the curtains. Returning to Albuquerque made her think more about all that she had written and while she finally dozed off, she was awake early, her sisters not stirring after she returned from using the bathroom. It was already 9:00 am and Jana felt ready to start the day. She pulled a sundress on and grabbed her notebooks and pen, carefully opening and shutting the door behind her, trying not to let any light in.

Outside, the sun was bright and she wished she had remembered her sunglasses. She knew the pool wasn't opened yet but she walked over and shyly asked the man cleaning it if she could sit under the umbrella. It was the first time someone had been there working when she had gone to it so early.

"Sure," he said, a Hispanic man with dark hair and a mustache. "I'll be done in ten minutes if you want to swim." He waved his free arm, the other one sweeping debris from the pool. "It's a beautiful day. Albuquerque is full of beautiful days. You should spend it here."

Jana smiled and opened her notebook at the patio table by the deep end. She first wrote her daily journal entry– not having been able to to do it in the car the previous day– and then tapped her pen on her notebook while she thought about what she wanted to say.

"Ah, a writer," the man said with a smile as he pulled out the blue telescopic pole from the pool with the leaf basket at the end filled with leaves and other trash that didn't belong in the pool. "My first wife wanted to be a writer," he said.

"Did she write?" Jana asked, feeling curious.

He emptied the basket into the trash can by the shallow end and laughed, shaking his head, the big set of keys clipped onto his jeans jingling as he moved and said, "No. Sadly, talked about it and she told great stories. But she never did what you're doing– taking the time out of the day. I think had she done that earlier in her life, she might have developed a habit. It's sad because of what she might have become."

"What happened to her?" Jana wondered, imagining her mother poking her in the back that she was asking too many questions.

"Mental illness. She left and never came back." His eyes looked sad, not the sparkle she saw when she had shown up. "I miss her but I couldn't stop her."

He shrugged his shoulders and pretended to tip a hat he wasn't wearing. "Enjoy your day! And keep writing!"

Someone had left the previous day's *Albuquerque Journal* on the table and Jana flipped through it, for no reason other than curiosity. She saw that since they had left it had rained two inches over several days, explaining why the air felt more damp than before.

She pushed the newspaper away and began to flip through the notebook pages she had started to rewrite and scratched her head. This was getting to be a bigger mess by the minute.

"Good morning," a voice above her said and she looked up to see her father looking down at her, a styrofoam cup of coffee in his right hand and that day's newspaper in the other.

"Hi Dad," she said, smiling, but surprised she didn't hear him.

He slipped into one of the other chairs. "How are you up and not the rest of the group?" He teased, looking over at the pages filled with writing. "Or did you feel inspired?"

"I think I felt inspired," she laughed. "When are we leaving?"

He shrugged his shoulders and looked out at the pool, still only partially in the early sun. "No telling what time everyone will be up."

She watched him, he watched the pool. She didn't say it but she was a little sad the trip was ending. She wasn't sure how things might be at home. Could she ask the same questions? Her dad had shared so much with her and wasn't it only fair that she shared with him, too? She knew that he didn't have to share with her, that he had chosen to share and yet she also knew that sometimes it was easier to share when a person wasn't in their usual environment, as if because one wasn't staying there long, one didn't have to worry about the secrets the walls would keep. And maybe blurt out questions to someone else one day.

She thought maybe it was time to ask one or two so she took a deep breath and dove right in.

"Don't you think it's harder to leave someone when you've spent more time with them, gotten to know them better?"

Mike turned his head toward her and didn't respond at first.

Jana wasn't sure how much she missed Scott. She wondered if Scott had been any other boy she knew– and there were a few she considered friends– would she be missing them in the same way? And yet, she felt as if Scott understood something about her, something that she hadn't sensed from any other boy. His outward support of her writing was part of what made him different.

She had thought about asking Katie about this but realized these weren't things Katie considered. If one asked Katie, she'd shrug her shoulders and say if he was cute and could carry on a conversation, she was happy to be with him. But Jana felt something else. Scott was cute and he could more than carry on a conversation. She liked that he had helped her try something new in her life. Jana felt a little more confident about playing tennis knowing how she had been able to surf a wave. Something about that made her feel stronger, not just physically but mentally, too.

"What was the highlight of your summer?" She could already picture the teachers asking– as they always did, their way of getting to know the students.

Jana knew exactly what her answer would be. "I learned to surf."

How many other of her classmates would be able to say that? she wondered, giving herself a pat on the back.

Her dad shrugged his shoulders. "Yes, it makes sense. The more you get to know someone, the more attached you get. Would you have preferred I didn't get you up that second day?"

Jana immediately backtracked. "Oh, Dad. Of course not." She paused and then said, "Thank you. You gave me something that day, maybe one of the best gifts I'll ever get by giving me that experience."

With that he smiled, laughed, and touched her hand. "Good. My intention wasn't to make it harder for you to leave. We can't ever think about life that way. We need to be all in or we aren't truly living."

"So…," Jana said, watching the pool, "kind of like Katie is all in about her relationships but yet she doesn't want to get her hair wet in the pool?"

Her dad laughed again. "Yes, like that."

But Jana didn't say that she kind of understood it. After all, it took Katie quite a bit of hair gel to make it move– or rather not move– the exact way she wanted it to.

Traffic breezed by on Route 66, giving background noise to their quiet conversation.

And– finally– in that moment she thought she could ask him the one question that had dogged her since she asked her mother that day– was that only a week and a half ago?– on the first night of their trip. "Dad, do you think you need to have lots of bad things happen to you, or hurts, to be a good writer?"

She didn't mean to but she let out a sigh after she asked it, as if she could finally let it go. And she hoped to get a good answer, realizing that it wasn't Donna who was going to answer it. Surely she had forgotten.

"Hmmm," Mike said, "that's one to think about. But you're the writer, what do you think?"

"Well," Jana said, not really aware of the adult kind of conversation they were having, or recognizing how much their relationship had changed over course of the trip, "everyone says you do and they seem to base it on someone like Hemingway who ended up drinking and killing himself. But I don't get it. Why can't you write a good story without suffering? Is everything about pain and heartache?"

She could see that her dad was listening, absorbing everything that she said. Jana waited for him to respond. But another thought came to her in the meantime. "Why does it have to be about suffering? Why can't people write about how they get to happy places?"

"Well," Mike said, leaning forward toward Jana. "I think that many times a book– having read a few in my life– is just a piece of someone's life. How many books do you read that are about someone's entire life unless they're some type of biography? So the ending will depend on where the story ends, where that person is. If you wrote a story about this trip for instance," he said– and now he seemed to be thinking out loud– "Where would it end? Would it be a happy ending?"

"What part of the trip?" She asked him, thinking it could go in several angles.

"How about you and Scott?"

"That's unknown."

"But are you suffering over it? Did you learn from it?"

She worked at absorbing all the questions he was asking her.

"Or do you think something else– maybe a different story– might come from this experience. Perhaps it inspires you to write something but it doesn't mean that you're retelling any of this particular story."

Jana nodded her head, something finally making sense, that there were pieces of the trip that would become part of her writing. They went quiet again, she sat back in her chair, watching the traffic pass by.

"I have an idea," he said suddenly, picking up his coffee and standing up. He waved his free hand. "Come with me."

"Where are we going?" She asked, trying to catch him as he excitedly walked quickly across the parking lot to the car.

He looked at his watch said, "It might be too early"– mostly to himself– and drove the car to the edge of the motel property. "Hmmm, I think we go left." He turned the car and Jana watched as they passed the other motels, enjoying the scenery and transporting herself back to the early 1960s, as some of it still looked.

Mike turned right onto a street called San Mateo and drove about a mile south, turning into a little hamburger stand called Blake's Lotaburger. Jana noticed the area of town wasn't much better than where they were staying, strip malls looking dated, houses not so kept up.

The little white stand sported a fresh coat of paint and what looked like a new sign. And yet it looked like it had been there for years.

"What is this?" Jana asked, taking in all the details.

He parked in the dirt lot and Mike looked at his watch. "Hmm. We still might be too early." He reached over to touch her shoulder and smiled. "The best burgers in town. Your mom doesn't particularly like this kind of thing but I should have just brought you here last week anyway."

A man was behind the open window, wearing all white, clearly prepping for the day.

"Hello," Mike said, leaning on the counter.

Jana watched her dad, it was as if he was in his element, an element she'd never known about and now she wished she'd had. She felt as if she had missed out on time with him.

The man walked over and said, "We're not open yet, sir." He looked the clock on an inside wall. "Another hour."

"Listen," her dad told him, "I know. We live in Chicago though and we're just passing through on our way home." He stood back a moment as if to take in the whole building, small as it was. "I ate here in the early sixties and wanted to share it with my daughter."

The man listened, then he thought for a moment before he said, "Why not. How about an Itsa Burger with green chile?"

"Absolutely," Mike said, pulling out his wallet. "And two Cokes."

"Put the wallet away, this one's on us," the man said, turning toward the grill. "Let me give you a piece of Albuquerque to remember." He nodded his head at Jana.

She smiled, watching her dad, he looking pleased with himself, taking the two Cokes in the paper cups with straws to a stone table under an umbrella. "Sometimes it pays to ask. And be nice to people."

"Dad," Jana said shyly, still afraid to broach certain things with him.

Her.

He took a drink and smiled. "Hmm?"

"Why don't you find Gloria?"

She said it. She blurted out the one thing that she had wanted to know. Her dad's face fell almost to the ground– a look of surprise that she had been brave enough to ask such a question that might have altered the course of her own life– although he picked it up as the burger guy brought over two bags with their burgers– and packets of French fries– in them.

"Thanks for remembering us," the man said, looking pleased with himself that he had done a good deed for the day. Early in the day, no less.

"Thank you," Mike said, opening the bag and smelling the burger. "That's green chile!" He laughed.

"That's the best part of living here," the man said, "And the sun." He swept his arm up toward the sky.

After they each held their green chile cheeseburgers in hand, Jana smelled what her dad was talking about.

"It's the roasting that you smell. They roast the peppers after harvest and freeze them just for this."

"And enchiladas," She reminded him.

"Yes. That, too."

171

She took a bite of the burger, trying to keep all the parts– the meat patty, melted cheese, onions, lettuce, tomato, catsup, mustard– the entire gooey mess from slipping out of the two-sided bun.

Mike had taken a bite and chewed thoughtfully and then spoke. "I've thought about it, Jana. Many times. And especially being here."

He didn't look at her. She kept chewing and her eyes focused on the burger, part of her too afraid to be direct. She was still regretting what she had asked.

"But what would I do with that?" He shrugged his shoulders. "I made a commitment to your mother when I married her. It seems easier for some people than others even though it's not as if we've had many struggles that would get in the way." He looked around at the surroundings. "I don't know why I couldn't give up living in Chicago. I might have been happier here. But who knows."

He took another bite; Jana grabbed a few fries and placed them next to her burger, picking them up one at a time to eat. She listened to the cars driving by, the sounds of being outside on a summer day. She could feel the sun heating up outside the umbrella.

"If I found her, what would I do?" He asked, almost to himself. "I would be happy to know what happened to her. I'm sure she married and had children. That's what we all did." He let out a little laugh. "Not even if we wanted to, that's just what we did." He shook his head.

Jana took a drink of her Coke, still listening, not wanting to interrupt. It felt as if he didn't want to stop talking.

"But then I think I would be sad to see her. I'd be happy initially but like I said, what would I do with it? Eventually I think it would make me sad in some way, maybe to see how things turned out. Maybe as much as I want to know who she is and what her life is like today, I would be sad because I'm not a part of it. At some point I had to let it go and live in the moment because that's where happiness is. I thought I could come back to Albuquerque and it wouldn't affect me but that wouldn't be the truth." He shrugged his shoulders. "And yet it makes me happy to share with you, to see you grow, to see your appreciation for this place."

She felt him looking at her and something told her to look up. Jana put down her Coke, and dropped her hands into her lap, watching her dad.

"I know that it probably doesn't make sense to you," he said, his tone serious but warm. "If I were your age and I were hearing the same thing, I would be thinking just as you are. But as you get older– and, yes, I realize how annoying it is to hear that." Jana let out a giggle and smiled. "You'll see that life isn't as black and white as it's made out to be. There's definitely a lot of gray area. And while it's that gray area that can make life meaningful and textured, it's also what makes it so challenging to find happiness and peace. And let go of any longing we might feel."

"You know," Jana said, feeling the need to lighten the moment, "if Katie were here, she'd say how surprised she is that you're so deep."

He rolled his eyes and admitted, "I can't quite do it the way she does. She perfected that when she was in kindergarten."

They shared a laugh and finished their meal. "Aren't you worried Mom will be mad we ate without them?"

"You know your mom," he said. "She won't think she missed a thing when she finds out it's local. She's a perfect example of why places like the Twilight Sands don't exist anymore. She wants to know that every hotel she enters is the same, has the same soap, has the same layout." He shrugged his shoulders. "That's her choice and I was lucky to convince her to do as much as she did on this trip."

"But on the way home we're staying at interstate exits with Holiday Inns and eating at Denny's restaurants?"

He laughed, picking up their trash. "That's exactly what we're doing. The fun atmosphere of the trip is finished. Head to the exit door and return to 1986."

$\mathcal{B}$ ack in the car, everyone looking tired but ready to get home, Katie took the newspaper Mike had stuck between the edge of his seat and the console– never having scanned it because he and Jana had gone to Blake's instead– and she began to read the headlines, and anything she found interesting, out loud.

"Building a new hotel...yawn...," she said, Jana watching her sister's eyes roam the newspaper. "Both houses have passed a budget compromise...more yawn..."

"How can you read in the car?" Lisa asked, mesmerized. "It makes me want to puke."

"Then don't do it," Katie said, flipping pages. "Or"– and she nudged her head toward Jana– "throw up toward your other sister."

Lisa looked at Jana and shook her head. "I don't want to throw up at all," she whispered.

"Ah, here's something interesting," Katie said folding the newspaper in half. "Dear Abby. Let me see...Vietnam Vet paralyzed waist down....the sexiest man in the world! Good for her! They have kids, too. He's not that paralyzed."

"What does that mean?" Lisa asked, looking at Katie.

Katie whispered. "Ask Mom," she taunted.

Lisa looked over at Jana, who was the one to shake her head this time. "Maybe another day," Jana whispered, thinking it might be time to give Donna a break.

"There's even an article about Paul Harvey," she said loud enough so Mike could hear her.

"Ah, all this way," Mike said. "It will be nice to be home and have my radio friends back when I'm driving to work."

She kept reading and throwing out comments occasionally. "Too bad we spent all our money in LA, they had a summer sale at Benetton at the mall in Albuquerque," Katie said, eyeing Jana. "Colorful Italian clothing, it says."

"I like what I got in LA," Jana said, scrunching her nose.

"Yeah, me, too. Moving on...not very hot in Chicago with a high of 77 but– gasp– it'll be 91 in Oklahoma City today. Keep the air conditioning on, Dad!"

Jana turned back to the scenery out her side of the car. It was a quick exit out of Albuquerque, unlike the seemingly hours it took to escape the city of Los Angeles. They'd passed through the Sandia Mountains via Tijeras Canyon and now they traveled on a fairly flat stretch of highway that took them back to Texas.

"Jana, this one is definitely for you," Katie said. "It's an article about that new country music dude, Randy Travis. He said it was hard to quit his job even as his career took off because he'd been working so hard at it for so long but when it happened, it happened so fast."

Jana smiled at her sister.

"You'll have sold a million books and we'll be telling you that you have to quit your job washing dishes and cooking catfish."

"As if I'd have a job doing that," Jana laughed, thinking of the image.

"Yeah," Katie said, thoughtfully. "I think it might be more plausible that you'd be working at Benetton. Hmm. You'd have to quit in the middle of the summer sale. I'm sure they could find someone to replace you though."

Jana looked up to see her dad smiling in the front seat, his sunglasses keeping her from seeing if he was getting any glimpse of the girls and their conversation. She thought her parents shared a quick smile before her dad turned his eyes back on the road.

Was everything different now? Jana wondered, the sky clear and the sun beating down on the sparse landscape. In her own perspective, she thought it was. She felt as if the trip had broken down each of their exteriors.

It wasn't that they had been never been close like some families she knew, Jana just saw that this trip somehow opened them all up. Something had cracked their exteriors, maybe to put it in bookish terms, had allowed them to open up their books and reveal what was inside. That was particularly true of her father. And maybe the least of all Lisa who was still Lisa and hadn't yet been molded so much by the world as by her relationship with Katie.

But as her dad had said earlier that morning, it was time to take the next exit and return to 1986. Jana shut her eyes and the next thing she heard was her dad calling out, "Goodbye Land of Enchantment! Maybe we'll see you soon again! Hello Texas!"

*****

That's exactly what they did– reemerging into 1986, arriving that night into Joplin, Missouri, not far over the Oklahoma border, to a fairly new Holiday Inn. With an indoor pool.

"Why is it inside?" Katie asked, looking at the big structure, not like the small motels they'd been staying along the way. "I don't want to swim inside in the summer."

"Ah," Mike said, searching for the pieces of paper in the maps where he had placed their reservation number. "But if you have indoor swimming, you can swim all winter and then more people might want to stay here. Purely a business decision."

Like her sister, Jana, too, was disappointed, but knowing he had done it to appease their mother, who was tired of the little motels along the way.

Soap, Jana thought, Mom wants the same soap in all her motels.

Their rooms– next to each other as usual– overlooked the pool area and the girls instantly dropped their things and headed to the indoor pool, their parents standing on the railing two floors up where they stayed, watching.

"At least it's a big pool," Katie said, shrugging her shoulders and jumping into the deep end with the big beach ball that she had just blown up for Lisa.

Jana was surprised how obvious she found the change from what she thought was like a time warp back to present day 1986. She didn't think it would be that obvious but it appeared to happen as easily as the landscape changed and they left behind the scrub of the Southwest and entered the plains states again, the grass growing high after good June rain.

Earlier that day, with so much time to think in the car, and feeling somewhat bored with the tapes she had brought and had listened to more times than she could count, she put her Walkman and headphones away and found herself thinking about her dad, while he continued to drive the family back toward Chicago and resume their lives where they left off two weeks ago.

Everyone else in the car was sleeping– Lisa leaning on Katie who had her head on her pillow against the car door and their mother's head tilted toward the car door in the front passenger seat. Jana wished she were alone with her dad, where she felt most comfortable asking questions.

For now though, she thought about him as a twenty-two year old, about that trip he took to California with Danny and how much his life had changed since that trip. While being twenty-two felt like years away, Jana knew her parents would tell her that it would come faster than she thought, especially as Katie would take her college entrance exams this coming school year– the SAT and ACT– and they would begin looking at colleges.

Jana didn't know how much this trip would change her. She wouldn't know that until they arrived home and she transplanted herself back into her life. But would it be life as she knew it? She peeked down at her tote bag and saw her two notebooks, one completely filled and one partially full.

She felt inspired, she felt like she found energy to not just keep going– not that it had been an issue before– of what she wanted her life to be. Meeting Scott had given her hope that someday she would meet a boy who would not just like her at the same time she liked him but someone who would appreciate who she was. And help her be the person she wanted to be.

What if her dad hadn't taken that trip on Route 66? Jana wondered. How would that have altered her own life? Would she have been able to come up with the story she wanted to tell? She wasn't sure. Maybe it could have come from somewhere else. But they might never have taken this trip if her dad didn't feel a need to return to Albuquerque. And then Jana would have never met Scott. Or learned to surf.

She longed to ask her dad his thoughts on this– did he sense the change it made in his life? What if he had decided to stay in Albuquerque? It was like a board game where one has several different directions that they can go. One doesn't know the outcome but Jana was learning that was part of life. You made a choice and you went with it.

They took full advantage of the indoor pool in Joplin, especially because it was pouring rain outside, a storm that came out of nowhere.

"Nothing like swimming in a thunderstorm," Katie joked, looking at the crackling lightning and thunder outside the large glass windows. She glanced behind her to see if Donna was nearby, but she was in the room next door already, probably reading the last book she had brought in the stack, clearly on a mission to finish before they arrived home.

After another long day in the car, the girls laughed and giggled and Jana wasn't really sure they were aware that it would be their last night before they would be home and into their own routines again.

Later, Katie and Lisa played a little miniature golf and Jana stayed with their things to write in her journal.

"Are you ready to go home?" Mike asked her, sitting in the lounge chair where Katie had left her beach towel. He realized it was damp and threw it over another chair to dry– even though Jana doubted it would with the warm, humid air of the pool area. All she could smell was chlorine and the humidity was definitely higher inside than outside, even in the Midwestern summer rain.

Jana shrugged her shoulders. "I guess. Mom said she'll get me some tennis lessons so I can try out for the high school team in the fall. And I've got babysitting."

Mike looked at her and nodded. Then he looked out at the pool. "And Scott?"

Jana looked down at her pink notebook and started to doodle with the black pen. "I don't know," she said. "It almost seems like a distant memory now."

"I told myself I would never be the parent who told his kids everything so they never figured anything out for themselves." He was still looking at the pool. Then he turned back to Jana and shook his head. "I can see now my dad was trying to help me but at the time I knew I had to learn it for myself."

She nodded, having no idea what he was talking about.

"I'm really happy that you had that adventure– shall we say– in Santa Monica. I know that it's something you'll never forget."

It was her turn to look at the empty pool, lit up in the twilight hours of the day.

"But I also know that you'll have many more adventures to come. And each one of those will help you learn and grow as a person. What I didn't realize was how much each part of life is like a building block. Everything that happens to us helps make us stronger for what's next."

He paused and Jana found herself speaking. "Dad, I liked Scott a lot. And I didn't like leaving." She stopped and looked at him, seeing a kindness in his eyes, one she didn't ever remember before, but one telling her that they had shared something on this trip that they might never have had they not taken the trip. She shook her head and let out half a laugh. "But I couldn't see myself with him. At least not right now. There's so much I want to do and I'm not sure where I'll land."

She could see her dad smiling at her and she continued.

"I want to be so much. I know lots of girls especially who want to get married and settle down and have kids. But I want something else."

"And that something else is right here," her dad said, pointing to the notebook she was writing in. "Each time you experience something, it helps you to weave a story together."

She found herself overcome with emotion although she didn't really understand it. She nodded.

"You just keep writing and the rest will fall into place."

Mike stood up and leaned over and hugged Jana, a hug she didn't remember since the days when she and Katie were much younger– even before Lisa was born– and Donna would open the front door of their house and send them out to greet him when he arrived home from work. She hated to let go in those days.

But the older she got, something had changed. Here was that hug again. She welcomed it and hoped it wouldn't be the last one.

On this trip, Jana also noticed how her mother had changed. When they left she had been so concerned with the girls, about sunscreen and not letting them out of her sight. And yet by the time they had hit Albuquerque, Jana also saw that she had begun the process of letting go– even Donna admitting it– that day in the Laundry Basket Laundromat.

Jana didn't think she would ever know what her mother felt about Albuquerque and Mike's true reason for taking them there. Jana also knew she probably needed to leave that unsaid, that as her own life unfolded in front of her, there was much she would never know and it was better to leave certain things between the people most involved by them.

But Jana could imagine that her father wanted to share something of it with their mother. Not about Gloria but about the experience. And yet her mother probably felt insulted that he would share something of his past that she didn't want to know about.

Just thinking about it made Jana's head spin. Relationships looked easy from the outside, she thought, but she was starting to see– even just by watching everyone else and not having experienced much herself– how hard it was with two people with two different life experiences to come together and somehow meet in the middle.

Jana could see how particularly hard that was for Katie who wanted all the boys to come over to her side and see everything her way. That wasn't how relationships worked though. And how could she not want to know more about their experiences, Jana wondered, thinking about Scott and how she wished they would have had more time to share. She wanted to see where he lived, to experience more of his life. And yet she knew she was lucky she'd had what she did.

The next morning they left early after breakfast at the Denny's down the road, traveling through Missouri and then back into Illinois.

For the last time on the trip– Mike had taken Interstate 55 until it ended, dumping them off in Joliet– Jana looked at the brown curls on her mother's head, softened now from the three weeks since her perm. They would be home in an hour

She hoped her mother was happy. Jana knew she had worked hard and her worry was always because she wanted the best for her family. And yet Jana wondered if there was something in her past she didn't share. Jana knew– yet again– that it was a privilege her dad had shared so much with her. It would have been easier not to.

And she knew he didn't share because he couldn't share with Donna. No, he shared because he wanted to give Jana all the tools he could that might help her create the life she wanted to have. Especially because Katie's ears turned deaf every time he offered advice to her.

It was nearly 6:00 pm when Mike pulled the car into the driveway of their white house with the forest green shutters. The humidity had long returned in Oklahoma, everyone feeling somewhat crankier the closer they got to home.

"It's definitely time for the trip to end," Mike had mumbled as he stopped outside St. Louis to fill the car up with gas. "I do believe my girls have had enough."

The night before they had eaten quietly, Katie eyeing a pay phone on their way in of the restaurant. "How much would a long-distance call be?" She asked no one in particular.

"Too much," Donna said, "We'll be home tomorrow and you can catch up with your friends then."

The car wasn't even unpacked when Katie heard the phone ringing in the house and made sure she was the first one inside to see who it was. Conveniently, for her.

"How does she do that?" Mike asked Donna, handing her a suitcase. "How do her friends know when we'd be home?"

Donna laughed and shook her head. "Are you sure she's ours? She doesn't seem to resemble both of us much."

"And yet we know you carried her around for nine months."

Jana watched the interaction of her parents, as her outside self. She thought about how she kind of liked it that way. Donna definitely looked more relaxed, more at ease, more likely to let the girls wander on their own. Not totally on their own but more than before.

When they had left, especially as Mike had shared with Jana about Gloria, Jana had wondered– maybe even worried– that her mother didn't want to take the trip because she knew what had transpired in Albuquerque in the years before she met Mike. Jana still didn't know if her mother knew or not but that didn't matter.

What mattered most was that she, too, seemed to have gotten something from the trip outside of the new dishes that she had just carried into the house and was starting to unpack on the glass-topped dining room table with the caned chairs that Jana always worried someone would fall backward in and hit the ground. Jana snuck a peek at her mother on her way up to her room with her yellow and white striped tote bag.

Donna was smiling as she looked at the plates, running a hand over them as if she had never seen them before.

We'll have happy dinners on them and we'll all remember the trip, Jana thought.

Everyone had something to take in– except Katie who had grabbed the cordless phone and was in her room with the door shut– and Jana had walked back outside, glad to be home to her own room, her own bed, her own space. But in some ways she was sad the time was over.

Something told her that her dad might never be that open and honest with her again. She knew it had something to do with where they were, especially because he had been right about leaving Albuquerque. He entered back into the present, maybe not just for Donna, but also because he had his job to return to, a job that was about selling the present and the future, not the past. Time would tell how the trip had changed their relationship. If it had changed it.

As he handed her a small bag, he and Jana held it at the same time for a moment and she said, "Thank you, Dad."

"For what?" He asked, looking a little perplexed.

"For the trip." She knew she didn't have to say more and the smile on his face indicated that he knew exactly what she meant.

"You're welcome."

When they had finished unpacking the car, Jana went up to her room and shut the door. She changed into her pajamas– not caring how early in the evening it was– and opened her notebook. Sitting on the floor with her back against her bed as she usually liked to sit in her room, she looked at what she had last written. She tapped her pen against the half-filled page of her loopy cursive handwriting and looked around her room, not at her white closet doors but at the future.

She couldn't see it. And she couldn't see the ending for her story yet.

Maybe I can't see the ending because this is where I'm at and this is all I'm supposed to know. She played with the wire coil that had been smashed and now didn't allow the pages to lay right in the notebook. Let it go, she thought. You can finish it another day when you know the ending. There isn't a hurry, is there?

She closed the notebook, grabbed the pink one from the trip, and placed them in a drawer in her desk knowing that one day she would return to them. She'd know how to end it when it was time. Everything was playing out exactly as it was supposed to.

Michelle L. Rusk

www.ingramcontent.com/pod-product-compliance
Lightning Source LLC
Chambersburg PA
CBHW051257250626
47155CB00009B/3322